A collecti...
the worla... ...*...ers*

International bestselling author

PENNY JORDAN

has appeared on the Sunday Times *and the*
New York Times *bestseller lists, and sold*
more than 80 million copies of her novels.

**"Women everywhere will find pieces of
themselves in Jordan's characters."**
—*Publishers Weekly*

Available in the

Queens of Romance

collection

17th March 2006

7th April 2006

21st April 2006

5th May 2006

Collect all 4 superb books!

PENNY JORDAN

Her Lover, Her Husband?

Containing

Back in the Marriage Bed
& The Marriage Demand

M&B™ and M&B™ with the Rose Device
are trademarks of the publisher.
Harlequin Mills & Boon Limited, Eton House,
18-24 Paradise Road,
Richmond, Surrey TW9 1SR

ISBN 0 263 85032 3

062-0406

Printed and bound in Spain
by Litografia Rosés S.A., Barcelona

Back in the Marriage Bed

PENNY JORDAN

CHAPTER ONE

ANNIE paused halfway up the stairs of her pretty Victorian cottage, a softly tantalising smile curling her mouth in secret appreciation, a dreamy, distant look hazing the normal clarity of her widely spaced intelligent grey eyes. She had had the dream again last night, the one that featured 'him'. And *this* time, *last* night, he had been even more deliciously real than ever before. So real, in fact...

As her cheeks pinkened betrayingly and her eyelashes modestly swept down to conceal the expression her eyes might inadvertently betray, Annie could feel the sharp thrill of remembered pleasure running hotly through her body. Last night when he had held her, touched her... A fierce shiver openly tensed her body and a little guiltily she hurried the rest of the way upstairs.

She only had an hour to get ready before leaving to collect Helena and her husband. The three of them were going out for a special celebratory meal, and by rights it was *that* she ought to be thinking about, not some impossibly wonderful and totally unreal man she had created out of her own imagination, her own dreams...her own *need*...

Her frown deepened a little. For a woman of twenty-three without a man in her life, without a *lover* in her life, the sheer intensity of the sensuality of the periodic dreams she had about the fantasy male she had mentally labelled her perfect lover, her soul mate and other half, were becoming increasingly explicit. A sign of her loveless, manless state, or an indication of the power of her imagination? Annie didn't know. What she did know, though, was that since she had first started dreaming about him none of the real men she had met had had the power to compare with him, nor to touch her emotions.

She was looking forward to the evening ahead. Helena was not, after all, just her closest friend and a substitute mother figure to her; she was also the woman, the *surgeon*, who was responsible for saving her life. No, Annie corrected herself quickly, what Helena was responsible for in many ways was *giving* her life, giving it back to her after others, less determined, less compassionate, less seeing, had said that...

Tensely Annie swallowed. Even now, nearly five years after the event, after the accident which had so nearly cost her her life, the mere thought of how close she had come to death had the power to strike an icy chill of terror right through her.

Perhaps illogically, the fact that she had no memory, either of the events leading up to the accident itself nor the weeks when she had been in a coma, made her fear of how easily she might not have survived all the more intense.

As she pushed at her bedroom door the slight awkwardness of her arm, which was the sole physical legacy she now had left of the accident, showed itself in the way she had to open it. Her arm had been so badly crushed, so badly damaged, that the senior registrar on duty when she had been rushed into the accident unit had been on the point of having her prepared for an amputation when Helena, who had only dropped in at the hospital to see another patient, had happened to walk through the unit and had been called over by him for a second opinion.

As the hospital's senior microsurgeon Helena had immediately taken charge, deciding it might be possible to save Annie's arm.

Her face had been the first one Annie had seen when she had first regained consciousness, but it hadn't been for many, many weeks after that that she had learned, not from Helena herself but from one of the nurses, how lucky she was that Helena had chanced to be in the hospital when she had been brought in.

It had been Helena who had spent hour after hour at her bedside talking to her whilst she lay in a coma, dragging her with the strength of her will and her love back to the world of the living, and Annie knew that she would never, never cease to revere and love her for all that she had done.

'You aren't the only one who has gained,' Helena often teased her gently. 'You have no idea how much higher my professional stock has grown since it's become publicly known that my personal surgical procedure saved your arm. Your arm is worth more than its weight in gold to me, Annie…' And then her face would soften as she'd add, far more tenderly, 'And you, my dear, are more special to me than I can find the words to say. The daughter I never thought I would have...'

Both of them had cried a little the first time Helena had made this loving claim, the moment and the words especially meaningful to them both. Helena, the highly qualified and skilled surgeon who had lost her own womb and her chances of motherhood at a very young age, and Annie, the girl who had been abandoned as a baby and then grown up in a children's home, always treated well but never loved in that special one-to-one way she had so often yearned for.

Two years ago, when Helena had finally accepted the proposal of marriage from her long-term partner Bob Lever, Annie had been more pleased for both of them than she had been able to find the words to say.

Previously Helena had always refused to marry Bob, claiming that one day he might meet a woman who could give him the children she couldn't and that when that day came she wanted him to feel free to go to her, and it had taken the combined efforts of both Annie and Bob to persuade her to think differently.

In the end it had been Annie's gentle reminder that since Helena had unofficially adopted her as her 'daughter' she no longer had any reason for refusing Bob's proposals.

'Very well. I give in,' Helena had laughed, waiting until they had finished toasting her acceptance of Bob's proposal before adding, tongue in cheek to Annie, 'Of course, you know what this means, don't you? As your ''mother'', and at my time of life,

Annie, I shall soon be urging you to find yourself a
mate and produce some grandchildren for me.'

It had been after that, and relaxed by the excellence of the Christmas dinner she and Helena had
cooked together and the wine that had accompanied
it, that Annie had been able to tell Helena the extraordinary intensity of the dreams she had been having.

'When did they first start?' Helena had questioned
her, immediately very professional.

'I'm not sure... I think I must have been having
them for a while before I actually *knew* I was,' Annie
had told her, shaking her head and laughing at her
own confusing statement.

'You see, when I did start to realise I was having
them they seemed so familiar, as though he had been
a part of my life for always... It was as though somehow...I...I knew him...' She had stopped speaking
to frown and shake her head as she tried to grapple
for the right words to describe the extraordinary com-
plexity of the feelings within her dreams, to convey
to her friend the reality of the man who featured in
them.

Now, though, as she headed for her wardrobe to
remove the new dress she and Helena had bought
especially for this occasion the previous month, she
caught sight of her reflection and gave another small
smile. She had been so lucky that her face hadn't
been damaged at all in the accident. Small and heart-
shaped, it still looked pretty much as it did in the
few photographs she had of her childhood. Her hair
was still the same blonde colour—an inheritance
from her unknown parent, along with the elegance

of her bone structure. Maturity, and the much stronger sense of self she had developed, meant that she no longer agonised over who and what her parents had been. It was enough that they had given the most precious gift there was—the gift of life itself.

All she knew of the accident was what she had been told, what had been said during the court case, which had resulted in the driver who had knocked her down on the pedestrian crossing she had been halfway over being convicted of dangerous driving and his insurance company being compelled to make a very large payment to her indeed.

Annie knew there were those who thought enviously that a weakened right arm and being out of action for almost a year were only minor inconveniences to have to put up with. Certainly the driver's insurance company's legal team had thought so, and Annie was the first to agree that because of the accident she had gained enormously—not because of the insurance company pay-out but because it had brought Helena and Bob into her life.

As the lawyers for the insurance company had been quick to point out, her injuries had not prevented her from going on to complete the degree course she had been just about to start when the accident happened, nor had it precluded her from obtaining a job. Indeed, for many people, the fact that she was only able to work part-time at the moment, job-sharing with another girl, would be a plus point and not a minus one.

Oh, yes, the lawyers for the defence had been very, very persuasive, but the evidence had been damning.

There had been five witnesses who had each seen the way the car had been driven across the pedestrian crossing and straight into Annie. The driver had been drinking—a stress-related problem which he now had under control, according to his defence.

Annie sighed. There had even been a tearful appearance by his wife, who'd said that without her husband's income, without his ability to earn a living, if he lost his licence for too long a period, the lives of her and her three small children would be made very hard indeed.

Annie's tender heart had ached for them, and still often did, but, as Helena had told her robustly, *she* was not the one who was responsible for their plight.

Even so, she was glad that the driver of the car had been from out of town and that there was no chance that she was likely to bump into him locally—or his family.

It seemed odd to her now to think that she had not lived the whole of her life here in this small, sleepy cathedral city, with its history, its castle, its small university and its river—the river which had once, many, many years ago, been the major source of its wealth and position. Now, though, the boats that used the pretty marina were strictly pleasure craft; the merchant vessels which had once brought their exotic wares to the port belonged to another era altogether.

Annie couldn't remember just why she had chosen to apply to Wryminster's university for a place, nor when she had arrived in the city. She had clearly not had time to make any friends or to confide her dreams or ambitions to them. The accident had hap-

pened just before the week of the new term—her first
week, her first term—and the only address the authorities had been able to find on Annie had been
that of the children's home where she had grown up.

According to what Helena had been able to find
out she had been a quite clever child, and something
of a loner. It had been Helena who had taken her
home when at last the hospital had discharged her.
Helena who had mothered her, cared for her, *loved*
her. And Helena, too, who had encouraged her in her
need to become properly independent, she and Bob
helping Annie to find her perfect little home not too
far from their own house.

As she slipped the new outfit she and Helena had
bought together from its protective wrapper Annie
expelled a small shaky breath. She had come so far
to reach this day, had *had* to come so far… The outfit
was a soft icy blue, a perfect foil for her skin tone
and her eyes. She had fallen in love with it the minute she had seen it, although it had taken a lot of
persuasion and coaxing from Helena before she had
finally given in and bought it.

In soft fine wool crêpe the trousers showed off the
slender length of her legs and the narrow delicacy of
her hips whilst the almost full-length coat added a
breathtakingly stylish elegance to the ensemble.
Beneath the coat there was a pretty embroidered top
to add a final touch of glamour.

'I won't get my money's worth out of it,' Annie
had predicted, shaking her head as she'd paid for it.
'I don't go anywhere I can wear something so expensive.'

'Well, perhaps you ought to start,' Helena had smiled. 'Sayad would do anything to get you to agree to a date.'

Sayad was a very, very dishy anaesthetist who had recently joined the hospital staff, and he had made a bee line for Annie the moment he had seen her.

'He's nice,' she had responded, quickly shaking her head. 'But...'

But not her dream man. Oh, no—nowhere even near her dream man. Where Sayad was merry and open-faced her dream lover was dark-browed and almost brooding; a *man* where Sayad was still in some ways, despite his age, part boy. Without knowing *how* she knew, she *knew* that her dream lover would have an air of authority and masterfulness, an aura of such strong maleness that Sayad could never in any way really compare with him.

Despite her reservations about the cost of her new outfit, she had given way in the end because tonight was a special celebration: her close friends Bob and Helena's wedding anniversary and Bob's birthday.

At Helena's insistence, following the successful conclusion of the long drawn-out legal battle she had endured before winning substantial damages for her injury, she was taking a few months' sabbatical from her job. Earlier in the week she had said her temporary goodbyes to her colleagues at the multinational petrochemical company, Petrofiche, whose head offices were situated in what had originally been a very large country house several miles outside the city, over a happy girlie lunch.

For this evening's meal she had booked a table at

the area's most prestigious restaurant on the river, insisting that on this occasion *she* was going to treat Helena and Bob, and that she would pick them up in her newly acquired and rather swish Mercedes car.

The car had been a real step forward for Annie. She hadn't been able to drive when she had had her accident, and for a long time afterwards she had remained terrified of even being near a car never mind driving one. But eventually she had forced herself to overcome her fears and she had successfully taken her test. The weakness in her arm meant that she felt much more comfortable driving an automatic car than a manual, and so, aided and abetted by Helena and Bob, she had finally given in and allowed herself the luxury of her new smart car.

It didn't take her long to get ready; she preferred to use the minimum of make-up and, as Helena often told her enviously, she was lucky enough to have naturally good skin. If her mouth was a little too full for her own liking, well, she had learned how to tone down its sizzling second glance male appeal with pastel-toned lipsticks. Her hair, silky and straight, she always wore long and simply styled, setting off her delicate bone structure.

Once on, the new outfit looked even better than Annie had remembered. She had finally, this last year, with the court case at long last behind her, started to put on a little extra weight and it suited her.

Giving her bedroom a proud appraisal, she walked over to the door. Her small Victorian cottage, bought out of the award the court had given her, had been very run-down when she had found it, and she had lived surrounded by builders' rubble and very often the builders themselves whilst it was being restored and renovated, determinedly refusing Helena and Bob's pleas for her to move back in with them until the work was finished. She had wanted to be on the spot, to prove her maturity and her independence and, most of all, to prove to *herself* that she was capable of managing on her own.

The large double bed which dominated the room couldn't help but catch her eye. Even now she wasn't quite sure *why* she had bought it, *why* she had so instinctively and automatically picked it out of all the beds in the showroom, heading for it almost like someone on autopilot, or someone who was sleep-walking.

All she had known was that it was the bed she had to have.

'Well, it will certainly suit the house,' had been Helena's comment when she had taken her to see it, and she had admired its reproduction Victorian styling.

In her dreams she and her dream lover were always in this bed, although in her dreams... Guiltily Annie reminded herself that she was going to be late picking up her friends if she didn't make a move.

Her face slightly more pink than it had been, she headed downstairs.

'Goodness, this place looks busy this evening,' Helena commented as Annie carefully reversed her car into the single parking space left in the restaurant's car park.

'Yes, they did say when I originally booked the table that they were expecting a busy evening. Apparently Petrofiche are having a dinner for their new consultant marine biologist.'

'Oh, yes, I heard they'd found someone to take Professor Salter's place. They've headhunted him from one of the Gulf States, or so I've heard. He's extremely highly qualified and relatively young—in his thirties. It seems he's actually worked for Petrofiche in the past.'

'Mmm… It's odd to think of a marine biologist working for the petrochemical industry,' Bob cut in.

Helena gave him a wifely smile and then exchanged a conspiratorial look with Annie as she teased him,

'I suppose *you* think of marine biologists as people who make underwater films of sharks and coral reefs…'

'No, of course I don't,' Bob denied, but his sheepish look gave him away.

'These days all the large multi-nationals are keen to ensure that their customers see them as greener than green and very environmentally aware,' Annie told them both. 'And because of the effect any kind of oil seepage has on the world's seas and oceans, and their life forms, for companies like Petrofiche it makes good sense to use the services of such experts.'

They were out of the car now and heading towards the restaurant. Originally a private house, it had been very successfully converted to an exclusive restaurant, complete with a conservatory area and a stunningly beautiful garden which ran down to the river. As they walked past the wrought-iron gates that led to the private garden they could see inside it, where skilful lighting illuminated several of the specimen trees as well as the courtyard area and its decorative statues.

The restaurant was owned and run by a husband and wife team in their late thirties, and as she recognised them Liz Rainford gave them a warm, welcoming smile.

'I've kept you your favourite table,' she whispered to them as she signalled to a waiter to take them through to the dining room.

Liz was on the committee of a local charity that Annie helped out, by volunteering for fund raising duties when she could, and Liz was aware of the history of Annie's accident and her relationship with Helena and Bob.

'I know tonight's a special night for all of you.' She smiled.

Their favourite table was one that was tucked quite discreetly in a corner by one of the windows, through which one could see down the length of the garden and beyond it to the river, and as their waiter settled them in their chairs and produced their menus with a theatrical flourish Annie gave a small sigh of pleasure.

Sometimes she felt almost as though she had been reborn on that morning five years ago when she had opened her eyes in her hospital bed to see Helena looking back at her. Although now she could remember her childhood and her teenage years, they were somehow in soft focus and slightly unreal, their edges blurred, so that occasionally it was hard for her to remember that those years, those *memories*, actually did belong to her.

It was the effect of the huge trauma her mind and body had experienced, Helena was quick to say, to comfort her when she worried about it; her mind's way of protecting her.

The restaurant was full, with the doors to the conservatory closed to protect the privacy of the party from Petrofiche dining inside it. The girls in the office had been talking about the new consultant when Annie had been at work earlier in the week.

'He's got his own business and Petrofiche is just *one* of his clients,' Beverley Smith, one of the senior personal assistants, had told them importantly. 'He'll only be coming in here a couple of days a week when he isn't out in the field.'

'Mmm... I wonder if he needs a PA. *I* certainly wouldn't mind a couple of trips to the Barrier Reef,' one of the other girls had remarked enviously.

'The Barrier Reef!' another had scoffed. 'More like Alaska. *That's* the current hot-spot for marine biologists.'

Annie had listened to their good-natured bantering with a small smile.

Although she was regularly invited out on dates by male members of the staff she never accepted. Helena had warned her gently that she was in danger of allowing her dream lover to blind her to the reality of real live potential mates, but Annie was quietly aware that there was more to her reluctance to accept dates than merely a romantic figment of her own idealistic dreams.

It was almost as though, in some way, something deep within her told her that it would be wrong for her to start seeing someone. Quite why she should think this she was at a loss to know, and, indeed, her feelings were so nebulous, so inexplicable, that she felt too foolish to even confide them to Helena. All she did know was that for some reason it was necessary for her to wait...but to wait for what? For whom? She had no idea. She just knew it was something she had to do!

CHAPTER TWO

'OH, WE didn't order champagne,' Annie began as the waiter suddenly appeared with a bottle and three glasses, and then stopped as she saw the look of smiling complicity Helena and Bob were exchanging.

'This was supposed to be *my* treat,' she reproached them as the waiter filled their champagne flutes.

'Yes, I know, but it *is* our celebration,' Bob reminded her fondly.

Annie agreed quietly, her eyes large and dark with the emotional intensity of her thoughts, tears just beginning to film them as she turned to Helena and told her huskily, 'If it hadn't been for you...' She stopped, unable to go on, and the three of them sat in silence as they each shared the others' emotions.

It was Bob who broke the emotional intensity of the moment, picking up his glass and lifting it, announcing in a firm voice, 'To you, Annie...'

'Yes, my love. To you,' Helena joined in the toast.

As she looked at Annie's flushed face Helena marvelled at the recuperative powers of the human body and its capacity for endurance. Looking at Annie, it was hard to equate the healthy young woman she was now with the comatose, badly injured accident victim she had seen lying inert on the hospital trolley as she'd hurried through the Accident and Emergency unit.

Later, whilst they were waiting for their pudding course, Annie excused herself to the other two.

'I'm just going to the loo,' she announced, getting up and walking towards the cloakrooms in the foyer. She was just about to walk past the entrance to the conservatory when the door opened and a party of four men came out. Two of them Annie recognised as executives from the company she worked for, the third she didn't know, and the fourth...

Her heart gave a stunned leap inside her chest wall, shock rooting her to the floor where she stood as she stared open-mouthed at the fourth member of the quartet in total disbelief.

It was him! He... The man... From her dreams... So exactly identical to him that she could only stand and stare in silent shock. Her dream lover come to life! But how could that be possible when he was only a figment of her own imagination, a creature she had conjured up within her own mind? No, it *wasn't* possible. She must be imagining it...hal-lucinating... She had drunk too much champagne she decided dizzily.

Quickly she closed her eyes and counted to ten, and then she opened them. He was still there, and what was more he was looking at her. She felt as though her blood was quite literally draining from her veins, leaving her empty, her body cold and in danger. Panic filled her. She tried to move and couldn't. She tried to speak but no sound emerged from her paralysed throat... A hideous, horrible sen-sation of fear invaded her. She *wanted* to move. She *wanted* to speak. But she couldn't. With horrible certainty Annie knew that she was going to faint.

When she came round she was in Liz's private quarters and Bob and Helena were hovering anxiously over her.

'Darling, what is it…what happened?' Helena was asking her worriedly as she chafed her hand. Helen's fingers were on her pulse, Annie recognised shakily, and she could see the professional beginning to take over from the concerned friend. Determinedly she forced herself to sit up.

'I'm all right,' she insisted. 'I just felt faint, that's all,' she whispered, still too much in shock to be able to tell Helena what had actually happened.

'I'm sorry,' she apologised to Liz as she ignored Helena's protests and swung her feet to the floor, gritting her teeth against her giddiness as she made herself stand up. 'I don't really have much of a head for vintage champagne,' she excused herself, giving the other woman a brief smile.

Of course there was no question of either Helena or Bob allowing her to drive home, nor of her being allowed to return home on her own. Instead she was put to bed in the bedroom which had been hers whilst she was recuperating, with Helena fussing round her and announcing that she felt it might be a good idea if she were to have a full check-up.

'There's nothing wrong with me,' Annie insisted. 'I just had a bit of a shock, that's all.'

'A shock? What kind of shock?' Helena demanded anxiously.

'I…I thought I saw someone I…' Annie paused

and shook her head, her mouth dry as she told her,
'I must have made a mistake, imagined it. I know,
because it just isn't possible that...'

'Who was it? *Who* did you think you saw, Annie?'
Helena probed.

'It...it wasn't anyone. It was...just...just a mistake,' Annie repeated stubbornly, but as she reached
for the cup of tea Bob had brought her she started to
tremble so violently that she had to put it down
again.

Covering her face with her hands she admitted
shakily, 'Oh, Helena...it was so...so surreal. I
don't...I saw *him*...the man...from my dreams... He
was...' She stopped and shook her head. 'I *know* that
I *can't* have done, that he just doesn't exist, but...'

'You're getting yourself all worked up,' Helena
told her firmly. 'I'll give you something to help you
relax and go to sleep, and then in the morning we
can talk about it properly.'

As she lay back against the pillows Annie gave
her a small weak smile. She knew that her friend was
right, of course.

Several minutes later Helena, who had left the
room, came back with a glass of water and two tablets for her to take. She watched with maternal tenderness as Annie dutifully swallowed them down.

'I'm sorry if I spoiled your evening,' she whispered drowsily to Helena as the tablets started to
work.

Now that she was beginning to feel calmer she
couldn't understand why she had overreacted so fool-
ishly, just because of some minor and no doubt imag-

ined similarity between the man she had seen in the restaurant and her own fantasy lover. And anyway, now that she *really* thought about it, there was no way her dream lover would *ever* have looked at her the way the man in the restaurant had, with that look of implacable cold hostility in his dense, darkly blue eyes, that blanked-out look of icy contempt and banked-down anger.

Wearily Annie felt her eyes starting to close, and ten minutes later, when Helena quietly shut the bedroom door behind herself, Annie was deeply and completely asleep.

'I suspect that the emotion of the evening and the memories it stirred up are the root cause of what happened,' Helena announced to her husband Bob as she went back downstairs to join him.

'Mmm… There's no way the man she saw *could* be someone she knew, is there?' Bob asked her curiously.

'Well, it *is* a possibility I suppose,' Helena agreed. 'After all, as you know, there are still some missing pieces from her memory. She can remember arriving here in Wryminster, but she *can't* remember *when* she arrived. It's difficult to imagine that anyone who was involved with her to the extent they would *have had* to be involved with her to be responsible for dreams of the intensity of those that Annie has been having could ever be cold-hearted enough, uncaring enough, not to get in touch after the accident. After all, it was reported in the local papers.'

'No, it does seem improbable,' Bob agreed.

                    *   *   *

Upstairs in her sleep Annie started to smile, her body quivering with a mixture of nervousness and excitement.

'God, but you feel so good… Will you let me look at you as well as hold you, little Annie? I want to so much…'

Annie tensed a little as the warm, knowing male hands began to gently undress her, nervous at first, her heart thumping anxiously, but then, as pleasure and excitement took over from her initial apprehension, her tension started to fade, her body beginning to relax as she started to respond to the soft verbal praise of her lover whilst he, oh, so slowly and carefully, laid her body bare to his gaze, peeling back the protective layers of her clothing, freeing her flesh to the warmth of his hands, their warmth, like their strength, a benediction as well as a nerve-thrilling wonderful new sensation.

He knew that this was her first real experience of a man's love, her first time, and he had told her, reassured her, that the choice, the decision was to be hers, that he would, if she asked him to do so, stop and allow her to change her mind. But she didn't *want* to change her mind, nor did she want him to *stop*. She wanted…

She gave a small gasp of delight as his touch set fire to her desires, igniting all the passion she had somehow known she was capable of feeling but which hitherto had been locked up inside her, hidden away in a secret place to which only he had the key.

She loved him so much…wanted him so much… What had been unthinkable with anyone else was not just 'thinkable' with him, but desirable…must-haveable… Her whole body shook with the force of what she was feeling…with her longing for him…her love for him. He only had to look at her and she melted.

Just the way he said her name was a form of poetry greater than even the greatest love sonnets. Just the way he looked at her more beautiful than any love song ever sung. The way he made her feel was so intense it was scary… He thrilled her, excited her, made her want to laugh and cry at the same time, filled her with such happiness that it made her feel afraid. *He* made her feel almost immortal, and yet, at the same time, he filled her with such a sense of her fragile vulnerability, her own frightening dependence on him and his love, that she was consumed with terror at the thought of losing him.

He stroked her breasts, watching her as she quivered in instant response, her eyes darkening, her lips parting.

'Has anyone ever told you that you have the sexiest mouth in the whole world?' he asked her softly, rimming it with his fingertip and smiling as she made an instinctive movement to catch hold of it.

'Not like that,' he whispered to her. 'Like this…' And then he slid his fingertip into her mouth, coaxing her to fasten her lips around it and slowly suck on it.

In her dream Annie moaned out loud in shocked delight, her body moving restlessly as it sought the intimacy of its lover's embrace.

The evening sun slanted through the wide windows. Beyond them, if she opened her eyes, Annie knew she would see the purple haze of the distant hills, and if she stood close to them she could look down on the mellow wash of the river. Even at this distance she could hear its soft rhythmic whisper, almost feel the insidious pull of its tide, just as she could feel the urgent tug of the female tide within her own body. She drew a sharp breath as she felt the male hunger in the hands that caressed her.

'Tell me now if you want me to stop,' he was whispering huskily, *insistently*, to her. 'Tell me now, Annie, otherwise it will be too late.'

But she knew she would say nothing, that she wanted him too much, loved him too much, even though the things he was doing to her, *with* her, were a world away from her own childish experience, limited to a few fumbled kisses.

'I'm much, much too old for you,' he had already told her, but somehow, instead of putting her off, his bold confession had only heightened and intensified her desire for him, imbuing him with a magical, almost mystical worldliness, a male knowledge and awareness that galvanised her body into excited little shivers.

And now it was nearly here, the moment of supreme revelation, the moment when...

Annie gave a sharp, piercing cry and she suddenly woke up, her body drenched in perspiration, her mind racing. As she sat up in her bed she covered her face with trembling hands.

Her dream had been so strong, so real, and the

man in it, her dream lover, had been so—so scarily alive.

Shakily she tried to draw a calming breath of air into her lungs, and then she closed her eyes, reliving the moment when she had traced with her lips the shape of the tiny scar she had seen on her lover's temple, the same scar in exactly the same spot that the man in the restaurant had had. How many times had she dreamed of that scar and not really known it?

She didn't know. She only knew that a small fierce stillness had gripped him as she touched it. It was as familiar to her as her own reflection. But how could that be? What was happening to her? Was she experiencing some kind of sixth sense, some kind of special awareness, some kind of inexplicable glimpse into the future? Were they perhaps fated to meet, and was this—these dreams—fate's way of warning her of what was to come, of what was to be? Her whole body started to tremble.

She had been so very close to death, and, although she was extremely loath to acknowledge it, never mind discuss it openly, had experienced the sensation she had read avidly and secretly about that was reportedly so common to people who shared her near-death experience: that feeling of rushing towards a wonderful welcoming place, being propelled through darkness into an indescribable sense of awesome light, then that sudden awareness of being turned back, pulled back, that voice that was not actually a voice announcing that it was not yet her time.

Had that experience somehow or other, illogical

and implausible though it might sound, given her the ability to sense, to feel, to experience a special, wonderful event in her life that had yet to take place?

Had the secret yearning she had carried all her life, to share it with someone who loved her, affected her to such an extent that she was already living in her dreams what she had yet to live in reality? Was her dream lover, in fact, not so much a figment of her imagination as a very factual and real figure from her future?

Impossible, implausible... Yes, maybe, but then there were many mysteries that defied logical explanation and analysis.

The fear she had felt earlier in the evening, the sense of shock and panic, had given way to an excitement that was almost euphoric. Her dream lover wasn't just a dream. He was real. He was... Ecstatically Annie closed her eyes, hugging her thoughts, her love, to her heart just as tightly as she yearned for him to hug and hold her.

It was a long time before she finally got back to sleep, and when she did finally succumb her exalted state had convinced her that the evening's meeting with the real-life physical embodiment of her dream man had been an act of fate for which her dreams had been preparing her.

'Annie, how are you feeling this morning, my love?'

A little groggily Annie focused on Helena as she walked into the bedroom carrying a fragrant mug of coffee.

'I'm not sure,' Annie admitted. 'Those pills you gave me really knocked me out.

'Helena,' she demanded, her voice changing as she sat up in her bed and looked at her friend and mentor with fixed determination. 'Helena, do you believe in…fate?' she asked solemnly.

'I'm not sure just what you mean,' Helena responded cautiously.

'The man—the one I saw in the restaurant last night,' Annie told her in a low voice. 'At first I thought I must be imagining it, that he couldn't possibly be the same man I've been dreaming about… But then, last night, I dreamed about him again, and I knew…'

She took a deep breath and told Helena huskily, 'I think that we must have been destined to meet somehow, Helena, and that he and I…' She paused and shook her head, responding to her friend's silence with a wry, 'Oh, I know how far-fetched this must sound, but what *other* explanation can there be? I don't pretend to know why I should have dreamed about him or why I should feel as though I already know him. I just do. Please don't tell me that you think I'm being silly,' she pleaded.

'I won't,' Helena promised her quietly, pausing to sit on the bed and stroke the soft tumbled hair back off Annie's face with one hand as she placed the mug of coffee on the bedside table with the other.

Annie was so very dear to her, very precious, so much the daughter, the child she herself had never had, but she was also, in Helena's opinion, a very vulnerable young woman. The gravity of her accident and her injuries had meant that the energy that other young women of her age would naturally give to the process of maturing had in Annie's case had to be given to her physical recovery, recuperating her health.

It wasn't that Annie in any way lacked intelligence—far from it. She had obtained her degree and she had a concern for the world and the people in it which made her, in many ways, older and wiser than her peers. But it was a fact that because of the length of time she had spent recovering from the accident Annie had not had the opportunity to mature as a *woman*, to experiment sexually, to make mistakes, errors of judgement, to indulge in all the youthful follies that people normally did on their journey through the turbulent years that led from one's late teens to one's mid-twenties.

Now it seemed that she preferred the fantasy of her dream lover rather than dating a real live man, that she was stubbornly determined to believe in fate rather than reality.

'You *do* think I'm being silly, don't you?' Annie accused Helena flatly as she saw the hesitation in her friend's eyes.

'Not silly,' Helena corrected quietly. 'But perhaps…' She stopped speaking, and then smiled ruefully at Annie before asking her gently, 'Has it occurred to you that this man may have been so familiar to you simply because he *is* familiar?'

'From my dreams, you mean?' Annie checked, nonplussed.

'No. Not from your dreams,' Helena stopped, and

then said quietly, 'Annie, he may have been familiar to you because you do actually know him.'

'*Know* him?' Annie looked perplexed. 'No, that's impossible.'

Helena waited before reminding her softly, 'There *are* still some gaps in your memory, my dear. The weeks leading up to the accident as well as the event itself, and those weeks after, when you were in a coma.'

'Yes, I know.' Annie's forehead creased in a small frown of distress. 'But I couldn't have known him…not the way I feel about him…the way we are… If I had he would have…' She stopped, shaking her head. 'No. It isn't possible,' she told Helena immediately and positively. 'I would have known if he… If I… If we… No,' she reaffirmed.

'Well, I must admit it *does* seem unlikely,' Helena acknowledged slowly. 'But I felt I ought to mention the possibility to you.'

'I understand,' Annie assured her, giving her a warm hug. 'But if he had known me he would have come forward when you advertised, wouldn't he? And besides…' A small secret smile curled her mouth, her eyes suddenly glowing with private happiness. 'I know that if he…if we…' She stopped and shook her head again. 'No. I would have known,' she told Helena calmly. 'I'm sorry I gave you such a shock by fainting like that last night,' she added more prosaically. 'I think it must have been the effect of seeing him so unexpectedly on top of the champagne.'

'Well, it *was* a very emotional evening,' Helena responded.

'You've been so good to me,' Annie told her, lovingly reaching out to cover the older woman's hands with her own.

'Everything I've given to you you've given me back a thousandfold, Annie,' Helena told her lovingly. 'And you are going to give Bob and me our grandchildren,' Helena teased her, deliberately lightening the atmosphere before giving a small exclamation. 'Heavens! Bob! I promised I'd help him with our packing for this conference we're flying out to attend tomorrow. Never mind,' she added with a naughty grin. 'He's so much better at it than I am!'

Annie laughed. 'Four days in Rio de Janeiro... How wonderful.'

'Not as wonderful as you'd think,' Helena countered ruefully. 'The conference goes on for three days, and when you've taken time out for recovering from jet lag and for being dragged all over the place by Bob to see the local ruins...'

'Stop complaining,' Annie teased. 'You know you love it. When the three of us went to Rome last year *I* was the one who had to go back to the hotel for a rest!'

'Yes, that was wonderful, wasn't it?' Helena agreed, getting up off the bed as she told Annie tenderly, 'Don't rush to get up. You might *feel* fine but your body's still in shock.'

'It was just a faint, Helena, that's all,' Annie assured her friend, but she wasn't totally surprised when, later in the day, Helena insisted on driving her to the hospital so that she could be checked over.

'Mothers!' the junior house doctor wisecracked after he had given Annie the all-clear. 'They do love to fuss.'

'Don't they just?' Annie said with a grin, then blushed a little at the admiring looks the young man was giving her.

CHAPTER THREE

'Now, you're sure you're feeling all right?' Helena checked as Annie dropped her and Bob off at the airport.

'I'm fine. Stop fussing,' Annie told her with a good-natured smile as she hugged them both and kissed them goodbye. 'And to prove it I'm going to go home and make a start on that gardening I've been threatening to do for months.'

The garden of her small house was long and narrow, and enclosed at the back by a high brick wall which ensured her privacy but gave the garden a rather closed-in feel.

For Christmas, amongst the other gifts they had given her, Bob and Helena had given her a gardening book with some wonderful ideas plus a very generous gift voucher for a local garden centre, and Annie, who had been studying the book intently, had now come up with her own design for the garden based on the principles in the book.

The first thing she needed, she had decided, was some pretty coloured trellising to place against the walls, and so, after she had watched Bob and Helena's plane take off, she headed back to her car and drove towards the garden centre.

Several happy and productive hours later Annie climbed back into her car again. She had chosen and

ordered her trellising, and made arrangements for it
to be delivered, as well as getting from the man in
charge of the fencing department the telephone number of someone who would come out and fix it in
place for her.

As she started her car engine Annie was humming
happily to herself. It was a bright sunny day, a brisk
breeze sending fluffy white clouds scudding across
the sky, and on impulse, instead of taking the direct
route back to her own home, Annie opted instead to
head towards the river.

The prettily wooded countryside on the outskirts
·of the town was criss-crossed with narrow country
lanes, confusingly so at times—especially when one
descended down through the trees and lost sight of
the river, as she had just done, Annie recognised as
she came to an unmarked fork in the road and
paused, not quite sure which road to take.

Instinctively she wanted to take the right-hand
fork, even though logic told her the left must lead
down towards the river. With a small mental shrug
Annie gave in to instinct and then wondered just
what she had done as the road she had chosen nar-
rowed virtually to a single track, winding up a sharp
steep hillside banked with hedges so thick and high
it was impossible for her to gauge just where she
was. And yet even though she knew she had never
driven up it before Annie felt that the road was somehow familiar.

She gave a small gasp as she rounded a particularly sharp bend and saw in front of her the entrance
to a large Victorian house. On the top of each brick

gatepost was an odd metal sculpture. The sculptures were made from the harpoons used on the ships of the man who had built this house from the money he had made from his whaling fleet. And *how* had she known *that*? Annie wondered in bemusement as she stopped her car just inside the drive to the house and switched off the engine. She must have read it somewhere, she acknowledged. She had read avidly in the long months of her recovery, books on every subject under the sun, including some on the local history of the area.

And yet… Unsteadily she got out of her car, her heart starting to beat very fast as she walked towards the house. The rhododendrons flanking the drive obscured the sunlight, throwing out dark shadows so that when she actually stepped back into its full beam it dazzled and dizzied her, making her rock slightly on her feet and close her eyes, only to open them again as she felt something coming between her and the warmth of the sun.

'You!' she whispered, her whole body shivering in a mixture of shock and delight as she saw who was standing in front of her. 'It's you,' she whispered a second time, her eyes glowing with bemusement and happiness as she stepped towards the man who had come out of the house to stand in front of her.

Close to and in the daylight he was so exactly the man from her dreams that the awesome nature of the impulse that had brought her here to him held Annie motionless in an invisible bubble of iridescent joy.

It was true. She had been right. There *was* something fateful, fated about him…about them…

Her eyes focused on him, eagerly absorbing every detail of him and mentally checking them off against her own private blueprint. His eyes were exactly the same dark dramatic blue she had dreamed of, his skin the same taut sheeny tan, his hair the same inky almost blue-black. Everything about him was just as she had dreamed—*everything*. Even his mouth. Especially his mouth!

His *mouth*. Annie shivered in sensual delight as she looked at the hard male curve of his upper lip, the sensual promise of his much fuller lower one. If she closed her eyes she would be able to recreate the sensation of it closing over her own, hungrily coaxing her lips to part whilst he caressed them, filling her with his life's breath whilst she…

'So you came.'

His voice reverberated through her, its tone unexpectedly harsh, even a little terse, but wholly recognisable and familiar.

The intensity of her emotions made her shudder as violent spasms of recognition racked her. She had travelled such a long way to reach this moment, this heartbeat out of infinity.

'Yes,' she whispered in response, her voice cracking against the dryness of her throat. 'You…you knew that I would?' she asked, her emotions so heightened that she felt as though she had suddenly entered an extra dimension of awareness.

Behind him she could see the open door to the house. Beyond it, she knew, lay a large hallway, with a table on which would be a bronze of the man who had originally commissioned the house, and into the stairway that curled upwards from it would be carved all manner of sea creatures, both real and mythical; leaping dolphins, graceful whales, octopuses, sea horses and mermaids.

'I...' His voice sounded terse and strained, as though he too was aware of the enormity of what was happening, and as she looked at him and saw the way his gaze suddenly shifted, as though he couldn't quite meet her eyes, she was overwhelmed by a sudden flood of fiercely protective love.

Instinctively she moved towards him, her hand resting lightly on his arm as she whispered protectively, 'It's all right...everything's all right. I'm here. We're...'

Beneath her fingertips she could feel his muscles bunching, clenching, and as she looked up into his face she could see the tight white line of his mouth. Her own body registered the aftershock of what he was feeling in the rush of almost seismic shudders that jolted his body.

'Can we...can we go inside?' she asked him hesitantly.

The house drew her, compelling her to walk towards it. It was almost as though she knew it already, its shape, its rooms, its history, even its scent... Just as she knew *him*...

Now it was her turn to shudder and to tense, but she was already inside the hallway and he was right behind her, blocking out the light from the doorway.

'I never thought this could happen,' she told him simply as she let her dreamy-eyed gaze absorb the wonderful reality of him.

He was tall, much taller than her, but she had known that, and broad too. She already knew just how he would feel and look beneath that soft checked workshirt he was wearing, without those old faded jeans that hugged the taut strength of his thighs. There would be a small scar just inside the right thigh, a tiny indentation, the relic of a boyhood accident. She would place her lips to it and he...

She was trembling wildly now, unable to stop what she was feeling, what she was wanting. A shudder of almost orgasmic sensitivity ripped through her as she watched him. She loved him so much!

'Can we...can we go upstairs?' she asked him huskily, her eyes never leaving his face as she waited for his response.

It seemed a lifetime, an aeon before he replied, both his mouth and his voice oddly stiff as he eventually responded, 'If that's what you want.'

'Yes,' she told him boldly. 'Yes, it is...what I want.' *I want...I want you. I love you.* She ached to tell him, but events were moving too fast to give her time to make such an emotional statement.

Instead...

She started to release his arm and turn towards the stairs, and then, impetuously, she reached up and touched his face with her fingertips, absorbing through them the longed for human warmth, the human reality of his skin, not a dream lover's flesh any more but that of a real man, a real lover.

Although he was clean shaven she could feel the rasp of his skin where he shaved, a prickle of such intense maleness against the acute female sensitivity of her own fingertips that she almost cried out in the raw shock of it, snatching her fingers away as though they had been burned, her eyes wide and dark, almost haunted as she looked up to his.

'You want me,' he said rawly. But it was a statement rather than a question. Still Annie nodded her head, mute, dumb, now that the final moment, the final acknowledgement of what lay between them, of what fate had ordained for them, was actually here.

Her glance darted over his face as nervous as that of a woodland fawn. His eyes…navy blue now, and smouldering with heat; his cheekbones…taut and hard where the flesh stretched across them, his mouth…

She felt giddy, dizzy with the force of her own longing. The silence, the tension between them stretched out like the thinnest of ice over the deepest, coldest and most dangerous water there could be, inviting only the most reckless, only the most foolhardy, to dare its danger.

'Come here,' he commanded her with soft force.

Immediately she did so, closing the gap between them as she moved, almost swayed into the burning inferno of his body heat, the breath driven out of her lungs in a soft, yearning gasp of delirious pleasure as his arms finally closed around her and she turned her face up to his for his kiss, her own lips so soft, swollen, parting with moist longing.

'Oh, yes… Yes… You want me…'

She heard him etch out the sharp, stingingly sensuous words against her mouth, his voice creamy with satisfaction and male pride as his arms made a tight, imprisoning band around her and he bent her back over them, so that the cradle of her pelvis was thrust up tight against his own body.

And then his mouth finally came down on hers in a kiss that her shocked senses registered as being so raw and branding, so determined to imprint on her his stamp of possession, so intent on taking her and breaking her in the most primitive of man to woman embraces that she almost sobbed aloud in an appeal for his awareness of her vulnerability, her lack of experience, her unknowingness. And yet in some confusing way she *did* know, did recognise.

'Was that good?' she heard him asking her in a low, satisfied voice when he finally released her kiss-bitten mouth, and then, before she could answer, before she could move, he was lowering his head again, to make the same hot, mouth-biting love assault on the erect peak of her nipple, his fingers expertly pushing her clothes out of the way of one soft sweetly pink-apexed breast whilst his lips, too hungry to wait, eagerly caressed the other through the thin fabric of her bra and shirt.

For a moment Annie felt almost as though she was going to die from the shock of pleasure that sheeted through her, its intensity such that it made her catch her breath and feel as though her life itself was momentarily held in suspension. Behind her closed eyelids she could see the same brilliant whiteness she remembered from her moment of near-death: pure, burning, intense, soul-touching...like the very best kind of love itself.

Quickly she opened her eyes and focused on his

downbent raven-dark head. The warm flesh of his
exposed nape was a tantalising contradiction of his
stance towards her and her reaction back to him, that
of a man to a woman at its most sensually intense.
That exposed nape was so very much that of a vulnerable boy, a child...the child they would one day
have...

Immediately Annie tensed, as though somehow
something had touched an exposed raw nerve within
her memory. The pain, initially so intense that it had
shocked her into protective immobility, was fading
now, but it still had the power to frighten her.

'What is it? Not second thoughts?' he was asking
her almost brusquely as his lips relinquished possession of her nipple and he lifted his head to look in
her eyes.

In his own there was something, an expression, a
darkness, that made her look away from him.
Somewhere deep within her a pain, a *wariness* was
stirring, but she quickly suppressed it. Nothing...
nothing...could be allowed to spoil this special *magical* coming together. Nothing!

'I...' she began slowly, wanting to find the words
to tell him how she was feeling, to ask him to help
her smother the sharp needle of pain she could feel
threatening her, to disarm it of its potential harm.

But instead of listening to her he shook his head
and said smoothly, 'I thought you wanted us to go
to bed. You *do* want that, don't you, Annie?'

Annie! He knew her *name*. Her heart slammed
fiercely against her ribs, her whole body convulsed
by the sweetly searing surge of her shock.

'I…I want us to make love…' she managed to tell him shakily, before adding breathlessly, so that he would know that her intuition, her knowingness, her acknowledgement of their shared fate matched his, 'Upstairs…in the room…the room…'

'I know which one,' he assured her, and if her ears thought they had caught a rough, searing note of anger beneath the sensual smoothness of his low-toned voice she quickly assured herself that she had to have imagined it.

They walked upstairs together, one step at a time, her body pressed close to his, his arm around her as she leaned helplessly into him. On the half-landing she stopped, automatically gazing through the window towards the river.

'This house was built by a whaling captain,' she told him huskily.

'Yes, I know,' he agreed tersely, his arm dropping momentarily away from her.

'I…I dream about it sometimes,' she told him, searching carefully for the right words to tell him what she had experienced. 'About…the room… and…and about you…'

Without saying anything else she moved back into the protection of his body, only realising that she had been holding her breath a little nervously when his arm finally rose and held her.

They had reached the top of the stairs and were standing in the doorway to the room before he said the words that made her heart turn somersaults of joy inside her body.

'I dream of you too.'

He dreamed of *her*. She *wasn't* alone in her be-lief…her recognition. Flooded with joy, she turned to him, holding his arm with her hand as she de-manded, 'You recognised me, then, the other night…in the restaurant?'

The abrupt, almost reluctant inclination of his head he gave in assent made her ache with female protec-tiveness. He felt embarrassed, almost afraid to reveal his vulnerability to her. Oh, how much she loved him. How wonderful it was that they had found one another.

'It's going to be so good,' she told him tenderly. '*We* are going to be so good…'

Inside the room everything was just as she had dreamed. The large windows with the view of the drop down to the river and the fields and hills on the other side of it. The floor, wooden, polished, bare. The walls, bare too; the windows with their filmy ethereal curtaining. The bed…

Annie shivered as she saw it, unable to take her gaze off it as her eyes widened and focused unblink-ingly on the oh, so familiar iron bedstead. Unlike hers, this, she knew immediately, was original. Very slowly and gently she reached out and touched the frame at the foot of the bed. The metal felt warm to her touch, warm and worn slightly with age. The bed was bigger than hers, much bigger, and piled high with creamy white traditional linen bedding. As she reached down and smoothed the edge of one of the covers she could almost smell the scent of lavender being released by her touch.

'This bed…' she began, dry-mouthed.

'It's a marriage bed,' he told her quickly, and she could almost taste the bitterness in his voice. But before she could question it, turning to him, her eyes quickening with surprise, he was reaching for her, the fierceness, the immediacy of his desire surprising her. She had expected passion, intensity, and even male possessiveness, but this fierce, heated *now*ness he was exhibiting, this silent, hungry concentrated way in which he was reaching for her, holding her…

'Open your mouth. Kiss me properly. You know how,' she could hear him insisting rawly as the fierce, biting intensity of his own kisses threatened to bruise the already swollen softness of her own mouth.

But willingly she complied, wanting only the pleasure she knew she would have in pleasing him. Her breath was drawn into his mouth, mingling with his in a small sobbing moan of acquiescence as he started to imitate the hot, pulsing tide she could feel within her own body, and within his, with small, pulsating thrusts of his tongue. Somehow they were undressing, her own fingers revealing a dexterity, a knowledge she hadn't guessed they possessed.

There was nothing for her to fear, of course. From her dreams she already knew him as he knew her. In them there was not a curve, a corner of one another's bodies they had not explored and enjoyed.

Even so… A fine shudder of female nervousness and shyness ran through her. The merest delicate frisson of sensation, but she knew he could feel it, knew that it was transmitting itself to him where his fingertips touched her flesh.

'You're afraid…'

He made it sound almost as though the thought of her fear pleased him, and Annie's tension increased.

'No,' she denied, her body and her eyes suddenly softening as she told him lovingly, 'How could I ever be afraid…with you?'

It was as though somehow she had unleashed a catalyst, a power, a primitive force that was beyond the control of either of them, because suddenly he had picked her up and was carrying her to the bed, kneeling over her as he laid her down on it, his eyes hot and dark, the colour and heat of a tropical night sky, the flesh of his face drawn so tightly over his bones that she felt compelled to reach out and touch it…him…

A primal sound, a groan, a warning growl, a low, mating purr—Annie did not know which—rasped deep in his throat as he turned his mouth to her hand, nibbling at the tender flesh on the mound of Venus beneath the base of her thumb.

Quivers of hot cataclysmic pleasure melted through her.

'Yes… Yes… Oh, yes,' she heard herself moaning as he continued to undress her, her body arching, moving to accommodate the increasing speed of his hands as the hot ache deep within her flesh manifested itself in a series of revealing uncoordinated jerky movements when she tried to get closer and closer to him. If she closed her eyes she could feel his heat, sense his need. Deep within her mind she already knew his possession, knew the hot, silken sheathed reality of him, the taut, urgent thrust of his body within her own.

A quiver, an ache, a wild yearning need possessed her.

'I want you. I want you,' she told him recklessly over and over again as her own eager fingers tore buttons from their buttonholes, eagerly pushing away the too intrusive fabric of his clothes where they came between them.

In the enclosed cocoon of the bed under the gradual darkening of the evening sky beyond the window she could smell his scent, her nostrils dilating as she deliberately nuzzled closer to him, wanting to absorb more of it…of him…

His chest, where his shirt had fallen open to reveal it, was tanned and taut with muscles, its hard male planes softened with a silky shimmering of fine body hair, so fine, so male, so *him* that it made her fingertips quiver just to touch it, to touch him. She could feel his muscles contracting beneath his skin where she touched him, and her hands spread out in fascinated female delight to span the power of his chest in response to the mute invitation he was giving her. His nipples, dark hard nubs of flesh, puckered into hot hard points of arousal when she touched them, and on a sudden wanton impulse she touched her fingers to her own lips and then to his body, circling each nipple deliberately with her moist fingertips and watching the way his body jerked in fierce quick spasms of reaction.

'Annie stop—you don't know what you're doing to me…' he began, and then groaned. And although

Annie heard the words, and registered the male pride and desire they carried, she was too lost in the pleasure of what she was doing to heed them.

If she were to touch him with her mouth where she had just touched him with her fingers would he…? She bent her head towards him and gasped in shock as he suddenly manacled her wrists with his own hands, pushing her down against the bed whilst he leaned over her.

His jeans, the jeans *she* had unfastened, had moved lower on his hips, revealing the immaculate white flash of his underwear and with it the visibly open evidence of his desire for her.

Annie found that her mouth had suddenly gone very dry and that her body was tensing, aching…wanting. The tremors of need shuddering through her were so intense that she knew he must see them as plainly as she could see him, see them, know them, take pleasure in them…as she was doing in all the signs there were of his arousal and response to her.

Even in her dreams it hadn't been like this, hadn't had this intensity, this needing, this knowing, this immediacy, and she knew without knowing how she knew that her dreams had only been a pale shadow of what would be reality.

'You want me,' he repeated, and as she smiled at him Annie suddenly felt so powerful, so womanly, so desirous and desirable, that when he released her hands it was the most natural, the most beautiful act in the world for her to stand up, reach out and tug down his jeans, her gaze lifting to his, meshing with his as her hands slid over his thighs towards the white glimmer of fabric that kept him hidden from her.

And then, when just for a heartbeat she hesitated, she heard him growling fiercely, 'Do it… Do it…'

His words were both a command and a plea, and a teasing female smile curled Annie's mouth as she moved to obey them. But it was a smile that died away, wiped out by the rolling flood of emotions that stormed her when she finally saw him naked.

Dreams were…just dreams. And *this* was…*he* was…reality. A small, sharp sob escaped her as mingled pain and pleasure arced through her, and without thinking what she was doing she made to wrap her arms around him, to rest her face against him, the tears of emotion that were clouding her eyes spilling over onto his skin.

'No.' The sharp rejection in his voice shocked and bewildered her as he started to thrust her away.

But the look on his face as she looked enquiringly towards him, searching his expression for an explanation of his rejection, locked her own breath in her throat and made her heart hammer so furiously with reciprocal emotion that she couldn't even begin to articulate what she wanted to say.

She forgot the tight grip of his hands on her arms, forgot too the initial thrust of rejection and shock she had felt when he had first given that harsh cry of denial. In a face that was bleached of all its colour his eyes glittered with such a look of raw torment that Annie couldn't drag her gaze away from them.

It was, she recognised, like looking into his soul

and seeing laid bare there all of man's strongest and most self-weakening emotions. Pain, anguish, anger, longing, need. She could see them all, and as she witnessed his vulnerability Annie felt her heart melt with love and tenderness towards him.

Why he should be exhibiting such strong and in so many ways contradictory emotions she had no idea. What she did know, though, was that he needed her comfort and her compassion, and automatically she reached out to him, wanting to give them to him, wanting to wrap him protectively in her love, to soothe and reassure him.

Emotional tears of protective love filled her eyes as Annie stood body to body with him.

'I love you,' she told him softly. 'I've always loved you and I always will.'

Something flashed in his eyes, an emotion, a response so brief and intense that it was gone before Annie could seize on it to recognise it, but she could hear the fury in his voice as he stepped back from her, demanding savagely, 'How can you say that?'

He was angry...questioning her love. Why, when he must know as deeply as she did, that...?

'You don't want me?' she questioned him shakily, her mouth starting to tremble and her face colouring. He gave a brief look at his own self-betraying body before telling her with raw sensuality, 'Does it look like I don't? Of course I damned well *want* you,' he told her savagely. 'And you want me too, don't you, Annie? Oh, yes, you want me.' He answered his own question, his voice as thick and soft as cream as he took control of the situation from her, reaching for her and drawing her into his arms, his kiss so delicate and tender, so tantalising and erotic that beneath her breath Annie gave a small moan of female longing, instinctively pressing her body as close to his as she could get it, revelling in the hot, silken naked feeling of his flesh against her own, shivering, shuddering as she responded helplessly to her own need for him.

Just to be with him like this, to be free to see, smell, touch the reality of him, not just dream about him.

Her feelings threatened to overwhelm her with such a flood of wanting that she had to close her eyes, her body suddenly so weak, powerless to resist the eroticism of her own thoughts.

'Oh, yes, you want me,' she heard him saying thickly to her with soft male satisfaction as he licked and nuzzled her skin. 'You want me and you're going to have me, Annie. All of me...all of me whilst *I* take all of you...'

It was everything she had dreamed of and more. A hot, silken, perfect meshing of limbs and mouths and then ultimately of the very essence of their two selves.

She had dreamed so often of this intimacy, had thought she had known all there was to know of it, and in many ways she did—in many ways she knew him so well already that her body was perfectly prepared for him, perfectly ready and eager. But in others...

A soft moan of pleasure escaped her lips as she looked down at their entwined bodies through half-closed eyes to watch as he moved up, over her and then within her quickly, but not before a staccato of gasps of shocked ecstasy as she saw how big he was, how perfectly he filled her, saw how wonderful…how good…how meant to be they looked together. And then she was past thinking, past observing, past *anything* other than simply being, responding, loving.

Adoringly Annie raised her face towards his, her lips parting for his kiss, her hands reaching out to draw him closer as he seemed to hesitate. Each thrust of his body within her own took her, drove her towards the wonderful rainbow-coloured place that was just so tantalisingly out of reach. And then suddenly it was there, and she was a part of it, transmuted by love and passion into a quicksilver explosion of heat and pleasure as he took her through the rainbow to a place beyond it, a sphere, a universe, a love-produced paradise of pleasure she had never, ever imagined existed.

As the final echoes of her orgasm slowly faded away Annie stretched luxuriously, so dizzy with happiness that it was impossible for her to find the words to say how she felt. Instead she simply reached out and lovingly touched his face with her fingertips, her eyes huge and dark with emotion, her mouth trembling.

'I love you so much,' she told him chokily. 'I hadn't realised… You were just a dream to me before…before…' she added huskily. 'And I thought that my dreams were so wonderful, so perfect that they would be impossible to match, but now…you've shown me just how far short of reality my dreams really were.' And then, her eyes filling with love-induced tears, she reached for his hand, tenderly placing it against her lips as she whispered a tremulous, 'Thank you. Thank you so much my love…my true love…my only love…'

If it hurt a little that he didn't return her words of love to him with his own to her, Annie reminded herself that he had just *shown* her how he felt, just physically revealed his emotions, his love, and that men were notoriously shy of putting their emotions into words.

Her last thought before she fell asleep was that she was the most fortunate woman who had ever lived.

As he looked down into Annie's peacefully sleeping face, Dominic Carlyle wondered grimly how she could possibly sleep so peacefully, so apparently guiltlessly and innocently.

Angrily he turned away from her and reached for his discarded clothes.

Well, *she* might be sleeping happily, but there was no way he could. What on earth had possessed him? She no longer meant anything to him emotionally. How could she? His eyes closed, his mouth momentarily compressing as he had an unwanted memory of the look in her eyes just before she had finally fallen asleep, worn out by their lovemaking…just after she had made that extraordinary gesture of reaching for his hand. He swallowed fiercely. It had just been a piece of play-acting, that was all, like everything she had done. It had to have been—there was no other way he could either understand or account for her extraordinary behaviour.

As he walked naked towards the bedroom door, his discarded clothes in one hand, he paused to turn his head and look back towards the bed and Annie's sleeping figure. She was lying facing him, her body curled up as though it was still curled against his own. A savagely contemptuous smile twisted his mouth. Even in her sleep she had to go on pretending... *Why? What* had made her do it? All that idiotic stuff about fate she had come out with...all that... Quickly he stopped, reminding himself that there was only one way he was going to find out the truth and that was by asking Annie herself.

As he opened the bedroom door and headed for a spare room he was shaking his head, wondering how on earth she had the gall to do what she had done. To simply walk back into his life and behave as though nothing had happened...as though the intervening years had never been.

CHAPTER FOUR

IRRITABLY Dominic sat up in bed and reached for his watch. Four o'clock in the morning. There was no way he was going to be able to get back to sleep. He felt too on edge, too charged up, his mind too full of anger and memories.

He had scarcely been able to believe it when he had seen Annie in the restaurant where he was being wined and dined by the executives of Petrofiche, in celebration of his acceptance of the position they had offered him as consultant marine biologist, and then, when she had actually arrived at the house…

Had she known that he was coming back? He had never intended to keep the house, but his work in the Middle East had kept him out of the country and it had made sense for him to let the house rather than try to sell it at a time when property prices had been in steep decline. And then, when he had finally acknowledged that he would be an idiot to turn down what he knew would be a dream-come-true career opportunity simply because it would bring him back to the place where he had first met Annie, he had acknowledged that it made sense to move back into the house himself now that the tenants had left.

How on earth had she, Annie, been able to walk back into his life like that? And not just his life. His body started to heat as he remembered the intensity of their recent lovemaking. No, not lovemaking, he corrected himself sternly. What *they* had just shared…what they had just *done*…had simply been an act of release. Sex…that was all. Annie… He closed his eyes, his mouth sad.

She had behaved tonight, talked tonight, as though… As though *what*? He moved uncomfortably in the bed, the bedclothes an irritating reminder of the softness of her against his naked skin, an unwanted reminder… All that rubbish she had spoken about fate and loving him. She couldn't possibly have expected him to believe… She couldn't possibly have thought…

Throwing back the bedclothes, he swung his feet to the floor and then walked naked across to the window. Like those of the bedroom he had left Annie in, it looked out across land secluded enough for him not to need to worry about his nakedness.

Annie!

It was almost exactly five years since they had first met. She had been eighteen and he had been a decade older, but of the two he had been more vulnerable, the one who had fallen so deeply, so intensely in love with her, virtually at first sight, that he had followed her back to the cheap boarding house where she'd been staying.

She had been confused and wary when he had first approached her, trying to appear worldly and in control of the situation and yet in reality coming across as so adorably unsure of herself that he had ached to take hold of her and protect her, to warn her against the danger of allowing herself to be so attracted to a man like himself.

It had taken him several days of constant visits and patient cajoling to persuade her to go out with him, and then only to a coffee bar, where she had insisted on them sitting at a table in the window. He remembered that whilst a part of him had applauded her caution another, the more deeply male predatory part of him, had known that the place he really wanted to be with her was somewhere much more private. But, since he was not in reality a caveman, he had acceded to her uncertain nervous insistence that they stay somewhere public.

They had talked on that first date of a wide variety of different things, the single hour he had coaxed out of her stretching to nearly four, plus the long, long walk back to her boarding house, where he had extracted a promise from her that she would see him again.

Falling in love with any woman, never mind an eighteen-year-old just on the verge of her adult life and her first term at university, had been so very much not a part of his plans for his life that his feelings for Annie had totally confused and shocked him.

Prior to meeting her he had signed a contract committing him to work in the Middle East for the sultan of a small Arab state. In career terms it had been a wonderful, once-in-a-lifetime opportunity—and one he had eagerly accepted.

The few months he had had at his disposal before his departure for the Middle East he had intended to use dealing with the practicalities of letting out his

Wryminster house during his absence and then visiting a few friends who lived in various parts of the country.

Logic had urged him to sell the house—it was far too large for one single man—but, like Annie, he had no close family. The house had come to him via an inheritance from an elderly great-aunt, and out of sentiment he'd felt that he wanted to keep it.

Grimly he turned away from the window.

He had known within a week of meeting Annie that he was recklessly and irreversibly in love with her, and within two that he had no option other than to marry her, much as his conscience had urged him not to do so.

She had been young...too young for the kind of commitment marriage entailed and too inexperienced to judge what kind of a man she really wanted to share her life with. But she had also been alone, and vulnerable, and he had ached with pain at the fear of rejection and aloneness he had seen in her eyes when he had gently told her that he was shortly to leave the country. And the truth was that he had wanted, needed, to commit himself to her just as much as she had seemed to want him to.

The love she had claimed to have for him had turned out to be nothing more than a teenager's infatuation. Was she to blame for mistaking it for something more or was he?

Angrily he started to frown. What was he doing? Even now he was still looking for excuses for her...explanations... Why?

She might only have been a very young woman,

but she must have known that he was not a young boy and that his feelings...his love... She had to have known—but that hadn't stopped her walking out on him without any explanation, without giving him the opportunity to talk to her...to... To what...? To persuade her to stay?

He had been over and over this argument with himself so many, many times before, and he still wasn't any closer to resolving it. If he had been at fault in rushing her into a marriage then surely she too had been at fault for not telling him that she had made a mistake and that she wanted it to end. That way... That way—what? That way he would have used the power of the sexual passion between them to persuade her to change her mind? Would he have done that? Or would he have been able to be strong enough to put her needs above his own and let her go?

He liked to believe he would have done the latter, but perhaps Annie had been afraid he would opt for the former and she would not be able to resist him or the intensity of their shared desire for one another.

And about that there had been no mistake, no error. He had never experienced anything like it before her and certainly never, ever after. But then after Annie he had never wanted to. After Annie that part of his life, that part of him...

Grittily he reminded himself as he recognised and redirected his thoughts. He had brought her back to this house for the first time after a long walk by the river. He had promised to take her back to her lodgings and had fully intended to keep that promise. But then it had started to rain heavily just as they were within yards of the house. Neither of them had had a coat and it had made sense for him to bring her here.

She had been open-mouthed with awe at the sight and size of the house, and he had seen the anxiety and defensiveness in her eyes as she had protested that her wet shoes would mark the polished floor. He had seen, too, and been hurt for her by her obvious feelings of inferiority. In order to try to relax her he had started to tell her something about the house's history and its original owner.

He remembered how fascinated she had been by the dolphins, tracing their delicate carvings with one forefinger, her eyes shining with delight as she turned her face up to exclaim excitedly to him about their beauty.

That had been when he had given in to his feelings for her, totally unable to resist his longing to take her in his arms and love her.

She had been a virgin when he had first made love with her. A girl. But it hadn't been a girl he had made love with earlier this evening. No, now she was a woman…all woman… He could feel his body starting to tense, to react. When she had buried her face against him and started to caress him…

Dominic made a savage low growl deep in his throat, but nothing could stem his memories now.

After their soaking during their walk he had insisted that she stay and have dinner with him.

'What would you most like to have to eat?' he

asked her, and she went shy and self-conscious again, shaking her head and looking adorably uncertain.

He had noticed whenever he took her out for a meal that she always looked to him for guidance before choosing from the menu, but it wasn't until he pressed her for a decision on what she would like on this occasion, explaining that they would need to go out and shop before he could cook for them, that she admitted that her upbringing had not prepared her for the kind of sophisticated lifestyle he enjoyed.

Previously she had talked briefly about her childhood, but that evening she was a good deal more forthcoming—due, he decided, to the potency of the very good wine he had bought to serve with the meal he intended to prepare for them.

His own parents had died when he was young, so their lack of a mother was something they shared. But his grandparents had been comparatively wealthy, and although he had found their care distant, and his life at boarding school formal and regimented, he had never, he recognised, been in the position that Annie was in, of having to be financially self-supporting.

After her admission that she wasn't either familiar or entirely comfortable with the lifestyle he obviously took for granted he was tenderly protective of her when he took her round the up-market delicatessen he drove them to so that they could shop for their evening meal. It touched him to watch her eyes rounding in awe as he picked the ingredients for their evening meal.

It both amused him and brought out in him an

almost paternal instinct he hadn't known he possessed to watch her face as they toured the food store
and he discreetly explained to her what the wide variety of cosmopolitan delicacies were and how they
were cooked and eaten.

'But who will cook it?' she asked him uncertainly
at one point.

Guessing what she was thinking, he quickly reassured her, 'I shall.'

And so he did.

Prior to meeting Annie he had considered himself
to be a confirmed bachelor, a man whose main attention, whose concentration, was focused on his career. It had been his dream from boyhood to be a
marine biologist, and thus to follow in the footsteps
of his parents, who had worked and died together in
a freak accident off the coast of Mauritius.

He liked women. Of course he did. But he con-
fined his activities to those members of the female
sex sophisticated enough to understand that he simply wasn't looking for a committed permanent relationship.

With Annie, though, his feelings had done a complete turnaround. He didn't just want her in his *bed*,
he wanted her permanently in his life.

They came back here with the food they had
bought, and true to his promise he cooked for her,
loving the way her eyes rounded with innocent
delight when he spoon-fed her little tastes of what he
was preparing.

'Aren't *you* hungry?' she asked him naïvely at one
point.

'Only for you,' he returned, watching the way she had blushed, almost dizzy with the intensity of his own desire.

After dinner they went into the drawing room, where he coaxed her to talk about her hopes and her dreams in between feeding her sips of champagne and strawberries covered in rich dark chocolate.

When she had finished eating one, with tiny, delicate little bites, there was a small fleck of chocolate left on her deliciously full upper lip. Unable to resist, he leaned forward to brush it away, smoothing his thumb over her mouth and feeling his body throb deep down inside in reaction to every tiny little tremble of her mouth. When he had dropped his hands to her face, cupping it to hold her still whilst he lowered his head to kiss her, she focused on him with a wide-eyed stare mingled with longing and uncertainty.

'It's all right,' he soothed her gently. 'I'm not going to hurt you…'

Him hurt *her*! Now, Dominic grimaced. What a joke! But he had never dreamed then what was going to happen. She had seemed so naïve, so adorably sweet and loving.

He had taken her to bed for the first time a month after they had met, coaxing her to shed her inhibitions along with her clothes, but in the end he had been the one who had come closest to losing total control, unable to hold back what he was feeling as he touched her, unable to stop himself from smothering the delicate soft-fleshed curves of her body with hungry, passionate kisses.

Six weeks after he had first met her they were married, and two weeks after that she had left him.

He had been totally honest with her from the start about the fact that he was due to take up his new job in the Gulf within a few weeks, and he had told her too, when he had finally persuaded her to marry him, that there was no way he could possibly take her with him.

'So…so how long will you be gone for?' she asked him bravely.

'Well, my contract is for three years. But,' he hurried on quickly when he saw her expression, 'I do get plenty of leave. For instance I will be home over Christmas for a month, and then again in the summer for two. After all, you've got your degree to get and the time will soon pass.'

'Are you really sure you want to marry me?' she asked him.

'Of course I'm sure,' he responded, not realising then that she was the one with the doubts.

'Are you really, really sure you want to marry me?' she pressed him urgently, on another occasion, and again he didn't recognise the cue she was giving him, didn't understand that she wanted him to ask if *she* really wanted to marry *him*.

Instead he told her firmly, 'Of course I am. I love you.'

'But we're so different,' she continued.

'Yes,' he agreed teasingly. 'You're a woman and I'm a man.'

'No, you know what I mean,' she insisted, flushing a little as she told him,

'At the home they taught us that it's the person you are that matters, and I know that that's true, but other people still do judge and our backgrounds are so very different—I...I don't even know who my parents were, and—'

He stopped her then, insisting, 'None of that matters.'

'Yes, it does,' she contradicted him. 'Your friends...your lifestyle...'

'*You* will be my life from now on, Annie,' he overruled her.

'You say that, but you're not going to be here,' Annie reminded him bleakly.

'I have to go. You know that,' Dominic told her, his voice slightly harsh with his own awareness of how much he was going to miss her.

'Yes,' she agreed quietly, and Dominic cursed himself inwardly, firstly for being responsible for her pain and secondly for his own selfishness.

He had, after all, known right from the start of his own unbreakable commitment to his Middle Eastern contract.

He tried to console her. 'It won't be so bad. I know it's going to be difficult for both of us, but other couples manage to survive such separations.'

'Yes,' Annie agreed, even more bleakly, before adding huskily, 'Sometimes I wonder if I'm destined always to be alone.'

'You aren't going to be alone,' Dominic instantly insisted, but her eyes remained shadowed.

'Perhaps it's easier not to have such strong feelings, not to love someone too much,' she whispered to him sadly later on.

Had it been then that she had started to distance herself from him? But she had seemed so happy when they had married, so much in love with him. Or had he, unforgivably, somehow assumed that his ten years' seniority over her had given him the right to know what was best for her?

The intervening years had changed him, he was forced to concede, as had the emotional pain he had suffered. And, whilst he knew he could never understand how Annie had been able to walk out on him without any kind of explanation, the bitterness he had originally felt had changed to a more rational acceptance. But a part of him still needed to have answers to the question she had left in his life.

His thoughts switched back to the past. Annie had married him. There had been formalities that had had to be dealt with, of course—authorities to be notified of their marriage, that kind of thing, and even the rings he had bought for her had had to be sent away to be altered because her fingers were so delicate and narrow.

He had carried her up to bed the first night of their marriage and he had made love to her with the windows flung wide open so that they could hear the soft whisper of the night and the river.

Their loving had been so intense that she had cried out, a sharp, high keening sound of female pleasure which had echoed on the stillness of the night. And for a heartbeat of time, or so it had seemed to Dominic, time itself had seemed to stand still, as though in awed recognition of the intensity of their love.

Afterwards she had cried, and his own eyes had been damp with emotion as well. But the closer it had got to the date for his departure, the more sad-eyed and withdrawn she had become, and mingled with his own agony at the thought of leaving her had been his guilt at the knowledge that he was responsible for her pain, that he had been the one to persuade her into marriage. And then had come the night when they had had their first and fateful argument.

It had been a sultry day, and his own temper had been on a short fuse. He had been dreading leaving her, and the thought had even begun to cross his mind that he might *have* to break his contract with the Sultan and look for work closer to home. But where? One of the oil companies operating in the North Sea?

In the Gulf he would be in charge of a team of divers and biologists hired by the Sultan to check on the effect of pollution on the area's seabed and life-forms. It was a golden, once-in-a-lifetime, opportunity to be part of the kind of research anyone in his position would have dreamed about. It was his intention to publish a paper on his discoveries once his work for the Sultan was completed, and he knew that if he turned his back on this opportunity he would never get another one like it.

But he still hated the thought of leaving Annie. For the past three days she had been crying in her sleep at night, and there was a tension between them that both of them seemed powerless to defuse.

Annie had been due to start her first term at university the week after he'd left, and on that particular day, in an attempt to give them both something else to think about other than his imminent departure, he had spent the evening discussing with her the career options that would be open to her once she had obtained her degree.

'I'm not sure I want to take up my university place any more,' she told him quietly. 'After all, we're married now, and…well…once we have children—'

'Children!' Dominic interrupted her blankly. The issue of whether or not they would have a family was not one they had as yet discussed. The experience of his own upbringing—his childhood belief that he wasn't important to his parents versus his now adult recognition of the demands their work had placed on them both—had forced him to acknowledge that not every adult was up to the huge responsibilities that being a parent meant, and to question whether or not he was himself.

Now he saw that Annie had a completely different viewpoint from his own, and he knew that he had to make her understand that they both needed time to adjust to their relationship to one another before they even began to discuss whether or not they would make good parents.

Certainly there was no question of them having a child whilst he was committed to his current contract. No way did he want a child to suffer through him in the way he had done as a boy—oh, no, no way!

'You don't want children?' she exclaimed in shock. 'But…but why not?'

'No. No, I don't,' he confirmed sharply.

'But why not?' Annie demanded, and Dominic cursed himself for the pain and disbelief he could hear in her voice, setting out as gently as he could to explain his feelings to her.

'Parenthood isn't just about having a baby, Annie. It's...' Desperately he struggled to find the right words. 'It's a very big responsibility. When we create a child we aren't just giving it life, we're giving it...*burdening* it, if you like, with ourselves...with our own personal history. And at the moment I feel that just isn't something I would want to burden a child with. We've got one another...isn't that enough?' he beseeched her, adding almost desperately as he saw the look in her eyes, 'I married you for you, Annie, and not for...for children.'

'Yes, I know,' she agreed, her voice becoming almost pleading as she added huskily, 'But sometimes things happen...a baby is conceived without being planned and...'

'No way...not for us,' Dominic denied immediately. 'I don't...' He stopped, then asked her gently, 'What are we arguing for? After all, there's no way you could be pregnant.'

One of the first things he had done, the very first time they had made love, was to assure her that she need have no fear of him being careless about contraception, and he had been touched and amused when, just before their marriage, Annie had hesitantly confided to him that she had read that sex could be more pleasurable for both of them if he did not have to...to 'use anything', and that because of that *she* had taken the responsibility for contraception into her own hands.

He had let her do it, partly because, if he was honest, he was just as eager to be inside her, skin to skin, flesh to flesh, as she was to have him there without a protective barrier between them.

'We can't have any accidents, Annie,' he reinforced firmly.

'But if we did?' she persisted with unusual stubbornness.

He frowned as he looked at her. Her face was flushed and her eyes unexpectedly determined as well as anxious. It was unlike her to argue with him, and the last thing he felt like doing when they had so little time left together was to argue about a hypothetical pregnancy. He rubbed his temple, where a pounding headache had been irritating him all day.

'*If* we did,' he told her tersely, 'then of course we would do the sensible thing, take the only reasonable option, and have the pregnancy terminated.'

'An abortion!' She gasped and went white. 'You mean you would want me to destroy our baby...to *kill* it...?'

'Annie, for God's sake stop being so emotional,' he demanded short-temperedly. 'When the time comes we can sit down together and discuss starting a family rationally and sensibly. Until that time does come, though, it would be crazy...impossible for us to have a child. Look at you,' he taunted her. 'You're still practically one yourself...'

'I wasn't a child when you wanted to take me to bed—or to marry me,' Annie immediately pointed out stiffly. 'And this is *my* body we're talking about. *Mine*, not yours. And I can tell you, Dominic, there's no way I could ever, ever destroy our child. And if you tried to make me then...then...'

'Then what?' Dominic demanded in exasperation. The ache in his head had gone from a single angry pounding to a pain that was jangling his already overstretched nerves to a rising crescendo so intense that he was having to grit his teeth to prevent himself from complaining about it.

'Then I'd leave you,' Annie told him flatly.

'Leave me? For God's sake, don't be so ridiculous, so childish,' he fumed. 'We've been married less than a month, Annie. You *aren't* pregnant, and...'

'But *if* I were? *If* I were you'd make me have a termination? Right?' she persisted emotionally.

Dominic sighed. 'It would be impossible for us to have a child right now.'

'Impossible? *Why?* Because *you* don't want one? Because—?'

'You know the position I'm in,' Dominic interrupted her shortly. 'I've got my career to think of, Annie, and...'

'Oh, yes, your *career*... I mustn't forget *that* must I?' she demanded, her eyes filling with tears. 'Nothing, *no one* must interfere with your precious career, must they Dominic?'

He guessed then—or at least he thought he had guessed—what was really wrong. Like him, she was dreading their imminent parting, and immediately his heart softened.

'Come here,' he commanded huskily, reaching for

her. But to his chagrin, instead of responding, instead of running to him and flinging herself into his arms, as he had expected, she deliberately took a step back from him, her face and her body freezing with disdain.

'Sex…is that *all* you can think about, Dominic? Well, I'm sorry, but I'm just not in the mood.'

And with that she stalked off, leaving him openmouthed, torn between anger and amusement.

He hadn't seen her display such haughtiness before, nor such obstinacy, he reflected later, when she refused all the tentative attempts he made to coax her back into a more loving frame of mind, and in the end, irritated both by what he considered to be her childishness and his own headache, he shrugged his shoulders, telling her pithily, 'If I were you, Annie, before I thought about having a child I would check on my own maturity…or lack of it!'

That night for the first time since their marriage they slept without touching. Several times Dominic was tempted to reach out and take hold of her, to end their discord by telling her how much he loved her and how much he was dreading being apart from her. But he had a stubborn streak of his own, and an even more well-hidden vulnerability as well, and a part of him needed to have her to be the one to turn to him, to tell him, *show* him, that he *was* wanted, that *he* meant more to her than the as yet unconceived child they had argued so hotly and painfully about.

But she didn't, and in the end, because of the pain in his head, he resorted to taking some of the strong painkillers he had been prescribed for such attacks, with the result that he overslept the following morning.

When he was finally able to drag himself out of his drug-induced sleep Annie had gone.

Gone never to return...

At first he simply assumed that she had gone into the city to do some shopping, but then lunchtime came and went, and then teatime, and it finally began to dawn on him that she might not be coming back.

He scoured the town for her, and the university, empty as yet, but he couldn't find any sign of her.

In the end, in desperation, he visited the lodging house where she had been staying when he had first met her, but the woman who ran the place was away on holiday with her husband, and her cousin, whom she had left in charge, didn't even recognise Annie's description.

He didn't sleep that night, nor the night after, expecting with every heartbeat that she would return. But when?

One day passed, and then a week without any sign of her, without any word from her, and Dominic began to think the unthinkable. Annie had left him, and all because of a stupid quarrel.

She's eighteen, a baby still, he tried to remind himself. Her reaction to their quarrel was excusable and understandable. She would come back once she had stopped sulking. Their love was too strong for her not to do so.

Ten days later, on the eve of his departure for the Middle East, he still hadn't been able to accept that she had actually left him, that she wasn't just playing a silly game with him to punish him. Right up until the moment the final call for his flight was given he still kept on expecting her to appear, to come running up to him, telling him that it had all been a mistake, that she loved him.

And even then he still didn't give up hope, asking the estate agents and the couple he had let the house to to let him know if she should get in touch.

But of course she didn't do any such thing, and in the end he had to accept that the reason she hadn't returned—no doubt the reason she had walked out on him in the first place—was that she regretted their marriage and considered it to be a mistake.

He didn't bother returning home to the UK that Christmas. What was the point? His birthday in March he celebrated alone, and all the birthdays that followed it, along with certain other special anniversaries: the one when he had first met her, the one when they had first made love, the one when they had married.

The years passed, and with them his initial shock of disbelief. All that remained was a natural irritation at not knowing why she had gone without an explanation. He had resigned himself to never losing the hurt, but the last thing that he had expected or envisaged was that she would simply walk back into his life, his home—his bed—as though nothing had happened…without any warning…without any real explanation, without any acknowledgement of what she had done. And he had certainly never imagined that she would behave in such an extraordinarily bizarre way.

His body tensed now, as he fought to quell the surge of aching longing that filled him. In the past, as lovers, *he* had been the tutor and she the disciple. But tonight… With the bitterness of the gall that only a man who has loved a woman more than she has loved him can feel he gritted his teeth against the ferocity of his jealousy at the thought of the relationships she must have had in his absence.

All that rubbish she had talked about fate and them being meant to be together had just been so ridiculous. Surely she couldn't possibly have expected him to believe her! So why hadn't he said something, stopped her—stopped himself? Because he was a man, *that* was why… She meant nothing to him on a personal level now—nothing whatsoever—and the first thing he was going to do when she eventually woke up was to demand an explanation of her reappearance in his life.

Yes. That was the first thing he was going to do. And the second was that he was going to get a divorce!

CHAPTER FIVE

ANNIE woke up with a small anxious start, peering quickly round the bedroom before smiling in relief as she saw the tall, familiar male figure standing in front of the window.

'It *wasn't* just a dream,' she breathed happily.

Dominic stared at her. What the hell was she playing at? Well, he could play as well.

'No, it wasn't a dream,' he agreed silkily. 'And I've got the scratches to prove it. Want to see them?'

As she blushed and lowered her eyelashes in faked modesty he admitted to himself that she was an excellent actress. Even he, *knowing* the truth, still found his heart giving a funny little erratic beat as he fought the temptation to move reassuringly closer to her.

Hardening his heart, he prepared to tell her that she was wasting her time trying to bamboozle him, but before he could say anything Annie pre-empted him, telling him shyly, 'I know this sounds silly, but I still can't quite believe that all this is real. That *you* and *I* are real,' she added for extra emphasis.

'What would you like me to do to prove it to you?' Dominic asked her urbanely. 'Come over there and—?' He stopped abruptly as he recognised that his words, designed to put her in her place, were instead having a very emphatic and very unwanted effect on his own body as his mind agilely leapt the chasm between his words and the events of the previous night, furnishing him in no uncertain terms with the knowledge of just how his body felt about renewing the intimacy they had so recently shared.

His *body* might want her but his emotions most certainly did not, Dominic assured himself sturdily, but for some reason he still found that he was moving closer to the bed and to Annie—because he wanted to ensure that she had no way of escaping when he confronted her and demanded an explanation of her behaviour he told himself firmly.

'I really ought to get up,' she was saying quietly. 'You must have things to do, and...'

'And so do you. What *are* you doing with your time, Annie? With your life?' he demanded aggressively.

For a moment she looked slightly taken aback, but her manner as she gathered the duvet around her body was so composed and quiet that Dominic felt reluctantly impressed.

'I...I work part-time for Petrofiche,' she told him hesitantly.

Dominic stiffened. No doubt *that* explained how she had known that he was returning to the area. She must have heard on the office grapevine about his appointment.

'*Part*-time?' he began critically, but Annie didn't appear to register the contempt in his voice because she had ignored what he was saying.

'Oh, this is a dream come true for me,' she told him huskily. 'I never thought... And then, when I saw you in the restaurant the other night... I never imagined that this could happen.' As she spoke she reached out to touch his hand, her expression one of luminous joy, her whole body trembling openly as she whispered, 'People say that reality can never match up to the expectancy of one's dreams, but now I know that they're wrong. My reality... *You*...'

She paused, visibly swallowing as she raised her head and fixed her gaze on him, her eyes wide and dark with an emotion that looked so real that Dominic had to remind himself just what she was, and how impossible it was for her to mean a word of what she was saying.

'*You,*' she emphasised, 'are more, so very much more than...than I ever dreamed you could possibly be. I can't believe even now that I've been lucky enough to find you...that fate should have picked us out for one another. I feel so...' She paused and swallowed, her eyes almost purple-grey with the intensity of the emotions Dominic knew she had to be faking as she continued huskily, 'I feel so, so blessed too. Last night,' Annie went on tremulously, drawing his hand closer to her, so he had to sit on the bed, 'was the most wonderful, the most beautiful, the most perfect night of my life.' She paused, and Dominic could hear the tiny emotional catch in her voice before she said, 'You made it that way for me. I love you so much...I...'

When her voice became suspended by emotion Dominic reminded himself that she was merely acting...lying...

'Oh, dear,' he could hear her saying, her voice rueful and husky with self-deprecatory laughter. 'I think I might be going to cry, and men hate weepy women, don't they?'

He had originally fallen almost as much in love with her gentle sense of humour as he had with her, but, like everything else about her, it was a fiction, he reminded himself sharply now as he made to pull away from her.

'I'm hungry,' he told her abruptly. 'I'll go downstairs and start breakfast.'

It made sense to wait until they were in less emotive surroundings before he confronted her, he told himself as he moved to stand up, but to his consternation, instead of letting him go, she clung tenderly to his arm.

'I'm hungry too—for you,' she whispered, her voice soft with love.

She blushed as he turned to look at her—a soft pink flushing of her skin that, like her downcast glance, *had* to be manufactured, he told himself.

'You want sex?' he demanded angrily, and then, before she could say anything, and without giving himself time to analyse either his anger or the way he was reacting to it, he turned back to her, once again sitting on the bed as he reached for her, wrapping her tightly in his arms, his mouth hard and punishing on hers.

Annie felt almost as though she might faint. To wake up this morning in the bed she had shared last night with the man she loved, to know that he was real, that their *love* was real, was almost too much for her to comprehend. And now to have him hold her, kiss her with such fierce hungry energy, to know, to *see* that he wanted her so much… She ached to reach out and caress him…intimately…but there were still some things, some intimacies she felt too shy to make the first move towards.

And then her hesitancy was forgotten as he suddenly pushed her back against the bed, growling against her mouth, 'You're the one who wanted this.'

'I do…I want you,' Annie whispered back. 'I love you…so much…'

She gave a small moan of delight as he pushed back the duvet, his hand and then his mouth hotly fierce against her naked skin, her naked breasts. In the clear morning light she could see the rosy crests of her nipples, her breasts still slightly flushed and swollen from the night's lovemaking.

As he touched her Annie felt a tremendous surge of longing kick through her body. Lovingly she reached out for him, tensing in shock as he pulled away from her, saying sharply, 'No!'

'You really *do* want your breakfast, don't you?' Annie teased him tenderly as she smiled up at him.

'I'll go down and start preparing it,' she heard him telling her almost tersely as he got off the bed and turned away from her, heading for the bedroom door.

Annie watched him go. Her body still ached for him, and yet beneath that ache lay a delicious contentment, a warm, positive memory of the night they had shared.

The bedroom had its own *en suite* bathroom which she quickly found, almost as though she knew already where it was. So much about the house was familiar to her that in certain other circumstances she might have found her instinctive familiarity with it slightly spooky. As it was she simply felt that it was all part of the extraordinary workings of fate.

Once downstairs, she found the kitchen as easily as she had done the bathroom, this time not so much by instinct as by the smell of freshly brewed coffee and cooking bacon.

'I've scrambled your eggs for you. I know that's how you prefer them.'

Annie stared as she was waved into an empty seat at the table and a plate of piping hot food was placed in front of her.

'I...I never eat a cooked breakfast,' she whispered. 'Only...'

'...at Christmas and other special occasions. Yes, I know,' she was told, her sentence finished for her.

Grimly Dominic watched her as confusion shadowed her eyes and she toyed with the plate of food.

'I can't believe that you can know so much about me without us ever having met,' she began slowly, and then she stopped, a brilliant smile illuminating her face as she told him blissfully, 'I'm so glad that we've found each other and that you love me.'

'*Found* each other,' Dominic derided grimly. 'You can stop pretending, Annie, the game's over. And as for me *loving* you... Just what the hell do you think I am? What kind of *fool* do you think I am? There is only one reason for what happened between us last night so far as *I'm* concerned, and it has nothing whatsoever to do with love. Quite simply I reacted to man's age-old need to scratch a certain itch.' He paused and waited.

Annie stared at him. Her heart had started to hammer shockingly fast, hurting her so much as it thudded against her chest wall that she could barely breathe.

'I don't understand,' she began painfully. 'What are you saying…? What do you mean…? I…'

'Oh, come on, Annie, get real. How much of a fool do you take me for? All that rubbish about fate… My God, but you're a cool one. Walking back into my life…crawling into my bed just as though the last five years have never happened.'

Annie felt as though a huge weight, a huge stone was crushing down inside her, preventing her from thinking, preventing her from speaking, preventing her from breathing, almost. But not preventing her from feeling fear and pain. No, not preventing her from feeling those.

'Please,' she croaked when she could finally force her vocal cords to unlock themselves. 'I don't understand.'

'You don't understand?' Dominic countered irritably.

She could see the way his chest rose and expanded under the pressure of his anger, but her fear of it and of him was somehow distant and vague, as though she simply didn't have the energy, the strength to come to terms with it as she battled with the enormity of the shock she was suffering.

'Do you think *I* understood when you walked out on me…on our marriage?'

Their *marriage*!

Without knowing she had done so Annie stood up,

and then gasped as the room spun giddily around her. In that instant she heard a harsh male voice speaking sharply.

'Oh, no, you don't. You won't escape by pulling that trick on me and pretending to faint. Annie... *Annie...*'

She heard him emphasise her name in raw fury as she finally slipped into the blessed relief of the darkness waiting for her.

When she came round she was sitting down again, but this time in a deep comfortable armchair in a large, pleasantly furnished sitting room. Like the other rooms of the house she had already seen it was somehow vaguely familiar to her.

A horrible, unwanted ice-cold sense of fear was beginning to fasten its death-inducing fingers around the tender vulnerability of her heart. A horrible, unwanted, uncertain sense of...something...

'I... We... We can't be married,' she whispered painfully. 'I...I don't know you. I don't even know your name...'

For a moment she actually thought he was going to strike her he looked so angry, but when she flinched he stepped back from her, throwing back his head and laughing savagely.

'Oh, my God, now I have heard everything. Last night you were claiming me as someone sent to you by fate, your one true love, and now you're trying to tell me that you don't know who I am. Tell me something, Annie, do you make a habit of going to bed with men you don't know? Is that another part of your personality I never knew existed? Just like your propensity for disappearing without explanation? Did you ever once—just once—stop to think how I might feel? How—'

Dominic could feel himself starting to sweat and he recognised how dangerously close to losing his self-control he was getting. He was becoming far too emotional. After all, what could her lack of love for him possibly mean to him now?

Annie could feel the pain welling up inside her, the awful, uncontrollable feeling of having stepped into a world of nightmarish terror, of having all her worst fears made real.

'We can't be married,' she repeated, her mouth trembling. 'We can't be...'

'Do you want me to prove it to you?' Dominic asked her tersely. 'Very well...'

Walking past her, he went over to an antique desk in the corner of the room, pulling open a drawer and extracting a small box from which he produced a piece of paper. He brought it over to her and held it in front of her.

'Read this,' he commanded acidly.

Her heart thumping, Annie did as he instructed. Her blood seemed to be freezing in her veins; her hands were deathly cold, her head light and hurting.

Slowly and carefully, as though she was a child, she read the words written on the certificate, lifting her eyes briefly from it to gaze into those of the man holding it with sick dismay before returning to read it a second time.

'Your name is Dominic,' was all she could say when he started to refold it.

Her mouth had gone dry and her heart was pounding sickly. There were so many questions she wanted to ask him but she was afraid to do so, afraid of his answers.

Twice now he had mentioned her walking out on him...disappearing. What kind of relationship must they have had for her to do that? Instinctively she knew it was simply not within her to walk out of the kind of commitment that marriage entailed. So what kind of marriage and what kind of man...? The kind of man who would take a woman to bed, as he had done her last night, simply for sex?

'I can't stay here. I have to go,' she began unsteadily, but Dominic was already standing over her, blocking her escape.

'No way,' he told her angrily. 'No way. Not until... Not until you've told me *why* you did it, Annie. Why you walked out on me.

'My God, it's the least you owe me, especially after that pathetic charade...that play-acting you put on for me last night. "I've wanted you so much",' he sighed, mimicking the emotion of her voice. '"I've wanted you so much...this is fate..."'

Annie winced as she heard the acid bitterness underlying the contempt of his words. What could she say? How *could* she explain. Every word he said felt like another blow to her sensitive emotions.

She tried to defend herself. 'It must have been... I would never...' She stopped, too proud, too shocked, too raw to tell him of her instinctive knowledge that everything she had said to him was true. *Was* true? She wasn't still dreaming about him, was she? Still...

'It must have been...?' Dominic was mimicking relentlessly. 'Can't you remember?'

Annie swallowed painfully.

'No, actually, I can't,' she told him quietly, raising her eyes to his.

They stared at one another in silence for several tautly tense seconds before he cursed and swung round, so that he wasn't looking at her when he demanded tersely, 'What kind of answer is that? What kind of *fool* do you take me for, Annie? You remembered well enough in bed last night. Every little touch, every little word...every single caress and kiss that ever meant anything to me...'

'That wasn't deliberate—' Annie began, and then stopped. What he was saying was too shocking...too painful. She desperately needed to get away, to be on her own and absorb properly what she had been told.

'Hey! Where do you think you're going?' Dominic demanded sharply as Annie took advantage of his lack of concentration and made a bolt for the door, running through it at full speed and almost colliding with the postman as she flung open the front door.

Dominic, who was right behind her, cursed as the postman waved a piece of paper in front of him, demanding a signature for a registered envelope. He could hear the engine of Annie's car firing, and then with a spurt of gravel she was speeding off down the drive.

She had done it. She had got away from him. Annie was trembling so violently as she drove the car out onto the main road that she knew she was not really fit to be driving, but there was no way she was going to stop now...not until she had got away from him and was back safely and securely in her own little house.

Tears were streaming down her face and her heart was pounding with shock and emotion. She wasn't Annie White, she was Mrs Dominic Carlyle—a married woman...married to the man of her dreams...

As she finally stopped her car outside her house Annie was laughing wildly in hysterical shocked disbelief. The man of her dreams... Maybe, but to him *she* was the *woman* of his worst *nightmares*!

CHAPTER SIX

'WE HAD a wonderful time. Bob says that we really should try to go again, and I said…' Worriedly Helena stopped talking as she recognised that Annie wasn't really listening to her.

'What is it? What's wrong?' she demanded.

'I…' Annie began, intending to deny that anything was the matter. She was an adult, after all, and surely capable of dealing with her own problems. But two nights of broken sleep coupled with the shock of discovering that she and Dominic were married had taken their toll.

'I've found out why Dominic, the man at the restaurant, seemed so familiar to me,' she told Helena bleakly.

Her anxiety increasing, Helena put down the mug of coffee Annie had poured for her and waited. Getting up from her small kitchen table, Annie walked over to the sink. She poured herself a glass of water and drank it to moisten her nervously dry throat, before continuing shakily, 'He's my husband.'

'What?' Helena stared at her.

'It's true,' Annie assured her, giving her a look of dry-eyed anguished despair. 'He showed me our marriage certificate.'

Half an hour later Annie had managed to tell her the full story of what had happened between Dominic

and herself—or most of what had happened! There
were some things, some betrayals of her self-esteem,
she could not even bring herself to admit to herself,
or to tell even her closest friend.

'Have you told him about your accident?' Helena
questioned her.

Annie shook her head.

'No. I...I couldn't... He says I walked out on him,
and... I...I don't know why he married me, Helena.
It's obvious how he feels about me now...'

'What about you? What do you feel for him?'

Helena questioned her gently, momentarily ignoring Dominic's feelings.

'I don't know,' Annie admitted. 'It's been such a
shock. I still can't believe...'

'You'll have to tell him about your accident,'
Helena told her firmly.

'Helena, I can't,' Annie protested. 'And to be honest I don't think he'd be prepared to listen. I feel
such a fool,' Annie told her. 'All those idiotic things
I felt and said about my dream man, over and over,
and all the time...'

'He was your husband,' Helena supplied grimly.

There was one more very important question she
had to ask Annie, even though she could see how
distressed and unhappy she was.

'When he...Dominic...told you that you were
married, did it...did you—?'

'Did I remember anything,' Annie interrupted her,
guessing what she was going to say and shaking her
head as she did so. 'No...nothing. I only wish I had,
then I could at least...'

She got up from the table and started to pace the small kitchen floor.

'I've got to remember what happened now, Helena…I've got to. Until I do…' She stopped, her voice and face so tortured that Helena longed to be able to comfort and reassure her.

'Why would I do something like that? Why would I just walk out on the man I was supposed to love and our marriage? I can't believe… I've got to know the truth—otherwise…'

'Couldn't Dominic throw any light on why you might have left?' Helena asked her.

'I… We didn't… He was so angry with me…'

Helena could see how distressed Annie was, and she didn't want to put her under any more pressure, so instead of asking her any more questions she started to soothe and reassure her. But privately she had already decided that Annie's husband would have to be told the truth of Annie's accident, and that if Annie didn't feel able to tell him herself then she would have to do so for her.

After Helena had gone Annie washed their coffee mugs, grimly forcing her hands to stop the slight trembling they seemed to have developed. Two anxious nights lying awake unable to sleep were beginning to take their toll on her, but she knew if she tried to sleep now she would be unable to do so.

What you need, my girl, is some healthy exercise—a good brisk walk, she told herself sternly. But deep down inside another voice, sharper and less comforting, was telling her instead that what she needed more than anything else was to be able to remember those lost weeks, that lost period of time. Not until she had done so would she ever be in a position to defend herself against Dominic's accusations, to refute his allegations.

From Petrofiche Helena had learned that Dominic was currently working from home, and she had decided to pay him a visit there without giving him any prior warning of her arrival, just in case he should refuse to see her.

His house and its setting were certainly very impressive, she acknowledged as she climbed out of her car and walked towards the front door. Why had Annie left her husband and her home? Dominic Carlyle held the key that could unlock the mystery, Helena felt sure. Was there some vital piece of information that he was withholding, or was he genuinely, as he had implied to Annie, as unaware of her reasons for leaving him as he had claimed?

Firmly Helena rang the doorbell and waited. She didn't have to wait very long.

'Dr Dominic Carlyle?' she questioned as Dominic opened the door.

'Yes?' Dominic agreed, frowning a little as he studied the set expression on the face of his unexpected visitor.

'I'm Helena Lever,' Helena introduced herself. 'Annie's doctor and friend...'

'Her doctor?' Dominic questioned, his frown intensifying as he invited Helena inside, closing the hall door on the room where he had been working and leading the way into the sitting room.

'Annie doesn't know I'm here,' Helena told him, shaking her head in refusal of the refreshments he was offering. 'But I had to see you because there's something I think you should know.'

Dominic studied her assessingly. She had all the hallmarks of a dedicated and very professional woman. She was Annie's doctor, she had told him, and suddenly an ominous chill of foreboding feathered down his spine.

'She's ill?' he questioned abruptly.

'Not in the physical sense,' Helena responded, equally curtly. The anxiety and concern she had heard in his voice had caught her somewhat off-guard. From Annie's description of what had happened she had expected him to be far more hostile.

'Annie was the victim of a serious road accident which resulted in her suffering from amnesia. Which is why—'

Helena stopped speaking as Dominic interrupted her, urgently demanding, 'What do you mean a serious road accident? We...'

Trenchantly Helena explained, concluding, 'So you see, when Annie told you that she did not know you were her husband she was telling you the truth. She has no memory of the accident or of the weeks prior to it. If you don't believe me there are medical records,' Helena informed him grittily, but Dominic was shaking his head.

He did believe her, but he was still in shock from the total unexpectedness of her revelations.

'Why the hell didn't Annie say something...tell me?' he demanded hoarsely. 'If she had...'

'If she had you would never have bullied and threatened her the way you did?' Helena offered crisply. 'No, I'm sure you wouldn't. No man worthy of the name would behave in such a way, would he?'

Helena could see from the slow dark burn of colour tingeing Dominic's cheekbones and jawline that she had made her point.

'Perhaps I was... Perhaps I did...overreact,' he admitted. 'But do you have any idea what it did to me when she simply walked out and disappeared?' he demanded, when Helena made no response.

'No,' she told him remorselessly. 'But I do know what it did to Annie when she was knocked down in the street and left in a coma, when she came round and it was discovered that she couldn't remember large chunks of her life...'

'When...when did it happen...the accident...?' Dominic asked her harshly.

As she witnessed his reaction to her comments Helena found herself relenting a little towards Dominic.

'Tuesday the twenty-eighth of September, just before midday, according to the witnesses,' she informed him. 'The date and the time are engraved on my memory—after all, I heard them often enough when I sat through the court case with Annie. She had to go to court to get proper compensation for her injuries,' she explained.

Dominic's face had gone pale.

'My flight left Heathrow later that afternoon,' he informed her, adding grimly, 'It's a date and time that are engraved on my memory as well. Right up until the flight was called I was still hoping that she would appear…explain… She'd been missing for ten days by then,' he added curtly. 'You say she has no memory at all of…of our marriage…of me…?'

Helena could see how hard it was for him to say the words, and she could guess how much it would hurt his pride to hear her answer.

'No, she hasn't,' she told him quietly.

'She recognised me, though,' Dominic persisted stubbornly.

'Yes,' Helena was forced to concede. 'In one sense that's true; she did. But not as a real person. Not as…'

'…her husband,' Dominic interjected for her. 'Is her memory ever likely to return? Can anything be done to…?'

'It may return. No one can say conclusively whether it will or not. And as for what can be done… Do you really think if there was anything…anything that Annie could do to remember, she wouldn't?' she asked him, shaking her head.

'When we were talking about what had happened, and about you, she told me that she would give anything, do anything, to be able to remember. I can appreciate how much of a shock this must be to you, but try, if you can, to imagine how it must be for Annie. Not only has she had to spend the last five years wondering, worrying about what the missing period of her life might contain, she now has to contend with the added trauma of discovering that she has a husband she can't remember, who she left without knowing why. I can assure you, Dr Carlyle, that

Annie is simply not the sort of person to walk out on a commitment she would consider as important as the commitment of marriage without having a very, very good reason.

'Perhaps you know more about that reason than you are prepared to say,' Helena probed, holding her breath as she saw the way Dominic's expression changed from one of intent concentration to one of inimical anger.

'I have no knowledge of any kind—secret or otherwise—as to why Annie left. We had had a quarrel, yes, a ridiculous, silly argument about whether we should or should not, at some future stage in our marriage, have children.'

Helena raised an eyebrow.

'You consider the issue of fathering children trivial?' she asked him wryly.

'No, I don't,' Dominic immediately defended himself grimly. 'Quite the opposite. My own childhood taught me the depth of a child's need to know it is loved and wanted by its parents. This was just a quarrel, a row. Caused, I believe, more by the fact that we were soon to part than any real disagreement between us about children.

'How is Annie?' he asked Helena abruptly, totally disarming her. 'I overreacted a little to…to certain aspects of…of her behaviour towards me, not knowing about the accident…'

'She's very shocked,' Helena informed him truthfully. 'But she also has a good deal of inner strength. She has needed to have it, otherwise she would never have survived.'

She glanced at her watch. It was time for her to leave.

'Annie needs your understanding, not your antagonism,' she told Dominic forthrightly. She hesitated. 'I haven't mentioned this to Annie because I don't want to raise her hopes, but it may be that your reappearance might just trigger something that could make her remember.'

Dominic had been in the middle of working on a very complex report when Helena had arrived, but after she had gone he knew there was no way he could go back to it. Although he had tried his best to hide it from Helena, her revelations had shocked him to such an extent that he still wasn't fully able to totally comprehend everything she had told him.

The thought of Annie being hurt, lying in hospital alone, afraid...in pain, close to death...filled him with such anger and pain that he simply couldn't keep still, pacing the floor of his sitting room. *Why* hadn't she said something to him? Told him herself? Why hadn't she explained to him that she was suffering from amnesia? Then he might have understood when she had kept going on about knowing him— about fate. Then he might...

He might have what? It was too late for him to have regrets now, to wish that he hadn't...

That he hadn't what? Taken her to bed? Taken advantage of her? In the light of what Helena had told him his own behaviour was little short of sheer outright cruelty.

But he hadn't known, he reminded himself. He had

thought, believed, that she was simply acting…playing him along… Had she really meant what
she had said to him? Had she really felt—been reliving—the happiness, the love, they had once shared?
Had she really believed that he was her soul
mate…that they were fated to meet…that she *loved*
him?

Well, if she had believed that she must be thoroughly disabused of that belief now. Nothing could
alter his own belief that in leaving him the way she
had she had deliberately destroyed the love they had
shared, but that did not excuse his own behaviour.
He would have to go and see her, Dominic decided.
He owed her an apology for the present, even if she
was either unprepared or unable to furnish him with
one for the past.

Wearily he recognised that he was in danger of
reactivating within himself emotions he had already
decided were no longer valid or necessary. But just
to think of Annie, his Annie, helpless and hurt, made
him feel…made him ache… Made him want… But
she wasn't his Annie any more, he reminded himself
savagely. She hadn't been his Annie from the moment she walked away from him.

Despondently Annie unpegged the washing from the
line, checking automatically that it was dry. She had
spent the last hours following Helena's visit in an
orgy of cleaning—a displacement activity to stop
herself from thinking about Dominic, from worrying
and forcing herself unsuccessfully to try to remember.

She knew that she must have loved Dominic—her dreams alone were proof of that—and presumably he must have loved her, although there had been little evidence of that love when... But, no, she must not think about that. She might have loved him but she had still obviously felt she had to leave him—and then, having done, so had recreated via her dreams an image of him as her perfect lover.

She knew better now, of course, but what she still did *not* know was *why* she should have dreamed of Dominic in the way she had, as her hero, her saviour, her special one and only person, when the reality was so very different.

'You walked out on me. You left me,' Dominic had told her, and she had no defence against this accusation because she had no memory of the events he had described.

Gathering up her dried washing, she hurried towards the house, trying to suppress the feeling of panic that was spreading through her.

By keeping herself physically occupied she might somehow be able to keep her anxiety at a safe distance, or so she tried to reason. She dared not stop, dared not allow herself even to think about the appalling and unbelievable nature of the situation she was in. She was a married woman. She was married to Dominic Carlyle—a stranger!

A fit of shudders ran through her body as her stressed nervous system went into revolt. Putting down the washing, she decided to make herself a cup of coffee. She had just filled the kettle and switched it on when she heard her doorbell. Assuming that her visitor must be Helena, returning to remind her of her invitation for Annie to return home with her, she went to open the door.

The sight of Dominic standing outside on her doorstep was so unexpected that she physically reeled with shock, only her own gritty determination keeping her body rigid as she refused to give in to the wave of sickening panic that swept her.

'What…what do you want?' she challenged him, dry-mouthed.

'I would like to talk to you,' Dominic responded politely, but Annie wasn't deceived. She knew now how deceptive that politeness actually was.

'Well, *I* don't want to talk to *you*,' she told him proudly, her chin tilting as she clung to the half-open door.

A couple of doors away one of her neighbours was walking down her garden path, and out of the corner of her eye Annie could see the interest they were attracting.

Instinctively she wanted to hide herself away from her neighbour's curiosity, and as though he sensed what she was feeling Dominic told her softly, 'I think you'd better let me in, Annie, unless you want other people to hear…'

He was leaving her no alternative other than to give in, Annie recognised.

Unsteadily she walked into the hallway, allowing him to follow her, needing the cool retreat of its privacy and semi-darkness.

Behind her, as he closed the door, she could hear Dominic asking, 'Are you all right?'

All right? She had to stifle the shard-like slivers of her own pain as her chest tightened and her throat threatened to close up.

'I was!' she told him coldly, when she felt in control enough to speak.

They had reached the end of the hall now, and through the kitchen door she could hear the kettle starting to boil. Automatically she moved towards it, tensing as she recognised that Dominic had followed her.

Don't come in here! she wanted to scream almost childishly at him. Don't come anywhere near me. I don't want you here...in my home...my sanctuary.

'Helena has been to see me,' he told her abruptly.

Annie could feel the shock of his words as though someone had opened her vein and let her blood drain away. The feeling was immediate and sickening: a cold wash of emotional pain coupled with a sense of blind panic and shock.

She felt the kettle she had just reached for slipping from her grasp. She cried out in alarm, instinctively jumping back as she dropped it and boiling water cascaded everywhere. She could feel her arm burning where the scalding water had touched it and she could hear herself crying out too. But it felt as though it was happening to someone else, as though somehow *she* wasn't really a part of what was happening.

She could see Dominic moving towards her. She could hear the way he was cursing as he demanded harshly, 'Let me see. You've scalded yourself.'

'It's nothing,' she denied as she fought not to give in to the fierce pull of her own emotions. 'Just a few splashes.' But it was too late. He was holding her arm and examining it, first his glance and then his fingers examining the long scar that ran from her wrist right up her arm. It had faded a lot now, but it was still—in her eyes, at least—something she preferred others not to notice. Her badge of courage, Helena called it.

'Why did you leave me, Annie?' she could hear Dominic demanding rawly, and suddenly everything was too much for her.

The shock she had been fighting to keep at bay ever since he had told her that they were married finally crashed through the barriers she had tried to erect, and she started to cry, her whole body shaking with the force of her emotions. She put her hands protectively over her face, as though somehow by covering her eyes she was concealing herself from him, and concealing too her own shame at her weakness as she sobbed helplessly.

'I don't know. I don't know… I can't remember. I *can't* remember…'

It was as though just making that admission, just acknowledging that weakness, had somehow opened the floodgates to all the pain and fear she had been bottling up right from the time of the accident.

She was shivering, shaking so badly she could hardly stand up, powerless to control what was happening to her. She could hear herself crying out in denial, as though she was being tortured, and then Dominic suddenly reached for her, wrapping his arms around her so tightly that his body provided a blanket that soaked up and smothered her distress as effectively as a blanket of foam might smother a sheet of flames.

'Right. That's it,' she could hear him saying as the shudders started to die out of her body and her tears subsided. 'There's no way you're staying here on your own. You're coming home with me.'

'No!' Annie denied immediately, pulling herself out of his embrace. 'I'm not a child. I'm an adult…a woman…and—'

'And you're also my wife,' Dominic reminded her sharply. '*You* may not be able to remember that you married me, Annie, but we are still man and wife.'

'We can get divorced…'

'Yes,' Dominic agreed. 'But so far as I am concerned, before we bring an official end to our marriage, there are questions I would like to have answered. There are things we *both* need to know…' he reinforced sombrely.

Annie looked away from him. She still felt weak and semi-shocked by the unexpectedness of her emotional breakdown. Breakdown! Meltdown, more likely. The small patches of flesh the water had splashed were still stinging painfully, and she felt dangerously light-headed, almost relieved to have Dominic take control.

'You're in shock,' he was telling her almost sternly. 'We both are, I suspect. This situation between us is something we need to work through *together*, Annie. I have no idea why you chose to end our marriage, and neither, it seems, do you.'

'What do you mean—it *seems*?' Annie challenged him immediately. 'Do you think I'm just pretending?

Do you think I don't *want* to remember? Do you think—' She stopped as she felt fresh tears threatening her. She felt weak and exhausted, both physically and emotionally, and what she longed for more than anything else right now was to be able to curl up somewhere dark and safe, to escape from all the trauma she was experiencing.

'That scald needs attention,' she could hear him telling her.

Tears burned the backs of her eyes.

'Leave me alone. I'm all right,' she told him. But she knew it wasn't true—she felt sick, dizzy, and her vision was starting to blur. In her head she could see Dominic's face—hear his voice—but not as they were now. Through the mists of her own confusion and faintness she tried desperately to catch the fading images but it was too late—already they were slipping away.

There had been a time, when she was first recovering, when she'd wondered despairingly whether she would ever be properly well, whether her inability to remember perhaps signified that her brain had been damaged along with her body. Helena had been quick to reassure her on that point, however, it had remained a slightly sensitive issue for her—one that had underlain her determination to obtain her degree and hold down a proper job.

Now, as she looked away from Dominic, she suddenly saw the blisters forming on her arm and recognised that she *hadn't* known she had hurt herself. Through the faintness threatening to overwhelm her she could hear Dominic saying grimly, 'Right, that's it. No more arguments. *You* are coming home with me.'

The emergency doctor they had seen at the hospital's casualty department might have told them that Annie's scalds were relatively minor, and that it was delayed shock which had been responsible for her near faint, but Dominic wasn't taking any chances. At his insistence she had been given both sedation and painkilling injections.

Now, as he headed for his home, the case he had returned to her house to pack for her stowed in the boot of his car, Annie dozed groggily beside him in the passenger seat.

Loath though he was to admit it, the vulnerability he had witnessed in her today had not just shocked him but also touched a nerve, an emotion he had thought he had long ago eradicated.

Because of this he knew he was behaving brusquely and distantly towards her, but if he didn't... That look of helpless pride and panic he had seen in her eyes earlier had almost been enough to...

It was because it reminded him of how she had once looked at him *before*, he told himself as he brought the car to a halt outside his house.

'Don't move,' he told Annie curtly as she started to reach for her door handle.

'I can walk,' Annie protested as Dominic came round and opened her door and reached inside to lift her out bodily. But even whilst she struggled to free herself from his hold waves of lethargy and weakness were sweeping over her.

The doctor in charge of the busy casualty unit, faced with Annie's protests that she didn't want any kind of medication and Dominic's implacable determination, had given in to the greater force, and now, as Dominic ignored her protests and swept Annie up into his arms to carry her into the house, she could feel herself slipping away into the comfort of a cotton-woolly world of nothingness.

Because of his impromptu decision to bring her home with him Dominic hadn't had any time to prepare a room for Annie, which meant that he had to carry her into his own room and place her carefully in the middle of his own large bed.

Studiously avoiding looking at her, he stripped off her outer clothes and pulled the duvet up over her underwear-clad body.

She had always been fine-boned, her body when he had first known her naturally that of a young girl, but now, although his senses told him that her curves were markedly those of a woman and not a girl, he was grimly aware of the fact that she was only just on the right side of being too thin, her ribs clearly discernible against the pale sheeny flesh of her midriff.

The Annie he had known had had a healthy appetite and an innocent enjoyment of her food that had made his body ache with the certain knowledge that her appetite for sex…for *him*…was just as innocent and enthusiastic. And there at least he had not been wrong. The first time he had taken her to bed—

Abruptly he stepped away. There were some memories it wasn't wise or safe to exhume, and that was most definitely one of them. But perhaps because of its very danger, he discovered, after he had made his way back downstairs and tried to recommence his abandoned work, it was one that wasn't going to allow itself to be sent away unrecognised.

Stifling a sigh of exasperation, he got up from his desk and walked over to the French windows, opening them and stepping outside into the garden. He was behaving as though he still loved her—but he didn't—couldn't—must not!

In the years they had been apart, the years of her desertion, her destruction of the love they had shared, he had used his anguish to ice-burn his feelings, his love, into a numbness he had refused to feel. Today, seeing the pain and fear in her eyes, he had felt the numbness starting to crack apart.

The knowledge that she had been hurt and close to death, even more than the discovery of her loss of memory, touched and hurt something deep within him he had thought incapable of being touched or brought to life ever again. It wasn't love, he reassured himself. How could it be?

No, it couldn't be love. But knowing that didn't protect him from remembering...

Unwillingly he looked up towards his bedroom window. In that room, in that bed—his bed—Annie lay asleep. Annie... His wife... In the bed he had once shared with Annie... His Annie... His love...

Morosely he looked back towards the river. She had loved to lie in bed at night with the curtains and the windows open so that she could hear the sound of the water. They had even once stolen out in the darkness so that they could swim there together, naked in the silent darkness.

She had demurred at first, protesting that the river would be cold and that they might be seen, but then they had started to touch one another and such things had been forgotten.

The water, he remembered, *had* been cold, but *they* had not!

'You look like a god, a river god,' she had told him tremulously, her hands trembling against his body, the cry she had given as his body surged powerfully into hers lost in the heated kiss of eager hunger they had exchanged.

Later that night, or rather early the next morning, she had reached for him in bed, tracing the sinewy muscles on his arms with her fingertips and her kisses and then, for the first time, becoming more demanding, more assertive as her lips had touched tentatively against his stomach before moving lower.

'Promise me you'll love me for ever,' she'd demanded.

'For ever,' he had told her, and he had meant it.

He moved back inside. He was a grown man now, with an intricate report waiting to be finished, and he had no business standing out here allowing his thoughts to drift into such dangerous waters.

No matter how much Annie's present plight might compel his compassion he *mustn't* allow himself to forget what had happened.

'I *can't* remember,' she had wept, and he had actively felt her fear and panic. But until she could remember neither of them would be fully free to walk away from the past—and from their marriage.

CHAPTER SEVEN

'How are you feeling now?'

'Fine,' Annie fibbed quickly, avoiding meeting Dominic's eyes as she stretched across the kitchen table to pour herself a fresh cup of coffee.

She had been here in his house for nearly three days now. Seventy-two hours. Which in her view was seventy-two hours too many. Granted, she had virtually spent the first twenty-four of them asleep, but she had recovered from the shock of her accident with the kettle now and she felt thoroughly ashamed of the way she had overreacted to the whole incident.

It was time for her to go home. She *wanted* to go home. She *needed* to go home, she reminded herself shakily. The realisation, when she had finally woken up, that she was asleep in Dominic's house and in Dominic's bed had sent a spasm of emotion through her that she still didn't feel strong enough to dare analyse.

She felt nothing for him other than anger at the way he had treated her—of course she didn't. But he had looked after her.

'I'm not hungry,' she had begun that first evening, when she had finally recovered from her shock and he had arrived in her bedroom—*his* bedroom, in reality—with a tray of food.

'Eat it,' was all he had said, but somehow his actions had touched her already sensitive emotions, and after he had gone her salty tears had mingled with the soup he had brought her.

'This is *your* room,' she had protested later, when he had come in to remove the tray.

'Our room,' he had corrected her shortly, stopping as he'd seen the way she froze.

'Don't worry, there's no way I want to insist on my husbandly rights,' he had assured her grimly. 'I've made myself up a bed in one of the other rooms.'

'Actually,' she continued determinedly now, but still avoiding looking directly at him, 'I feel so well that I really think it's time I went home and…'

'And what?' Dominic challenged her. 'No! There's still too much unresolved business between us, Annie.'

'I…I have things to do—my garden, the house,' Annie told him, and then stopped as she saw he was shaking his head. 'The neighbours will be wondering what's happened,' she insisted.

'There's no need for you to worry about any of that,' Dominic assured her calmly. 'I've already explained the situation to your neighbours. And as for the garden, I can speak to the people who do mine and ask them…'

'You've explained *what* situation?' Annie interrupted sharply, her heart starting to thump heavily with nervous tension.

'I've told them about your accident with the kettle and I've explained that, as my wife—'

'Your wife! You *told* them that we're *married*...'
Annie exploded in angry disbelief.

'Why not?' Dominic challenged her. 'After all, it's
the truth.'

'But we're getting a divorce,' Annie protested, and
added angrily, 'You had no right to do that. I don't
want—'

'People to know that I'm your husband?' Dominic
interrupted her cynically.

Annie shook her head. How could she explain to
him how mortified she felt about the prurient curiosity she feared she was bound to be the subject of
once people knew that she had a husband she
couldn't even remember marrying?

'You had no right to do that,' she repeated huskily,
before getting out of her chair and pacing the kitchen
nervously and then telling him sharply, 'I want to go
home, Dominic. I want to go home now.'

'*This* is your home,' he repeated grittily, adding,
before she could deny it, 'I had the house placed in
joint names after we got married, Annie, which is
one of the reasons I haven't been able to sell the
place—without your written agreement...'

'You can have it,' she told him quickly. 'I don't
want...I can't stay here.'

'Why not? What is it you're so afraid of?'

'Nothing...*nothing*,' she denied fiercely, turning to
face him as she did so.

'You're treating me as though I'm your adversary,
Annie,' Dominic told her grimly. 'Your enemy. I'm
not. All I want—'

'Is for me to recover my memory so that I can tell

you why I left you,' Annie interrupted him sharply. 'Do you think *I* don't want to remember? Do you think I'm pretending, lying? Have you *any* idea how it feels to be told that you're married...that you've shared a life...a love...with a man who...?'

Annie stopped as she felt the full weight of her own emotions threatening to overwhelm her. 'Of course I want to remember. But I can't,' she told him flatly.

'Maybe not—by yourself. But perhaps with my help—' Dominic began.

'Your help?' Annie stared at him. 'What do you mean?'

'You and I shared those missing weeks of your life, Annie. I can remember them, even if you can't. I can remember everything we did...*everything*—and I think that if we were to relive them...if I were to take you back through them...it just might...*just* might bring something back for you.'

'What do you mean "if we were to relive them"?' Annie asked him warily. What he was suggesting was ridiculous, and of course there was no way she was going to agree to it, but he was obviously determined to have his say.

'Oh, you needn't look at me like that,' he assured her immediately. 'I'm not some kind of weirdo who gets off on forcing a reluctant woman to have sex with him, Annie. This will be a return to the past *without* the sexual element of the relationship we shared. After all, that is something you *haven't* forgotten, isn't it?' he taunted her softly.

Hot-faced, Annie swallowed the angry words of

denial springing to her lips. He was talking about her dreams, of course, and she couldn't deny what he was saying—much as she longed to be able to do so.

'It wouldn't work,' she told him flatly.

'You can't say that until you try it,' Dominic insisted grimly. 'And you owe it to yourself to.'

Annie turned away from him, unable to make any response, knowing that what he said was true and remembering, too, how she had told him herself she would do anything to remember.

'Very well,' she agreed reluctantly. 'But I don't have to stay here…'

'Yes, you do,' Dominic corrected her. 'After all, you lived here with me.'

'Before we were married?' she demanded, her voice betraying her shock.

'Yes,' Dominic told her laconically. 'After all, we *were* lovers, and there was no reason why we should have lived apart.'

No reason, perhaps, but for some reason Annie felt shocked by his revelation.

'Look,' Dominic was telling her, 'you and I had two months together. All I'm asking is that you give me that time now, Annie. Two months, that's all. If, at the end of that time, you're no closer to remembering anything then I'll concede defeat and—'

'And we'll be divorced,' Annie interrupted him flatly.

'Yes,' he agreed in an equally emotionless voice.

Annie knew that she could have pointed out that since they intended to divorce anyway there seemed little point in delaying matters without any logical reason for doing so. But of course there *was* a reason, and she knew perfectly well what it was. Dominic's male pride was still smarting because she had left him. He wanted an explanation, a reason, and he was determined that she was going to provide him with one.

Her own reasons for wishing to remember her past were far more complex. She had dreamed about Dominic as her lover; her body remembered him as its lover. Before he had told her the truth about their marriage, their shared past, she had craved a closeness with him so strong that he had somehow broken through the locked doors of her memory. So *why* had she left him? Her inability to remember made her feel that a piece of herself was missing, threatening to resurrect all the insecurity she had known as an abandoned child. Only this time she was the one who had done the abandoning—why? She had to find out...

'You're doing *what*?' Helena demanded when Annie telephoned her to tell her what they were going to do.

'Dominic says that until I've remembered the past and him properly neither of us will be able to move our lives on,' Annie explained.

'Well, yes, I suppose he *does* have a point,' Helena acknowledged. 'And if it's what you want to do...'

The urge to tell her friend that it was the last thing she wanted to do was immensely strong, but somehow Annie resisted it. Dominic was determined to have his own way and she suspected that not even

Helena would be able to stop him. She was trying to tell herself that enduring the next two months was going to be a bit like enduring the uncomfortable treatments she had had to go through in hospital. The end result would be worth the pain.

'Well, I have to admit that I'm glad you're not living on your own. You're facing a very traumatic time, Annie—and, stubbornly independent though you are, and much as I understand how you feel, this isn't a good time for you to be on your own.

'I take it that a divorce is going to be put on hold for the time being?' Helena continued.

'For the time being,' Annie agreed shakily. 'It's just a temporary delay, that's all.'

Just a temporary delay. Just two months' delay. But no less than three days into it Annie was beginning to bitterly regret allowing Dominic to persuade her to agree to his plan.

Both Helena and Dominic were insisting that she was still not fully recovered and must not overdo things, and Annie was beginning to feel that time was hanging too heavily on her hands. Dominic, though, had been so busy that she had barely seen him—a fact for which she *ought* to be thankful, she knew, but somehow she wasn't. She felt tired and headachy, her lethargy caused, she knew, as much by the fact that she was not sleeping properly as much as anything else. She was reluctant to allow herself to go into a deep, restful sleep because she was so afraid she might dream about Dominic.

Dominic!

Living here with him was putting her under immense strain, and not *just* because of their shared past.

Just thinking about him made her body tense, a tiny convulsive shudder gripping her. She was far too physically aware of him. Far too physically vulnerable to him. There, she had forced herself to admit what she had been fighting so hard to hide from and deny these last few days. She had brought out into the open her own fear. Physically, she was…she found…she wanted… Closing her eyes, Annie willed herself to bring her chaotic thoughts and feelings to order. It was warm out here in the garden, with the sun beating down on her closed eyelids. Dominic was at work and she was on her own. A bee buzzed busily in the roses nearby.

The roses. She could smell their scent. A prickle of sensation ran through her body. Behind her closed eyelids she could see zig-zagging confusing images: roses flushed with the sun and heavily petalled, their scent filling her nostrils, but still unable to eliminate the sensually thrilling slightly musky scent of the man beside her. She could see his hand, his fingers as he reached for one of the roses.

'No, don't pick it,' she whispered to him. 'It will live longer out here…'

'You're such a baby…'

The warm indulgent sound of his voice echoed against her ears like the sound of the sea heard in a shell, audible, recognisable, but somehow at a distance.

She could feel his breath against her skin, her

mouth, as he leaned closer to her, and she held her own breath, knowing he was going to kiss her, her stomach muscles tensing on a shock-surge of excitement and anticipation.

His mouth feathered delicately against hers, the touch of his lips as light and delicate as the warm air against the roses, but she still quivered in mute delight. She could feel his hands moving up her arms, cupping the balls of her shoulders. Instinctively she moved closer to him whilst his tongue probed the softly closed line of her lips, as busily determined to taste her sweetness as the bee seeking the roses' honeyed pollen-dusted centre.

Her whole body quivered, her response mute no longer as she gave a soft moan of delirious pleasure.

'Dominic...'

Abruptly Annie opened her eyes. Where she had been pleasantly warm and relaxed she was now icily cold and tense, and yet despite the shivers shuddering through her she could feel sweat beading her forehead.

What was happening to her? Was she going mad, or was what she had just experienced a flashback to reality, the sharply jagged edge of a memory forcing its way into her conscious awareness?

Had Dominic once kissed her here, in this secluded rose garden?

'Annie?'

When she heard Dominic's voice she tried to compose herself, but as he looked at her and she saw his expression she knew she had not succeeded.

'What is it? What's wrong?' he demanded sharply as he reached her.

He made an imposing figure, standing there in his office suit and a crisp white shirt, looking both formidable and yet somehow virilely male at the same time. Or was it her own memories that were making her see him like that? Her memories... Automatically Annie closed her eyes.

'I...I think I may just have remembered something,' she heard herself admitting shakily.

Why had she said that? Why had she said anything? But it was too late now to regret her impulsiveness. Dominic was next to her, one hand reaching out to hold her arm as he exclaimed, 'You have? What? Tell me...'

'It was nothing...not really,' Annie started to deny it, reluctant now to describe to him the very sensual and intimate nature of her experience.

'You're lying,' Dominic challenged her. 'Tell me, Annie. I have a right to know.'

Annie swallowed. She was beginning to feel slightly giddy and disorientated—because of the heat or because of what had happened? She could feel herself beginning to tremble.

'I'm sorry,' she heard Dominic apologise unexpectedly as he felt her body tremor beneath his touch. 'I didn't mean to sound so aggressive.'

His apology melted Annie's resistance. Hesitantly she tried to tell him what had happened, beginning, 'It was the roses... I could smell them, and then suddenly...' She stopped and looked at him, unaware of the apprehension and the appeal Dominic could see so clearly in her eyes.

'Was there ever a time…?' she began uncertainly. 'Did we…?'

Dominic knew immediately what she was trying to ask.

'You loved this part of the garden,' he told her quietly. 'You often used to come here and…' He paused and looked away from her. 'I know how difficult and painful this must be for you, Annie,' he told her, in a much less controlled tone of voice. 'But unlike you I *do* have my memories of our time together and…'

He stopped, his hand dropping away from her arm. Oddly Annie discovered that she missed its warmth. Awkwardly she raised her own hand, without realising what she was doing, her eyes widening as Dominic looked at it and then reached out and clasped it with his, entwining his fingers with hers and keeping his gaze on their entwined clasped hands as he continued.

'I'm not altogether immune to those memories of that time…'

Annie could see his chest rise and fall as he took a steadying breath.

'It was here that I told you I wanted to take a mental photograph of you, to take with me when I left, and here that…'

'…that you kissed me and said that my skin smelled sweeter than any rose ever could,' Annie finished, shakily and gravely.

There was a small silent pause before Dominic nodded his head and said bleakly, 'Yes.'

'I...I've only just remembered that bit...when you told me about the photograph. Before I could only remember how you...that you had kissed me here,' Annie heard herself confiding.

'Yes. I kissed you here,' Dominic was agreeing. 'And you kissed me back, and... Oh, God, Annie...'

Suddenly she was in his arms and his mouth was on hers, and the kiss they were sharing was anything but a mere memory.

She ought to stop him, Annie knew, but instead her lips were clinging eagerly to his, and this time the warm sensual scent of man, of him, which was doing so much to destroy her self-control, was in no way imaginary—and perhaps because of that was having a much more dangerous effect on her senses.

Was it because of what she had remembered that she was feeling like this, that she was responding to him like this, wanting him like this? Annie wondered dizzily as his tongue-tip probed her lips and they parted for him.

'Dominic. Dominic...Dominic...' She was even unaware of saying his name until she heard him respond rawly against her mouth,

'Yes. Yes... I'm here...' And then his hands were cupping her face as his tongue probed deeper and more intimately, and their bodies clung and melded together as though they were, in reality, still lovers.

Some things could never be forgotten or wiped out. Some feelings...some needs... Annie's heart thudded frantically against her ribs as her legs parted automatically to make way for the tautness of Dominic's thigh. Instinctively she leaned into him, shivering with pleasure.

Soon he would kiss her throat, and then her breasts, gently peeling away her clothes so that he was free to do so... He would tell her that she was beautiful beyond compare, and her nipples would tighten into two hard, excited, imploring buds that he would suckle into full flower and then...

'No!' Her voice high and sharp with panic, Annie broke the kiss and pulled away.

For a split second she and Dominic stared at one another in shared anguish and shock, and then, equally immediately, both of them threw up protective shutters of wariness to conceal from one another their thoughts and feelings.

'You shouldn't have done that—' Annie began, but Dominic stopped her, interrupting her tersely.

'You shouldn't have let me,' he countered.

Let him! At least he hadn't said she shouldn't have responded to him, Annie tried to comfort herself.

Suddenly she felt very cold and tired, and as though he sensed it Dominic said almost gently, 'Look, I appreciate how difficult this must be for you. But it isn't exactly easy for me either, you know.'

'No,' Annie agreed shakily. 'But at least you can remember about...about us. I...' Tears filled her eyes, her voice becoming gruff with the frustration of her feelings. 'You're back earlier than I expected,' she told him, changing the subject.

'It's a nice afternoon. I thought you might feel like

going out,' he told her. 'But if you aren't feeling well…'

'I'm fine,' Annie told him untruthfully. She still felt dizzy and slightly disorientated, but whether that was because of what she had remembered of the past or because of what she felt now, here, in the present, when Dominic had kissed her, she didn't know. And neither did she want to know. Because she was afraid of what she might have to confront?

'Perhaps now that you have remembered something this might be a good time to see if you could remember a little bit more,' Dominic suggested quietly.

'What do you mean?' Annie challenged him warily. If he was going to suggest that he kissed her again then there was no way she was going to go along with his suggestion, but when he answered her sharp query his voice was gently reassuring.

'I thought we might go out for a drive, revisit some of the places we went when we were… together. It might just help to jog your memory.'

Cautiously Annie examined his suggestion.

'Do you really…? I suppose it won't do any harm,' she admitted grudgingly. She might not be sure that she wanted to go along with Dominic's suggestion, but she *was* sure that she didn't want to stay here in the intimacy of the rose garden with him.

At least there could be no memories associated with Dominic's car, she acknowledged with a small sense of relief as she reached for her seat belt. This was a new model and...

'What kind of car did you have...then?' she asked him, suddenly curious in spite of herself.

'Then?' he questioned as he eased the large BMW out into the traffic on the busy road. 'You mean when you and I first met?'

Annie nodded her head.

'You can't remember?' he pressed her.

She started to shake her head, and then, for some reason, she had a mental image of a rather battered four-wheel drive vehicle, its dark green paintwork mud-spattered and scratched.

'Was it a...? No! I can't remember,' she told him shortly.

Immediately Dominic sensed that she was fibbing. Well, two could play at *that* game.

'It was a small sports model,' he told her, casually and untruthfully. 'Bright red...'

'What?'

'You look surprised,' Dominic told her. 'Why? What kind of car did you expect me to have had?'

'Er...I don't know,' Annie told him, shrugging as she said uncertainly, 'I thought perhaps a Land Rover, or something of that type.'

'A Range Rover,' Dominic corrected her softly. 'A dark green Range Rover...'

They were driving through the town now, and into the town square, where Dominic swung the car into a parking space. 'Come on,' he told Annie, 'We're going for a walk.'

* * *

'Well?' Dominic demanded half an hour later, his hand very firmly clasping hers as he walked Annie for the third time along the narrow street where he told her they had first met.

'No,' she told him truthfully. 'Nothing. There's *nothing*.'

As she saw the look of disappointment in his eyes her own emotions filled her eyes with defeated tears.

'Do you think any of this is *easy* for me?' she challenged him. 'I *dreamed* about you,' she told him helplessly. 'I thought you were my *dream* lover. But *this* isn't a dream, it's a nightmare, and it's horrible, unbearable…and I don't want it…'

'Just like you don't want me?' Dominic suggested.

Annie didn't dare to look at him.

'This isn't going to work,' she said shakily instead. Out of the corner of her eye she could see a young couple walking towards them, the girl nestled up against her boyfriend, his arm protectively holding her close. Just as they drew level with Annie and Dominic they paused, stopping to kiss one another, lightly at first and then with increasing passion. The girl pulled away first, laughing breathlessly. Transfixed, Annie was unable to look away from them, the girl's laughter seemed to echo inside her head, making her feel giddy.

'Annie?'

She could hear Dominic calling her name and somehow forced herself to focus on him, dragging her gaze away from the young couple.

'I'm tired, Dominic,' she told him. 'I want to go home…'

A little to her surprise he didn't press her to stay, or make any further unkind comments, but instead of driving back to the house he drove out of town and through country lanes to a small pub she had visited on a couple of occasions with Helena and Bob. It was well known for its excellent home-cooked food but there was no way she could ever have visited it with Dominic because it had opened as an eating place only two or three years previously.

'We never came here,' she told him positively.

'No, I know,' he responded. 'But we both need something to eat and I thought it might help for us to be on mutually unfamiliar territory.'

I'm not hungry, she wanted to say. But suddenly, surprisingly, she was.

Their meal, accompanied by a couple of glasses of wine, had had the inevitable effect of relaxing her—perhaps a little too much, Annie acknowledged a couple of hours later when she opened her eyes to discover that she had fallen asleep whilst Dominic had been driving her home.

'Are you feeling okay?' he asked her as she focused bemusedly on him.

Perhaps it was the male amusement she could see in his eyes, or perhaps it was the certain something she felt she could see behind it. Annie didn't know. What she did know, though, was that his air of male superiority somehow irritated her.

'Yes, I'm fine,' she snapped, quickly sitting upright in her seat. 'A couple of glasses of wine doesn't turn me into…a…a drunk.'

'No,' he agreed, his mouth suddenly quirking up at the corners and his eyes gleaming with a look that sent a thrill of sharply warning emotion flashing through her body. 'But if my memory serves me right, and I know it does, what it does turn you into is a delightfully uninhibited and loving woman who—'

'Stop it!' Annie commanded him shakily, immediately putting her hands up to her ears to blot out the sound of his voice. She was feeling vulnerable enough as it was, without him making things even worse. Without waiting to see what effect her distress might have had on him, Annie reached for her door handle and opened the door of the car, hurrying towards the front door of the house.

She had almost reached it when Dominic caught up with her, his hand reaching for her as, to her astonishment, he apologised quietly, 'I'm sorry. I shouldn't have said that.'

'No. You shouldn't,' Annie agreed shakily, and then, urged on by her own sense of fair-mindedness, she added truthfully, 'I know how anxious you are for me to regain my memory, but making digs at me about things you can remember that I can't, in the hope of reactivating my memory...'

There was a small pause whilst Dominic unlocked the door, and then as Annie made to step through it he totally confounded her by saying softly, 'Who says it was your *memory* I was hoping to reactivate?'

He had been drinking too, she reminded herself as she struggled to find an explanation for his extraordinary statement. Even if he had only had one glass to her two, and even though he had always had a much harder head for alcohol. She could remember well how he'd used to urge her to finish her first glass whilst he had been on his… She stopped dead in the hallway. She *could* remember. Unsteadily she walked towards the kitchen, where she could see Dominic filling the kettle and then reaching for two coffee mugs.

'Okay, okay, I know I shouldn't have said that,' he began as she walked into the room, but then, the moment he saw her face, he stopped and put down the coffee mugs, walking quickly towards her and taking hold of her gently as he asked quietly, 'What is it? What's happened?'

Too bemused to question how he could so instinctively know that something *had* happened, Annie replied shakily, 'I'm not sure. It's…' She stopped and looked up into his face, her eyes wide and dark, huge with a heart-touching mixture of pride and apprehension as she told him uncertainly, 'It's nothing, really… Just…'

When she stopped she could feel his fingers tightening a little on her arms, communicating to her his own tension. 'I remembered that I was always still on my first glass of wine whilst you were finishing your second.' As she saw him frown she tried to explain. 'It was… I could see you…us…' she told him huskily. 'I could *hear* you… It was almost as though I was actually there…

'You're disappointed?' she guessed when he didn't speak. 'I'm sorry. I…'

'No, no...' Dominic was quick to reassure her. 'You mustn't be. I'm not... It's a start.'

'Yes,' she agreed a little bleakly as he released her arms. It was obvious that he had hoped she might have remembered more, and she herself was beginning to wish that she had...that she could... Her head had started to ache. Because of the wine?

She wished he wouldn't be so nice to her, so understanding. She far preferred it when he was angry and antagonistic towards her. That way... That way what? That way she could refuse to acknowledge those unwanted tendrils of emotion and longing that were beginning to curl their way around her heart? She was just suffering from confusion...*delusion*...imagining that...subconsciously remembering that they had once loved one another. But that had been in the past, a past that she couldn't remember...a past where she had walked out on him and that love.

'I'm tired,' she told him unsteadily. 'I think I'll go straight to bed.'

Dominic watched her walk away from him, his forehead furrowed in a small frown. She looked so vulnerable, so lost and sad, that he wanted to run after her, to sweep her into his arms and tell her not to worry, that the past didn't matter, that they could... That they could what? Start again? What the hell was he thinking? Just because he had seen her earlier as the girl she had been...just because when he had kissed her she had responded to him...reminded him...

But it wasn't *that* girl who had moved him to re-

morse and filled him with tenderness just now—was
it?

So he still had feelings for her…still reacted to
her? Still wanted her, dammit. So what? He was allowed to be *human*, wasn't he? And besides, none
of that meant…

None of that meant what? That he was falling in
love with her all over again? As a woman this time
and not a girl.

He took a mouthful of his coffee and grimaced. It
tasted sharp and bitter. Irritably he poured it away.
Wasteful, perhaps, but better that than suffering the
inevitable after-effects of drinking it so strong: the
insomnia, the heartburn…

Heartburn? Oh, yes, he had suffered enough of
that…more than enough!

CHAPTER EIGHT

RESTLESSLY Annie looked across the darkened bedroom to the window and then at her watch. It was just gone two in the morning and she had been awake for well over an hour, her thoughts racing round inside her head in an exhausting chase that led nowhere.

The recovered fragments of her lost memory taunted her, defying her to make proper sense of them, their real meaning tormentingly eluding her.

Somewhere deep inside her subconscious lay the answer to the question both she and Dominic wanted so desperately to have answered. But she was no closer to discovering just what it was. The brief memories of her marriage she had regained had only reinforced what her dreams had already told her— namely that her body yearned for Dominic as its lover, its mate, and that whatever her reason had been for leaving him—and it must have been a very strong and important one—it had not been strong or important enough to destroy her desire for him...

Her desire?

Impatiently she pushed back the bedcovers and slid her feet to the floor. There was no way she was going to sleep now. She might as well go downstairs and make herself the cup of tea her parched throat was crying out for.

A rueful smile curled her mouth as she reached for the familiar warmth of her cotton robe. It had been a present from Helena and Bob, a private joke of a gift, after she had commented on having seen it in a shop window. White cotton printed with little black heart outlines and written messages. For some reason it had attracted her attention. It was a girl's robe, really, rather than a woman's, short and demure, but she still loved it.

As she made her way quietly downstairs she paused to admire the carved balustrade, automatically stroking her fingers along the polished wood. The long months of her recovery had given her time, which she had used in reading and learning…in thinking, broadening her outlook in every direction. The uncertain young girl she had been, defensively concerned that others would reject her because of her background, had been replaced by a young woman confident in herself and about herself.

It still hurt, of course, to know that her mother had abandoned her and that she would never, ever know just who her parents were. But the mutual love and respect that existed between herself and Helena, the rapport and closeness they shared, had shown her that it was as herself that she was valued, *because* of what and who she was and not in spite of it.

In the children's home where she had grown up she had been too quiet and withdrawn to make many friends, or to have much appeal to the couples who had come to the home looking for a child to adopt or foster.

Annie paused as she reached the bottom of the

stairs, her forehead pleating in a small frown as she remembered one particularly painful incident from her childhood.

She had been about four at the time, one of two little girls being considered for adoption by a young couple who had already visited the home on several occasions. Annie had hoped desperately that they would choose her, but she had been too shy to vocalise her feelings to them when they had taken her out, praying desperately at night instead that they would choose her. But then had come the day when they had visited the home with an older couple— obviously the parents of one of them, Annie now realised. She had been standing outside the door, waiting to be summoned in to see them, when she had overheard a conversation between them all.

'I like Annie,' she had heard the younger woman saying. 'She is so sweet and pretty.'

'Annie?' the older woman had intervened sharply. 'Isn't that the child who was abandoned? I don't think you should chose her, Elaine. You don't have the faintest idea what her background is—other than... Well, I mean, circumstances speak for themselves, don't they? What kind of person would abandon their child? And you know what they say about bad blood! No. I think you should go for the dark-haired one. At least you know her background.'

As in any structured society there had been a hierarchy, a pecking order in the home, and Annie had already known that she was 'different' from most of the others, in that no one had any idea who she was or where she had come from. She had been found by an elderly woman, wrapped in a woolly jumper in the ladies' toilets at a town's busy railway station, and despite every attempt on the part of the authorities for someone to come forward and claim her no one had done so. At that moment she had known why. It was because she had bad blood!

In the kitchen she made herself a cup of tea and then walked back into the hallway, stopping as she reached the open door to the sitting room.

It had been in there that she and Dominic had cuddled up together in the evenings. Reading...talking...

Shakily she walked into the room, heading, not for the sofa but for the large chair alongside it, carefully placing her tea on the coffee table and then sitting down facing the sofa, staring searchingly at it.

What was she looking for? Some inner vision of Dominic and herself seated there?

She was, she discovered, holding her breath, willing herself almost to see them...to remember more... But already the memory was fading, stubbornly refusing to metamorphose into anything more meaningful.

Angrily Annie subsided into her chair. She felt as though her own memory was playing a deliberately tormenting game with her, feeding her just enough information to lead her on but then refusing to give her something more substantial.

There was a notepad and a pen on the table, and on an impulse she reached out and picked them up, settling back in the chair, curling her legs beneath her as she started to doodle idly.

Stiff, spiky-branched trees...a little house, four-square to the world, with curtained windows and smoke coming out of its chimney. She gave it a garden, picket-fenced and secure. Well, it didn't take much imagination to know what *that* represented. But what about the river she had also drawn, and the car? A large, boxy vehicle, not totally unlike a four-wheel drive—Dominic's Range Rover?

'Think… Think…' Annie urged herself. 'Remember…'

She started to write. Dominic's name, she realised when she had finished, with little sketched hearts over the 'i's instead of dots. Now why had she done that? She wrote down the word 'marriage', and then under it she started to write another list of words, her pen moving faster and faster as she did so.

When she finally stopped she was breathing as though she had physically exerted herself and her heart was pounding.

Nervously she studied the list.

Love. Trust. Respect. Joy. Sharing. Acceptance. Dominic.

Tears blurred her eyes.

Dominic grimaced as he stared at his alarm clock. He had woken up abruptly several minutes ago, as alertly and totally awake as though it was seven in the morning and not still three.

He knew there was no way he was going to go back to sleep. He might as well use the time to do some work. Slipping out of bed, he pulled on his robe.

*   *   *

Annie was concentrating so hard on her list that she
failed to see or hear Dominic until he was in the
sitting room, and her face burned bright pink with
self-consciousness when she looked up and saw him.

'I couldn't sleep,' she told him, almost defensively. 'So I came downstairs to make a drink…'

'Mmm… Me too…' Dominic told her, going to
stand beside her so that he could look down at the
list she wasn't quite quick enough to conceal.

'What are you doing?' he asked curiously.

'It's nothing…just… I just thought if I wrote down
whatever came into my head it might somehow…'

'May I see?' Dominic asked her, sitting down on
the sofa.

Reluctantly Annie handed over the piece of paper.
'I don't know why I bothered,' she told him. 'It was
a silly idea and… What is it?' she demanded as she
saw the way he was frowning as he concentrated on
the paper.

'Nothing,' he told her shortly, and then, as though
he recognised how curt he had been, he explained,
'It's the little hearts…above the ''i''s. Like these on
your robe,' he added, pointing out a similarity that
Annie herself hadn't recognised. 'That's the way you
always used to write my name. You used to say that
the hearts were ours.'

He looked back at the list and Annie studiously
avoided meeting his eyes when he eventually finished. She was aware of a very special subtle aura
of intimacy and closeness enclosing them, as though
both of them had briefly let down their defences.

'*What* went wrong between us?' she asked

Dominic helplessly. *'Why…?'* She stopped and took a deep breath before admitting shakily to him, 'Sometimes I feel I'm destined to have unanswered questions in my life, empty spaces…'

Her eyes clouded and Dominic guessed intuitively what she was thinking. Like her, he too was conscious of an unexpected closeness between them, a sense of them sharing their need to discover her lost past.

'You mean your parents?' he asked her.

Numbly Annie nodded her head.

'I often wonder if she, my mother, ever thinks of me.'

Her unguarded admission touched Dominic's feelings in a way he hadn't expected. He was in danger of responding to her as though he still loved her, he warned himself, and then proceeded to ignore his self-warning as he told her gently, 'I'm sure she does.'

It was and always had been his personal opinion that the mother who had abandoned Annie as a very new baby must have been a very young and very frightened girl, too immature and too afraid to admit that she had given birth, and Dominic felt equally sure that as she had grown up and matured she must have spent many sad hours wondering about the baby girl she had abandoned.

'I could never do that to my child,' Annie burst out passionately. 'Never. Not under any circumstances. Not for anyone…' She stopped and flushed. What on earth had provoked such an outburst from her?

'Can I ask…?' she began, and then stopped, before speaking again and very quickly, so she didn't lose her courage or change her mind. 'Will you tell me what it was like for us…being married?' she asked Dominic huskily. 'Perhaps it might help me to remember. I don't know…'

'It was…it was very good,' Dominic told her sombrely. 'In fact…' He paused and looked past her, as though he was able to see something she could not. 'It was more than very good, Annie,' he told her. 'It was…we were…'

As she heard the emotion in his voice and saw the brief sheen on remembered pain in his eyes Annie was overwhelmed with sorrow and remorse.

'Oh, Dominic,' she protested. 'I…'

She stopped and looked at him, his eyes…his mouth…his… Her heart lurched as her gaze was drawn inextricably back to his mouth.

'Annie…'

She could hear the protest in his voice, and the need, and then suddenly they were reaching for one another, touching, kissing, with an inevitability that Annie knew nothing could have prevented.

Annie felt herself being lifted tenderly out of her chair and drawn down against Dominic's body. She had no will to resist him; she could find no need, no reason. She felt his hand tremble slightly as he smoothed her hair off her face. They might have made love a hundred times before, but instinctively Annie knew that this was different, that this was special; what they were feeling, sharing, was not merely a re-enactment of their shared past.

This Dominic, who held and touched her now, was not a figment of her imagination, nor even her husband from the past. This Dominic was the man he was in the here and now.

In the light of the lamp she had switched on she could see his face, shadowed and mysterious and yet at the same time familiar. She traced the shape of his jaw, the curve of his cheekbone, and then stopped as she saw the way he was watching her. Time itself seemed to rock to a standstill—no sound, no movement, no breath even breaking the intensity of their silent communication with one another.

Very slowly and carefully Dominic lowered his head towards her. Automatically her lips parted, her eyes closing in sweet, sensual anticipation. His lips felt warm against hers, their caress so sensitising and arousing that she started to quiver. A soft moan broke the silence between them as his hands slid down her body, shaping the nakedness of her curves beneath her thin robe.

Now she understood why she had been so drawn to its small printed hearts. They *were* almost an exact replica of the ones she had drawn in Dominic's name. She pressed closer to him, her mouth softening enticingly beneath his.

Dominic shuddered as he felt the response of her mouth and her body. Beneath his touch her nipples had flowered into life, and he could see as well as feel their sharp outline beneath her robe. His body was even more flagrantly proclaiming its own arousal, and his tongue was pushing against the flimsy resistance of her softened lips.

What had begun as an attempt to show her just
how good their love had been had turned swiftly into
something far more potently dangerous, and rooted
in the present. The woman he was holding, kissing…caressing…wanting…wasn't the Annie of the
past, the girl he had married. The woman he was
holding now…wanting now…was Annie as she now
was, and the way he wanted her, the intensity with
which he wanted her, faded into insignificance his
memories of the way they had once been.

He had known already of the danger he was in,
and now it couldn't be denied any longer. He *was*
falling in love with her all over again, abusing the
power his position in her life gave him to use, what
on her part had been an innocent and anguished plea
for his help to satisfy his own need.

He had to stop before it was too late…before he…

Annie tensed in loss and bemusement as Dominic
tore his mouth from hers. He was breathing heavily,
and she could feel her own heart pumping fast in
aroused response.

'Dominic,' she protested yearningly, but he was
already distancing himself from her.

'We shouldn't be doing this,' he told her curtly.
'This isn't… We're playing with fire, Annie,' he told
her bluntly. 'It would be the easiest thing in the
world for me to take you to bed now, but…'

Annie felt her face start to burn with humiliation,
but much as she longed to be able to do so she knew
she couldn't deny his assertion. What was wrong
with her? Where was her pride? Why was she fling-

ing herself at him, virtually begging him to make love to her?

'You're right,' she agreed proudly, forcing herself to appear indifferent and unconcerned. 'To be honest,' she added as carelessly as she could, as she turned away to pick up the sheet of paper she had been writing on, 'personally, *I* don't believe it matters *why* our marriage ended. Even if I did remember, it wouldn't change anything. I think it would be best if we just went ahead and got a divorce.'

What would she do if he grabbed hold of her and told her there was no way he ever wanted to let her go? Did he *really* need to ask himself that question? Dominic wondered grimly.

Only now did he recognise that somewhere over the last few days his desire to understand why Annie had left him, to draw a line under their marriage, had been replaced by a far more urgent need to discover what had gone wrong in order that he could somehow put it right. It wasn't the past and formally ending their marriage he was focusing on, but the present, and the future he wanted to convince Annie they could have together.

'Best for whom?' he challenged her sharply as the fragile fabric of his hopes gave way under the weight of reality. 'Not for me. There are still answers that I need from you, Annie. And until I get them...'

He stopped and took a deep breath before continuing. 'Look, this isn't going to get us anywhere. I suggest that we will be able to discuss the whole subject more rationally when we've slept on it.'

He was right; Annie knew. Her own emotions felt

strung out, raw and over-sensitive. She ached for him in a way that both tormented and infuriated her. He had no right to be able to make her feel like this.

But half an hour later in her own room, waiting for sleep to deaden the intensity of her emotions, a tear crept down her cheek as she reflected unwillingly on the closeness she had felt between them before Dominic had destroyed it. Was that what it had been like between them? Had they been so close, so attuned to one another, so much in love with one another that nothing and no one else had mattered?

An aching sense of loss and loneliness filled her, a sharply acute feeling of grief and pain as she wept for the love that she and Dominic had somehow, between them, destroyed.

'Tell me again. Everything. All of it…right from when we met…' Annie demanded doggedly.

Dominic sighed, examining her pale set face. They had been treating one another with cautious reserve since the night he had so nearly given in to the temptation to make love to her, and it made his heart ache to see the way Annie was driving herself, pushing herself, to try to regain her memory.

They were walking by the river, and suddenly Annie gave a sharp exclamation as a couple of youths on bicycles came up behind her, sounding their horns and making her stumble in surprise.

Automatically Dominic reached out to steady her, frowning as he felt the way her body shuddered beneath his protective arm.

'Are you all right?' he asked her in concern.

'They gave me a shock,' Annie admitted. Her teeth had started to chatter together and she was trembling so violently that Dominic was loath to let her go.

'You said we met *when*?' she began to prompt him, but Dominic refused to be diverted.

'You're not well,' he told her sharply. 'And I think—'

'I don't care what you think, Dominic,' Annie interrupted him in a high, strained voice. 'All I care about is finding out why I left you and getting on with my life.'

Dominic's concern increased. He was worried that if he didn't take a stand the pressure she was putting herself under to try to remember was going to make her ill.

Every day now, several times a day, she insisted on him telling her the history of their relationship, demanding to know every tiny detail and listening to him with increasing desperation as nothing he said triggered off any memories for her.

'*Why* can't I remember?' Annie demanded helplessly. 'Why? Why…?'

She sounded and looked so tortured that Dominic automatically wanted to comfort her.

'Don't. Don't push yourself so hard,' he urged her, and then as she turned her head he caught sight of the tears on her eyelashes and it was too much for his self-control.

'Annie, Annie,' he groaned as he reached for her.

Frantically Annie tensed against the tormenting intimacy of his arms. His breath brushed softly against her skin and her body quivered helplessly in longing for him. She wanted him so much…loved him so much… How could she deny it?

'No, Dominic,' she protested defensively, but it was already too late, and her lips parted weakly under his as he brushed the tears from her eyelashes.

Obliviously they clung together, sharing the bittersweetness of a kiss that could have been that of tender new lovers. But she couldn't let him guess how she felt. Her pride wouldn't let her.

Somehow she managed to find the strength to push him away. As she turned away from him suddenly the world turned dark and swung dizzily around her.

'Annie…'

She could hear the anxiety in Dominic's voice as he called her name, but somehow she was distanced from it and in another place…another time… She had a vivid sharp memory of another occasion on which she had walked beside the river with Dominic. They had kissed then too, but then… Annie drew in her breath in a sharply painful gasp.

'Annie? What is it? What's wrong? Tell me,' Dominic insisted.

Hazily Annie focused on him. Her mental image of them had faded now. But not the memory it had brought.

'I…we were walking here,' she told him distantly. 'You kissed me, and then…' She stopped and looked back the way they had just walked, in the direction in which the house lay.

'And then I whispered to you that I wanted to take you home, to be where I could make love to you properly,' Dominic supplied rawly for her. 'And you looked at me and—'

'I don't want to hear any more,' Annie interrupted him. Her mouth had gone dry and her heart had started to race. The images Dominic's soft words were conjuring up were making her feel far too vulnerable.

It was only her pride now that was making her grit her teeth and see through her determination to make herself remember. Every day she spent with Dominic, every hour was making her more and more aware of the danger she was in. She might not know why she had left him but she certainly knew why she had fallen in love with him.

Only this morning, in an unguarded moment, he had made her laugh with his droll description of an incident which had taken place at work. And it had disconcerted her to discover that they shared not only the same taste in food but that they also read the same newspaper, liked the same kind of countryside, enjoyed the same TV programmes, felt passionate about the same issues.

'Come on,' Dominic told her abruptly. 'I'm taking you home. Oh, it's all right,' he assured her when he saw the panic crossing her face, 'I'm not about to re-enact our past and take you to bed. If I did…'

He stopped, and Annie stopped too, forgetting the danger of looking intimately at him as she lifted her gaze to his face and felt her heart thump and bang against her ribs in reactive punishment.

'You're exhausted. No, don't bother trying to deny

it. I can see it in your eyes. You're pushing yourself too hard...'

'You're the one who wants me to remember,' Annie told him shortly, but he refused to react to her defensive aggression.

'I thought we'd agreed that we *both* need to know the truth,' he said calmly. When she made no response he continued gently, 'Come on, let's get you home.'

Home! Quickly Annie blinked away the humiliating threat of her tears. She had been so awed, so thrilled—so overwhelmed when she had realised that Dominic's house was to be her home.

'Well, where did you expect us to live?' he had teased her lovingly.

'I... I,.. It's so big,' she had breathed.

'It's just a house, Annie,' Dominic had tried to reassure her. 'Bricks and mortar, that's all. Only with you to share it with me it can truly become a home.'

A home. *Her* home. The *first* real home she had ever known. And Dominic had gone out of his way to make sure she had felt that it *was* her home.

He had taken her shopping, insisting that she was to choose new decor for their shared bedroom, encouraging her to trust her own instincts and taste. She smiled wryly, remembering the hours she had spent poring over books she had bought, trying to find out what style of decor would be right for the house.

'The Chinese silk would have been wonderful, but I was afraid because it was so expensive,' she said now.

Both of them looked at one another, and then,

without any kind of hesitation, Dominic said easily, 'You mean for the bedroom curtains? Yes, it would have looked good. Especially if you'd given in and let me buy that four-poster bed.'

Annie closed her eyes in despair.

'What's wrong with me?' she demanded in a guarded voice. '*Why* can I remember something as unimportant as the curtain fabric I didn't choose when I can't remember the most vital thing of all?'

There was a brief pause before Dominic replied somberly, 'Perhaps it's less painful to remember why you rejected the silk.'

He didn't say anything else. He didn't need to, Annie recognised. What he had implied was that her rejection of *him* was something too traumatic for her to allow herself to recall, and she knew that he was probably right.

Out of all the questions she had asked him, she acknowledged, there was one she still had not been able to bring herself to ask, but now, suddenly, she felt she had to do so. Touching his arm tentatively, she asked huskily, 'Why do *you* think I left?'

At first she thought he wasn't going to answer her. The bleak expression hardening his mouth made her shiver a little.

'How many times have I asked myself that question?' he said, half under his breath. 'And not been able to give myself an answer. I can't think of any logical explanation. You were upset because I was going away. We had rowed about it. We'd been having a series of petty rows brought on by the tension of our imminent parting.'

'But I knew right from the start that you had to go.'

Annie had surprised herself by defending him. A wry smile touched his mouth. 'You're playing devil's advocate with a vengeance,' he told her. 'I *had* told you, yes, but that didn't stop me from feeling guilty about leaving you.'

'But you had no choice,' Annie insisted.

His mouth turned down at the corners.

'There are always choices. I could have broken the contract. I could have put you first...shown you... You were too young for the pressure of that kind of separation and...' Dominic paused, carefully searching for words that would not anger or offend her. 'Your background being as it was meant that you had more need to feel secure...wanted...loved. Perhaps more than I had made allowance for. Perhaps...'

'Perhaps that made me run away like a sulky child?' Annie supplied grimly for him, adding before he could stop her, 'A sulky child demanding attention and playing up to get it... Is *that* what I was like, Dominic?'

'No. Not at all,' he tried to reassure her.

'But that is what you think, isn't it?' she guessed. 'You think I *did* leave because you were going away, to punish you for leaving me. But that's so childish.'

'It's a possibility,' he allowed. 'You were very young, and at that age it's dangerously easy to mistake a crush for love.'

Annie frowned. Although his explanation sounded feasible, for some reason she couldn't accept it. It jarred on her, rubbed against her own inner knowledge of herself.

'Come on,' Dominic reiterated. 'You're exhausted. What you need is a hot bath and then bed. I'll bring you some supper up on a tray and—'

'Read me a bedtime story?' Annie finished dryly. 'I'm not a child now, Dominic.'

'No,' he agreed. 'You're not. And anyway, aren't bedtime stories supposed to have happy endings?' he asked, in a sharply bleak voice that wrenched at her own emotions so painfully she caught her breath.

There could be no happy ending to their own story. Not unless— Not unless what? Not unless Dominic told her that he didn't care what had happened in the past, that he loved her far too much in the here and now to ever let her go? Was that what she really wanted? What she wanted was him, Dominic—her lover, her husband, her fate, she recognised achingly.

'I've got to go into the office and the chances are that I'm going to have to work late,' Dominic told Annie as he finished his breakfast.

Annie averted her face. The sight and smell of his coffee was making her feel acutely nauseous, and her stomach heaved protestingly, just as it had heaved for the last three mornings in a row. 'Will you be all right here on your own?'

'I'll be fine,' she assured him. The scald wounds on her arm had healed cleanly, without any problems, and even Dominic was forced to agree with her doctor that she was now fully recovered.

Dominic looked across the table at her.

'There's something I want you to promise me,' he told her quietly.

Annie gave a small sigh.

'If I remember anything I promise you I'll tell you about it—' she began, but he stopped her with a shake of his head.

'No, that isn't what I was going to ask.' He made a movement as though he was going to reach for her, and then stopped himself, getting up to go and stand with his back to her in front of the window. 'I want you to promise me, Annie, that there won't be another disappearing act. Promise me,' he demanded harshly when she made no immediate response.

He was afraid that she was going to leave whilst he was gone. Bemusedly Annie stared at his dark-suited back. His shoulders were so broad, his stance so upright, his air so authoritative and male that it was almost impossible for her to believe that he was vulnerable in any kind of way, but his words were telling her a different story.

'If I don't promise?' she asked him huskily.

He turned round.

'Then I don't go,' he told her unequivocally.

Annie blinked in surprise. If it mattered so much to him that she stayed, then—she was letting her imagination and her own feelings run away with her, she warned herself. The reason he wanted her to stay was because he still wanted to get to the bottom of why she had left him.

'I…I'll stay,' she told him unsteadily. As she glanced towards the calendar on the kitchen wall she recognised absently that she had already been here with him for over a month. Over a month! Her stomach started to churn like a washing machine on full spin. Over a *month*! That meant…

Somehow Annie managed to make herself wait until after Dominic had gone before going over to the calendar and frantically counting backwards. Her stomach was heaving, panic and nausea vying for supremacy as the truth hit her in a sweat-drenched sheet of shock. Blindly she turned away from the calendar, her hands shaking as she reached for the telephone and started to dial Helena's telephone number. But then, before she had completed dialling, she quickly hung up.

No… No! She couldn't share her fears with anyone else yet…not yet…not until she was sure. She *could* walk down into the town. It wasn't very far and there was a chemist's shop at the bottom of the hill. It would have what she needed. Because Helena's car was off the road Annie had insisted that she borrow her own Mercedes, which meant that she herself was temporarily without any means of transport.

Three hours later she stood numbly in the bathroom as she stared in sick disbelief at the pregnancy test she had just done. Her second…and both of them were showing a positive result. She was pregnant. Dominic would be— Dominic! Suddenly the bathroom started to sway ominously round her. Instinctively she reached for the shower door to support herself, whispering a husky, 'No.'

A confused jumble of images were forming themselves inside her head: sounds, pictures, *memories*.

Somehow she managed to make her way to Dominic's bedroom before she collapsed across the bed. The shutter which had closed her off from the past, protected her from it, had suddenly lifted, and she knew now the answer to Dominic's question. Oh, yes, she knew!

She was pregnant with Dominic's child. Just as she had thought, feared she might be all those years ago. Then she had been wrong. But now...

Dominic's belief was that she had left him as the result of an immature desire to punish him for his having to leave her...that the love she had claimed to have for him had, in reality, been little more than a youthful crush, incapable of withstanding the pressure of adult emotions. But he was wrong.

Tormentedly Annie closed her eyes.

'You don't want children?' she had asked him then, in shocked fear.

'No, I don't,' he answered with cold emphasis.

She was so shocked, so afraid. For days she had been worrying about inadvertently missing one day of taking the Pill, knowing that a baby so soon in their marriage wasn't something they had planned, feeling overwhelmed by the prospect of everything that having a baby would mean and desperately needing Dominic's love and support. Instead the reaction she was getting from him threatened to destroy her—it was certainly destroying her trust in him.

'But why not?' she forced herself to ask him, never imagining for one minute just what she was going to hear.

'Parenthood isn't just about having a baby, Annie,' he told her. 'It's a very big responsibility. When we create a child we aren't just giving it life, we are giving it...*burdening* it, if you like, with ourselves…with our own personal history. And at the moment I feel that just isn't something I would want to burden a child with.'

Their own personal history. She knew what he meant, of course. He was referring to the fact that they—*she*—knew nothing of her own parentage, of what kind of inheritance, both genetically and emotionally, she might be passing on to her own child. Contaminating it with bad blood… That was what Dominic meant. He was afraid of giving his child…their child…her bad blood.

Annie felt as though a part of her had died. As though a part of her had been broken and destroyed. She had believed Dominic totally when he told her that it was her he loved…that her history didn't matter to him. But he had lied to her.

But worse was to follow. When she tried stumblingly to tell him of her fear that it could already be too late, that she might already be carrying his child, his reaction made her feel literally sick with fear.

'An abortion! You mean you would want me to destroy our baby?' she demanded, white-faced.

'Anne, for God's sake stop being so emotional,' Dominic replied angrily.

Annie moistened her dry lips. She couldn't take in properly what had happened. How, within the space of less than twenty-four hours, with a few short, sharp words, her love, her life, her future, her trust, had all been destroyed—as Dominic would insist on her destroying their child.

Numbly she tried to come to terms with what had happened. Dominic was talking to her, trying to reason with her, coax her, but it was as though there was an invisible barrier between them. She no longer wanted even to breathe the same air as him, never mind be physically close to him. He had claimed that he loved her but he had been lying. He didn't want his child…his children…to have her as their mother. He was worried about the inheritance she might give them. He was worried that she would contaminate them with the bad blood she carried.

Suddenly he was a stranger to her. A stranger who threatened the life of her child—a child she knew she would fight to protect to the last breath of life left in her.

There was no way she could abandon her child in the way her own mother had done her. Poor baby. Why should it suffer because she was its mother? She couldn't stay with Dominic now. For her baby's sake, she had to leave him. Round and round her thoughts circled, causing a whirlpool of fear and pain that sucked her down into its black centre.

That night in bed, she couldn't sleep. Dominic had taken some medication for a headache. Logic told her that her wisest course would be to wait until he had left the country before she disappeared from his life, but his departure was still more than two weeks away and she feared that there was no way she could continue to live with him for that length of time without betraying herself.

Driven by the desperation of her own emotions, she left their bed, packed a few necessities and left the house.

CHAPTER NINE

IT WAS over two weeks since she had left Dominic. In a very short space of time now he would be leaving the country, and once he did... Once he did it was unlikely that they would ever meet again.

She didn't know why she had come back here, to the town where she had been born. She had booked herself into the cheapest bed and breakfast she could find—after all, she was financially responsible for herself now. She had been to the library and re-read the newspaper story written when she had been found abandoned. The old lady who had found her had died many years before, and as Annie already knew there was no way back for her into the past to discover exactly who and what she was. Neither was there any way forward into the future for her now, as Dominic's wife.

She shivered beneath the thin cover on her bed.

Dominic!

She missed him desperately, longed for him despairingly, despite the hurt he had inflicted on her.

It was well past midnight. What was he doing? Was he thinking of her...wondering...worrying...? Was it possible for him to love her as a woman even whilst rejecting her as a mother for his children?

She was still awake when daylight came creeping across the sky.

In another few hours Dominic would be gone. Hot, heart-wrenching tears seeped between her closed eyelids. The thought of never seeing him again made her want to crawl away somewhere and die, but she couldn't. She had her baby...*their* baby to think of.

She had to see him...just one last time... Just see him, that was all... She wouldn't say anything to him—she couldn't. She would just go home and watch him leave—watch him as he walked out of their lives...hers and his baby's...the baby he thought she wasn't good enough to mother.

She was on the first commuter train to leave town, making her slow journey back across the country. In Dominic's car, with Dominic's hands on the wheel, she could have been there in a couple of hours. But there was no direct rail service from her home town, only a series of complicated connections.

She was waiting for the train that would take her on the final lap of her journey back when she made the discovery that her flight had been for nothing, that there was to be no baby.

By the time she had dealt with the emergency of her unexpected period and dried the tears she had cried for the life that wasn't to be she had missed her connecting train.

Numbly she boarded the next one to arrive. There was no baby now to keep her and Dominic apart, but there was still her awareness, her realisation of the fact that he didn't consider her good enough to have his children. If she could catch him before he left she could tell him that their marriage was over, that he was free to find a woman whom he did consider good enough.

The journey took longer than she had expected. The train she had missed had been an express, and the one she was on was a much slower one, stopping at every station. By the time she eventually got off Annie knew that Dominic would be on his way to Heathrow for his flight.

Not knowing what to do, she started to cross the road via the pedestrian crossing...and walked straight into the path of a speeding car.

Shakily Annie wiped the tears from her face with the back of her hand.

There was no point in weeping for the sorrows of the girl she had once been. Crying wouldn't do anything to help *her*—nor to help herself *now*, she recognised.

Her body felt stiff and cold, and when she looked at her watch she was shocked to see how many hours had passed since she had first walked into Dominic's bedroom.

Now, as she looked around it, she knew *exactly* how it had felt to lie here in Dominic's arms. *Exactly* how it had felt to be loved by him and to have loved him in return. To *have* loved him? She could still taste the bitterness of her own weak tears. No wonder she had found it impossible to destroy the feelings of love she had increasingly begun to feel for him. The reality was that she had never *stopped* loving him...not for one moment.

'You left me,' he had accused her, but the truth was that *he* had abandoned *her*.

She would have to tell him just what she had discovered, of course. He had a right to know... About the past, yes, but not about the present and the baby she knew for sure she was carrying this time. No, that was her concern and hers alone, and she intended it to remain that way. He had been right then, in calling her immature and a child, but she wasn't either of those things any more. She was an adult, a woman and as such she had no need of any man to help her bear the responsibility of the new life growing inside her.

She closed her eyes, determined not to allow herself to cry any more tears. What was the point?

Logically, she knew she should wait until Dominic returned home to tell him what she had remembered, but anxiety, and a certain instinct that if she was alone with him too long he might somehow discern that she was keeping something vital from him, urged her to get the whole thing over and done with as quickly as she could.

She would pack her things, get a taxi to take her to Dominic's office and then go straight on to her own home.

Grimly Dominic stared out of his office window. For all the good he was doing at work he might as well have stayed at home, because that was where his thoughts were—at home with Annie. Annie... His wife... His woman... The woman who had left him... His *love*...

It was no use. Grittily Dominic forced himself to face the self-knowledge he had been trying to avoid. He still loved Annie. Loved her even more as a woman than he had done as a girl—if that was possible.

In maturity she had become so much more of everything she had already been. He had to see her, talk to her…tell her how he felt and if, after that, she still wanted her freedom…

Quickly he strode out of his office, heading for the exit.

Leaving the taxi driver waiting for her in the car park, nervously Annie started to make her way across it, heading for the main office of the building. It was five o'clock, and staff were already starting to leave, streaming out of the building. Suddenly Annie froze as she saw Dominic amongst them.

'Dominic!' She said his name under her breath, so totally fixated on him that her senses couldn't register anything else. 'Dominic…'

Some instinct he couldn't name made Dominic turn his head.

'Annie…'

What was she doing *here*? He started to move towards her. She was standing, staring rigidly at him.

'Annie!' He called her name, and then cursed as she suddenly seemed to shudder, a statue coming to life.

'Annie…'

Out of the corner of his eye Dominic saw the car, and realised that Annie was standing right in its path, oblivious to its presence or her own danger. With a superhuman burst of speed he reached her, pulling her down on top of him as he fell to the ground and rolling her out of the way of the car's front wheels.

As he did so he felt the sharp thud of metal striking his own body and grunted in surprise. His body felt oddly numb...but somehow heavy... Somewhere in the distance he could hear screams...voices...the wails of a siren.

'Ah, so you're back with us again. Good, I'll go and tell Dr Spears.'

Hazily Dominic focused on the smiling nurse standing beside his bed.

'You've been sleeping for so long we thought we'd start to call you Rip Van Winkle,' she told him cheerfully as she pressed the bell above his head.

Where the devil was he? What was going on? And then abruptly Dominic remembered, struggling to sit up and ignoring both the admonishment of the nurse and the pain in his side as he demanded anxiously, 'Annie, my wife. Is she...?'

'She's fine.' The nurse smiled. 'And before you ask, so is the baby.'

'The baby? The *baby*...' Dominic could feel his heart starting to thud with heavy, adrenalin-fuelled beats.

'Oh, that's sent your pulse-rate up,' the nurse commented, examining the screen on the far side of the bed. 'Your wife was lucky that you had the forethought to do what you did. Otherwise it might have been a very different story, both for her and the baby.'

Annie was pregnant!

Dominic closed his eyes, his body suddenly drenched in sweat as he realised what he might have lost.

'Where is Annie...my wife...?' he asked thickly.

'Dr Spears sent her home. She didn't want to go. She'd been sitting here beside you for virtually twenty-four hours. But he insisted. With her pregnancy at such a very early stage it's important that she doesn't over-stress herself.'

Twenty-four hours. Annie had sat with him for twenty-four hours!

'How long have I been here?' he asked the nurse.

'Mmm...nearly two days. The impact of the car knocked you out, and then Dr Spears had to sedate you so that he could examine you properly. He was concerned that there might be some permanent damage to your back, but luckily for you there isn't. You've been drifting in and out of consciousness all afternoon, but I think you're finally with us this time.'

'I want to go home,' Dominic told her, moving to throw back the covers and climb out of the hospital bed. The nurse laughed.

'What? Wired up to one of our precious machines?'

As Dominic turned his head he realised what she meant, his forehead pleating in a frown as he looked down at the wires attached to his body.

'If I'm all right, what am I doing with all this?' he demanded shortly.

'You're being monitored,' the nurse told him dryly. 'It's what we do in hospitals. Although you probably don't feel it, your body's still in shock,' she told him in a kinder voice. 'Nothing was broken by the impact when the car hit you, but you are very badly bruised and you're going to find it very painful, if not impossible, to move properly for quite a substantial length of time.'

'How long is that?' Dominic asked her suspiciously.

'Well... Ah, here's Dr Spears,' she announced, smiling at the man who had walked into Dominic's room.

'All I want to know is how soon I can go home,' Dominic told the doctor when the nurse had left. 'I want to see my wife; she's pregnant.'

'Yes, I know,' the doctor confirmed, misunderstanding what Dominic had been about to say. 'Poor girl. I don't think she knew which of you to be the more anxious about at first. But once we'd reassured her that baby is tucked away safely, just where he or she ought to be, she was able to concentrate all her anxiety on you. I've sent her home now. She needed some rest.'

'She shouldn't be on her own,' Dominic told him fiercely. 'She suffered a bad accident herself some years ago and...'

'Yes, I do know,' the doctor told him gently. 'I was on duty when they brought her in. But I think you'll find you're worrying unnecessarily. The maternal instinct is very strong and it empowers a woman with a very special kind of strength.'

'I want to go home,' Dominic repeated.

'Not yet,' the doctor told him calmly. 'I want to see that bruising come down a little bit more first. Ah, good, here's Nurse with a painkilling injection for you.'

'I don't want...' Dominic began, but it was too late, the nurse was already skilfully inserting the hypodermic into his skin and within seconds he could feel himself starting to drift towards unconsciousness.

CHAPTER TEN

'DOMINIC will be able to come home today.'

'Yes, I know,' said Annie as she put down the cup of coffee Helena had just made her. 'They rang me from the hospital earlier. I'm going to pick him up this afternoon and—'

'When are you going to tell him about the baby?' Helena interrupted her to ask.

Immediately Annie looked away from her, her voice tense as she told her, 'I'm not.' She defended her decision when Helena didn't answer. 'There isn't any point. I've told you what happened before, what I remembered. Nothing's changed, Helena.'

'No, nothing's changed,' Helena agreed. 'You *still* love him. You've admitted that.'

'Yes. Yes, I do. But this baby…' She touched her stomach tenderly. 'This baby…*my* baby, has to come first, Helena.'

'The hospital are only releasing Dominic because they think you're going to be on hand to look after him. He's still very badly bruised.'

'Yes, I know,' Annie agreed. 'And I shall be. The baby doesn't show,' she told her quickly. 'It's not… I'm not… I owe him that much, Helena. After all, if he hadn't done what he did…'

'You don't have to justify your decision to me,' Helena told her dryly. 'Although I wouldn't be your

163

friend if I didn't counsel you to think again. This child is *his* child as well as yours, you know.'

'No, it's mine,' Annie insisted fiercely. '*He* won't want it; I know that already. I can remember how it was before.'

'That was five years ago,' Helena reminded her.

'Five years—fifty years. A leopard doesn't change its spots,' Annie returned grimly.

'No,' Helena agreed. 'But a man isn't a leopard and he *can* change his *mind*.'

'A man can,' Annie allowed. 'But *I* don't intend to change *mine*.'

It was nearly a week now since the accident, and every day she had gone to the hospital to see Dominic, remembering how important contact with the outside world had been for her.

He was on his feet now, and walking, despite the pain she knew he had to be suffering from his bruises.

There was still a dressing on his leg, where the flesh had been scraped raw, which had to be changed every day.

'Will you be able to cope?' the doctor had asked her the previous day.

But before she had been able to reply Dominic had announced sharply, 'She won't have to. I can do it myself.'

'Yes, I can cope,' Annie had answered him quietly, ignoring Dominic.

Now, with her pregnancy properly confirmed, there were things she had to do, plans she had to make. But they would have to be put on hold until Dominic was fully back on his feet—she owed him that.

'Lean on me,' she instructed him now, as he hobbled towards the door to his room. 'The car isn't very far away, but if you'd like a wheelchair...'

'What I'd like,' Dominic told her grittily, 'is to be treated like the adult I am and *not* a child. I *can* walk, Annie.'

Only the memory of how she herself had felt whilst she was recuperating enabled Annie to bite back the sharp words hovering on her tongue.

He looked surprisingly fit for a man who had been in hospital for close on a week. His skin was still tanned, his body still full of that sensual male power that made her own tighten and shiver slightly.

As he forced himself not to give in to the pain of his bruises Dominic wondered when Annie was going to tell him about the baby. Not once during her visits had she made *any* reference to it, and he was angrily aware of how inappropriate their current role reversal was. He was the one who should be taking care of *her*, cherishing her, guarding her, protecting her.

'Dr Spears said it might be more comfortable for you to sleep downstairs for the time being,' Annie announced once they were in the car—Dominic's car, not her own, because the seats were more comfortable and there was more leg room for him, even if she herself would have preferred to have been driving her own car.

'No way! For God's sake, I'm *not* an invalid!'

Dominic exploded angrily. 'I don't *need* molly-coddling Annie. In fact...'

'In fact what?' she challenged him sharply. 'In fact you'd prefer me to leave? There's no way that the hospital would have let you come home if they thought you were going to be on your own,' she reminded him.

Want her to *leave*! Dominic looked out of the car window. When they had told him how she had in-sisted on staying at his bedside until she knew he was going to make a full recovery he had thought...hoped... But in the days since he had re-covered consciousness, instead of drawing closer to-gether, instead of him having an opportunity to tell her how thrilled he was about the baby and how much he wanted them to put the past behind them and start again, Annie seemed to have thrown up a wall between them which she had no intention of allowing him to cross.

'We're here,' she announced unnecessarily as she turned into the drive and parked the car. 'You stay here. I'll go and unlock the door and then I'll come back for you.'

Dominic let her get as far as the front door before he opened his own car door and struggled out.

Standing on the gravel of the drive was, for some reason, much harder and much more painful than standing beside his hospital bed—and as for walk-ing...! Gritting his teeth, he started to move towards the house.

Annie finally realised what he was doing when she

had unlocked the door and turned back towards the car.

'Dominic!' she protested sharply, hurrying towards him and reaching him just as he sagged heavily to one side, breathing hard.

'I'm all right. For God's sake, stop fussing,' he told her curtly.

'You're *not* all right. You should have waited for me.'

'Waited for you?'

She watched his mouth twisting bitterly.

'What good would that do me, Annie? What good has it ever done me?'

If she didn't know better she might have thought that there was more than just physical pain she could see in his eyes. But what was the point in tormenting herself? Dominic had told her himself that he no longer loved her.

With only herself to consider she might have been tempted into the weakness of allowing the physical desire she could sense he still felt for her to have free rein, but the knowledge that soon she would have another, much more vulnerable life to consider had given her a strength she hadn't known she could possess. No matter how much her body might ache for him she could never now accept the shallow worthlessness of mere sexual satisfaction.

'Dr Spears gave me some painkillers for you,' she said calmly. 'Once you're in bed I'll bring you some.'

They were inside the house now, and as she looked at the stairs, and then at him, she told him, 'I've got to go back to the car for your bag, and then I'll help you upstairs.'

'No,' he told her swiftly. 'I *can* manage. If I lean on you it could hurt you.'

Hurt her? He was concerned about *hurting* her… *Now*! After what he had already done… Annie didn't know whether to laugh or cry, but he did have a point. If he should fall…

Helplessly she watched as he struggled painfully up the stairs. When he reached the top he leaned heavily on the balustrade. Anxiously she rushed towards him. She could see the pain etched into his face. Automatically she went to take his arm, ignoring his anger as she helped him into his room.

'Thank you. But I can undress myself,' he gritted. 'Unless, of course, you want to watch!'

Her face burning, Annie fled. She, more than anyone else, understood how pain and incapacity could sharpen even the sweetest temper, but the mere thought of him naked… Pink-cheeked, she hurried back downstairs. The thought of Dominic naked was not a thought she should allow herself to have, she told herself sternly.

It was later that night when a sound from Dominic's room disturbed her own sleep. Automatically she was out of bed, reaching for her robe, pulling it on as she hurried anxiously towards his door.

The anguished groan that reached her ears as she opened the door had her scurrying towards the bed.

Dominic was lying in the middle of it, the bedclothes pushed down to expose his naked body, the bruises still livid against his tan, the dressing on his leg a paler blur.

Hastily averting her gaze from the very visual evidence of his maleness, Annie leaned across him, intending to reach for the bedclothes to cover him up. But as she did so he suddenly opened his eyes and grasped her arm.

'Annie,' he whispered hoarsely. 'I was just dreaming about you.'

Annie licked her lips a little nervously.

'You're so beautiful,' Dominic told her softly. 'So very, very beautiful.'

His fingers were caressing her arm, making her shiver, making her...

'Dominic, stop it,' she protested. 'You aren't well. You shouldn't...'

'I shouldn't what?' he demanded softly. 'I shouldn't make love to my wife? They said at the hospital that I should do whatever I felt able to do, and I feel very, very able to make love to you, my Annie...*very* able!'

His Annie! She wasn't that now...not any more.

'Dominic,' she whispered in a paper-thin voice. But somehow she was still bending towards him, still allowing him to draw her down beside him to hold her, touch her, kiss her.

'I can remember the first time we made love here,' he was telling her, and Annie had to stop herself from responding. So can I.

She didn't want to tell him she was leaving him until she was sure he was well enough to look after himself. She didn't want to argue or quarrel with him at all, she recognised. Giddily he started to kiss her, and her head began to swim.

'It was so good between us…I wish you could remember,' he was telling her as he reached inside her robe and started to stroke his hand over her body. Was it her imagination or did they linger deliberately on the still flat plane of her tummy?

'I wanted you so much then,' he told her rawly. 'I want you just as much now, Annie.'

It must be the drugs that were making him like this, Annie decided as her breathing quickened and shallowed in response to the desire that he was arousing in her. She could feel her nipples peaking, hardening, aching for much, much more than the delicate brush of his fingertips against them.

'Dominic, no,' she told him as he rolled her gently onto her back and started to kiss her throat, then her breasts.

'Annie, yes,' he whispered back in response as his hands warmed her body.

It was her dreams…her memories…her longings brought vividly to life—and more. She ought to stop him—now—whilst she still could. He wasn't well and she wasn't… But instead of pushing him away she suddenly discovered that she was holding on to him, crying out softly to him…*for* him—too caught up in what she was feeling herself to be shocked by the raw immediacy of his fierce possession of her.

'Is this all right for you?' he asked as he entered her, full and hard, and yet somehow gentle too, as though…

'I want you to…' To stop, she had intended to tell

him, but suddenly her voice was suspended as her need for him overwhelmed her and she was crying out helplessly to him. 'I want you to love me, Dominic. I want you to hold me, fill me…love me—'

Briefly even her baby was forgotten in her desire to absorb and accommodate as much of him as she could, and when she felt him holding back she pressed closer to him, urging him on.

'Yes, oh, yes, that feels so good,' she encouraged him as her fingers tightened against his buttocks and her back arched. 'Oh, yes, Dom… Dom… Yes… Oh… Oh, yes, my darling—yes!'

'Dominic, your leg—your bruises,' Annie gasped in remorse several minutes later, when she had come back down to earth enough to realise what they had done.

'What leg…what bruises?' Dominic teased her.

She could feel the laughter rocking his body just as she had felt the passion moving it only minutes before. What she had done was wrong. Inexcusable. Tears blurred her eyes, but when she moved to pull away from him Dominic held onto her.

'No!' he commanded fiercely, his voice softening as he told her, 'I want you here with me, Annie. I need you here…please stay.'

Please stay! In the darkness Annie fought against her own emotions. He was only being like this because of the drugs he was on, because he felt vulnerable. She waited until she was sure he was asleep before sliding out from beneath his restraining arm and picking up her discarded robe. Her own bed felt cold and lonely…empty. Every time she closed her eyes she could see him…feel him…

Dominic frowned as he watched Annie through his study window. She was outside in the garden, where she had gone to get some mint for the lamb they were having for their meal. He had been home a number of days now, and she had still made no mention to him of her pregnancy. Since the first night he had been home and he had made love with her the atmosphere between them had been distant and strained. He couldn't blame her for *that*. She had every reason to feel angry that he had taken advantage of her kind-heartedness—of her. As he watched her walk slowly, reluctantly, back to the house and him, he made up his mind that if *she* wasn't going to broach the subject of the baby then he would have to do so.

'You aren't eating your lamb,' Annie protested as Dominic pushed away his meal without finishing it.

'No,' he agreed curtly. 'I'm not particularly hungry. Annie, there's something—'

'But lamb always used to be your favourite,' Annie interrupted him anxiously, and then stopped, ashen-faced, as she realised what she had said. She could see the way Dominic was looking at her—the anger in his eyes.

There was a long sharp silence before he demanded, 'You've remembered?'

'Yes,' she was forced to concede.

'When?' Dominic questioned her insistently, repeating the demand with even harsher emphasis when Annie turned her head away before answering him.

'It was…it was before your accident,' she admitted unwillingly, insisting, when he made no response, 'I *would* have told you…I was *going* to tell you, but…'

'But you preferred to keep it to yourself,' Dominic finished angrily for her. 'I wonder why?' he asked sarcastically. 'Or do I? Why *did* you walk out on me, Annie? *Was* it just because of a childish tantrum, or because you realised you didn't really love me?'

'No,' she told him quietly.

'No?' He continued to look at her before repeating harshly, '*No*? Is that it? I want to know everything, Annie.'

The flash of anger in his eyes made her quail a little, but she refused to let him see it.

'Everything? Very well, I shall tell you "everything",' she agreed proudly, her own eyes darkening with her own reciprocal emotions.

Now that it was here—the moment she had been dreading, the confrontation she knew they would have, the final hurdle she had to clear before she could finally draw a line under the part of her life that included him and walk away—the relief she had expected and hoped to feel was lost, submerged beneath the pressure of her other emotions.

It had been a mistake to give in to that wanton need she had had for him the first night he had been home. Making love with him had aroused all manner of needs, feelings—thoughts she simply didn't have the spare capacity to deal with.

'Well?' Dominic pressed through gritted teeth.

He wanted an explanation for why she had left him? Well, he should have one. She took a deep breath, and then, to her own dismay, she heard herself blurting out emotionally, 'I'm leaving you, Dominic. I can't stay here any longer. I don't owe you any explanations. There's no reason...no need for us to be together any more.'

'What?' Dominic demanded harshly, leaning across the table and placing his palms down on it, either side of her. 'I should have thought you and I had an *excellent* reason for being together. The baby,' he elaborated when Annie remained stubbornly silent. '*Our* baby.'

Annie gasped. He *knew*. How? When?

'They told me at the hospital,' he informed her, reading her mind.

'It isn't your baby,' Annie told him stiffly, looking away from him. 'It's mine.' She gave him a tight little smile. 'You see, I *haven't* forgotten.' She took a deep breath. 'I've remembered *exactly* why we quarrelled, Dominic, *and* what you said to me... about...about not wanting me to have your child— about wanting me to abort it.'

'What?' Dominic had gone white. He came round to her side of the table and grasped her upper arms, giving her a grimly emotional little shake as he demanded, 'You were pregnant *then*? You—'

'No,' Annie had to admit. 'No, I wasn't. But I *thought* I might be, and I was afraid. You told me

you didn't want me to have your child because of
my background, my bad blood. That's why I… I tried
to tell you but you wouldn't listen. You…'

'What? I said *no* such thing,' Dominic objected,
horrified. 'Annie…'

'You did,' Annie insisted. 'You said you didn't
want to burden a child with—'

'With a father who couldn't be there for it. A father who put his career before it, as my parents had
done. I know how it feels to grow up realising that
you're not totally loved by your parents—*that* was
the burden I was referring to, not…'

He stopped, white to the lips, shaking his head as
he protested,

'Annie, how *could* you have thought…be-
lieved…? I *loved* you. I…I didn't think either of us
was emotionally ready to be a good parent, it's true,
and perhaps I did overreact… But I never… If I'd
thought for one moment you'd believed you were
already pregnant… I simply thought you were in
danger of succumbing to an impulse—that you
wanted a baby because you were afraid of being
alone. I never…'

Her revelations had stunned and appalled him.
They had hurt him as well, he recognised, but he
forced himself to set aside that feeling, to remember
Annie as she had been then, to understand and remember how she had felt about her unknown parentage. He took a deep breath. Somehow he had to
find a way of reassuring her, convincing her…
showing her just how wrong she had been.

'Whoever and whatever your parents were doesn't

matter, Annie. What matters is that *you* are you—a wonderful, special, individual person who logically must carry something of both of them within your genes.'

He reached out and cupped her face before she could move away, his eyes dark with the intensity of his emotions as he told her fiercely, 'You may never have known them, Annie, but I know that I would be as proud to have them as my child's grandparents as I am to have you as its mother. What you are, *all* that you are, shows in everything about you—your honesty, your compassion, your courage, your intelligence, and most of all your love.

'I wish that I could say the same about my own genetic inheritance. My parents were thoughtless, selfish, stubborn, totally wrapped up in their own concerns. I was an encumbrance they didn't really want, a nuisance farmed out into the care of my grandparents, who looked on me as a duty…a responsibility. *That* was the genetic inheritance I didn't want my child to have.'

As she searched his face Annie knew that he was telling her the truth. Tears blurred her vision.

Dominic leaned forward. Sensing that he was about to kiss her, she panicked and pulled away. She needed time to absorb what he had told her, to accept it and to accept that she had misjudged him. That she had left him—destroyed their marriage and their love for nothing. Was there any way she could ever accept the enormity of that?

Silently Dominic let her go. It was symptomatic of everything that had gone wrong between them that even now they couldn't share their feelings—that there were barriers between them.

Love might grow quickly but trust was another matter. Trust was a slow-growing plant that needed nurturing. His fault was that he had not seen and responded to Annie's need for that careful nurturing—and hers... She owned no fault, he recognised. She had simply reacted out of fear to his crass thoughtlessness.

Annie didn't know what hurt most—knowing that the love she and Dominic had once shared was lost to her for ever or knowing that her own lack of self-esteem, her own fear of the unknownness of her background, had led to its destruction. But what was worse, much worse, than her own pain was the pain she was going to inflict on her child, who would now have to grow up without the benefit of the loving closeness of both its parents.

She loved Dominic totally, completely, irreversibly, irretrievably. She knew that now. She knew, too, that he still found her desirable. But desire wasn't love, and he had already told her quite plainly that his reason, his only reason, for wanting her back in his life was so that she could provide him with the answers he needed before he drew a line under their marriage and divorced her.

This morning he had walked downstairs unaided. It was time for her to go whilst she could still go with dignity and with pride.

She packed quietly and efficiently and then went to find him. He was in the kitchen.

'It's time for me to go,' she told him calmly. 'We both know the answer to your question now. The divorce should go through easily enough, and—'

'The divorce? *What* divorce?' Dominic demanded grimly. 'You're carrying my child, Annie. There's no way I'm going to…we can't divorce now.'

Annie's face paled. Deep down inside she had feared he would react like this, but she had told herself she was strong enough to resist the temptation he was offering her.

'Look,' he said, more gently, 'I know we've got some bridge-building to do. I know you need time. Trust isn't something that grows overnight, but I know we can make it work.'

Annie could feel herself start to quake deep down inside with the effort of trying to hold onto reality, trying to remind herself of what reality was, and the fact that he no longer loved her whilst she…

From somewhere she managed to dredge up the necessary will-power.

'I realise you are speaking out of some misguided sense of responsibility and…and duty, Dominic,' she told him. 'But—'

'It wasn't *responsibility* that made me want you in my bed the other night,' Dominic interrupted her trenchantly. 'And, forgive me if I'm being ungallant, I don't think it was *duty* that kept you there either.'

'That's not fair,' Annie gasped in outrage. 'What happened then was…was…'

'Was what?' Dominic encouraged her softly. 'Or shall I tell you what it was?' When she made no answer he continued in a sexy whisper, 'What happened then was what nature designed us to *have* happen, my Annie. What happened then was…'

She tensed as his voice dropped even lower.

'I've *never* stopped loving you and I don't think that you've ever stopped loving me. Consciously you may have forgotten me, pushed me to the back of your mind, but deep down inside you *couldn't* forget… Deep down inside you, your love, like mine, *couldn't* be extinguished. We owe it to the baby to give ourselves…our *love*…another chance, Annie.'

'No.' Immediately she shook her head in denial.

For a moment Dominic was silent, and then, just as she thought he was going to accept her denial of him and turn away, he cupped her face and said, so gently that it made her heart turn over inside her body, 'Do you know what I think? I think that you're afraid to…'

'I'm not afraid of anything,' Annie denied quickly. 'I can manage by myself, Dominic. I don't need…'

'…me?' he finished quietly for her. 'Maybe you don't, Annie. But this…' He touched her tummy gently. 'Our son or our daughter does. We both know what it's like to grow up alone, isolated…feeling different…feeling unloved…'

'My baby *will* be loved,' Annie insisted stiffly. 'I shall love it. You can't make me stay here, Dominic. You can't make me stay married to you.'

As he searched her face she instinctively turned away, trying to hide herself from him. He had been right when he accused her of being afraid—not that she would ever admit it to him. She *was* afraid…very afraid. How could she take the risk of believing him?

'No, I can't make you stay,' he agreed heavily as he released her.

What had she expected? What had she wanted? For him to physically hold onto her?

Without looking at him she edged round the kitchen door and then fled into the hallway, where she had left her things.

'I've never stopped loving you,' he had said. But how *could* she believe him? How could she be sure he wasn't just saying it to protect their child?

The door to Dominic's study stood open. Impulsively she tiptoed inside. The room was empty, the curtains blowing in the breeze. A piece of paper had been blown down onto the floor. Automatically she bent to pick it up, and then froze as she replaced it on the desk. In the half-open drawer she could see a photograph frame. Carefully she picked it up, studying the five-year-old photograph. It was her and Dominic on their wedding day. She remembered how Dominic had insisted that they had the photo taken. Tears filled her eyes, her fingertips trembling as she pressed them against the cool glass.

She had been so happy that day, so filled with joy and love. Dominic had, in truth, been her perfect lover, her dream hero...her love... But he was five years older now, and a different person. They were both different people. Different outwardly, perhaps, but inside, their emotions...their love...

She could feel the pain turning and twisting inside her. But if she gave in to Dominic now how would she ever know if he really wanted her?

Quickly she replaced the photograph, and then

closed the window before walking back into the hall-way and picking up her bags.

Her keys in one hand and her bags in the other, she opened the front door and looked towards her car.

Dominic! What on earth…? She swallowed hard, and then blinked. Dominic was standing beside her car, a heavy bag at his feet.

'If you won't live with me, my Annie, then I'm just going to have to live with you,' Dominic told her simply. 'Where you go—I go. There isn't any way there's going to be another disappearing act.'

'You can't do this,' Annie protested thickly. 'You don't want me…it's just because of the baby…'

'Really? Is that what you think?' Dominic asked her politely, so politely and so calmly that Annie was taken off guard. He dropped his case and came strid-ing towards her, saying softly, 'Well, I'll just have to prove to you how wrong you are, won't I?'

She had left it too late to turn and run. 'Dominic,' she protested. 'No. You mustn't…your leg…' But the remainder of her denial was lost against the soft-ness of his shirt as he swept her up into his arms and strode through the house with her and up the stairs.

'It was in this room, this bed, that we made love as only lovers can,' he whispered softly to her as he laid her on it. 'This bed where I *showed* you just how much I love you Annie. It was here, too, that you showed me your love—told me of it.'

'That was five years ago,' she protested sharply. 'And…'

'No. I don't mean *then*,' Dominic denied, smiling

dangerously at her as he reminded her, 'Our child was conceived in this bed...the night you told me I was your dream lover come true, the night you told me how much—'

'No!' Annie protested weakly, covering her ears, her face hot with self-consciousness.

'Yes,' Dominic insisted thickly as he took advantage of her occupied hands to cup her face and look down into her eyes. 'Both of us have unhappy memories...fears and doubts. But what we really feel for one another... Give yourself to me now,' he whispered to her, 'and then tell me if you dare that you don't love me...that you don't feel my love for you, that you and I don't have a future together.'

'Please don't do this,' Annie begged painfully. 'I don't want...'

'You don't want what?' Dominic asked her gently. 'You don't want this?'

She moaned beneath her breath as he kissed her and her resistance started to melt. She could feel the heat of her own desire licking through her veins, her flesh.

'You don't want me?' Dominic pressed as his tongue twined with hers and her body arched tautly against him. 'Or this...?'

He was nibbling at the vulnerable column of her throat, his hands stroking at her skin—her bare skin, Annie realised fatalistically as he skilfully swept away her clothes along with her inhibitions.

'You're a magician...a warlock...' she told him resentfully, her voice as clouded with her emotions as her eyes, her body already heavily languorous with her love and longing.

'I'm a man,' Dominic corrected, adding possessively, 'And you're my woman, my Annie. My love, my only love…'

She heard him groan as she felt the hot satin of his bare body against her own, felt him shudder as his need convulsed him.

'I love you so much,' he told her. 'Please, please love me in return. You're my life, my love…my past, my present and my future, Annie. Without you…'

His mouth brushed her nipples, taut and tender now with her desire for him, and she cried out, unable to resist the temptation to move closer to him, to wrap her arms around him and hold him captive against her body…within her body… She felt the ecstatic ripple of pleasure flow through her as he entered her, so gently, and she knew he was deliberately holding himself back because of the baby… their baby…

When she started to cry he licked away her tears, holding her, comforting her, telling her that she was crying away her pain, and suddenly she knew that it was true. She could almost feel the tide of her emotions turning, the happiness and the love flowing back through her body. Dream lovers were all very well in their way, but *this* was reality, and the reality was…the reality was…

'Mmm?' Dominic encouraged as he realised she was trying to speak.

'I love you,' Annie sighed mundanely, but to Dominic the simple words were as powerful as the most passionate love prose that had ever been written.

EPILOGUE

'WHAT'S the A for?' Helena asked curiously as she watched Annie inscribing the invitations to her six-month-old daughter's christening.

'Amnesia,' Dominic replied for her with a teasing grin. 'So that we can both remember how she came into being.'

'Oh, no,' Helena protested. 'Surely you aren't...?' She stopped as she saw the laughing shake of her head that Annie was giving her husband.

Helena and Bob had called round to see them to discuss the arrangements for the christening.

'We ought to ring them first,' Bob had warned her. 'You know what happened the last time we called unexpectedly. We quite obviously interrupted them in the middle of making love.'

'Yes, but that was four months ago, when Charlotte was eight weeks old and Annie had been given the all-clear by her gynaecologist.'

'I don't care. You only have to see those two to know that it's damn near impossible for them to keep their hands off one another,' Bob told her forth-rightly.

'Well, they've got five missing years to catch up on,' Helena had reminded him.

She had never seen a couple so much in love with one another. Annie was practically incandescent with it, and as for Dominic... She wasn't sure when she had seen him looking more proud—the day he and Annie had renewed their vows to one another, a month before Charlotte's birth, or the first time he had actually held his newborn daughter.

'The A is for Alice,' Annie told Helena, giving Dominic a stern look.

'Alice. Oh, that's my middle name.' Helena beamed.

'Yes, I know,' Annie told her lovingly, getting up to go and give her friend a hug as she saw the way Helena's face pinkened with colour and her eyes sheened over with tears.

'I'm too *old* to be her godmother,' she had protested when Annie had told her of their plans, but Annie and Dominic had overcome all her objections, and the truth was that she was thrilled at the thought of having her as her godchild.

'Charlotte Alice sounds lovely,' she approved, when she had her emotions back under control.

'Charlotte Amnesia sounds better,' Dominic argued. 'And we'd never forget it...'

'Ignore him,' Annie told her friend, picking up a cushion, which she threw at her husband.

As he caught it Helena heard him whispering to Annie, 'I'll make you pay for that...later!'

It was growing dark when Helena and Bob left, and as she turned in her seat to reach for her seat belt, as Bob drove down the drive Helena saw an upstairs bedroom light go on in the house behind them. She knew it was the light to Annie and Dominic's bedroom.

'For heaven's sake, Dominic,' Annie scolded her husband as he bundled her onto the bed.

'You're wearing far too many clothes—do you know that?' he whispered, mock naughtily.

'Helena and Bob will have seen the light go on, and they'll know…'

'They'll know what?' he asked her softly. 'That I can't wait to make love to my wife?' He laughed as he saw the way Annie was blushing. 'Besides,' he teased her. 'Wasn't it *you* who said just before they went that you fancied an early night?'

'An early *night*,' Annie agreed. 'Not— Oh…' She gave a small gasp as Dominic touched her, and then another, before protesting longingly, 'Dominic…'

'Mmm…?' he encouraged.

'It doesn't matter,' Annie breathed as her arms opened to wrap round him. 'Nothing matters. Only you…only… Mmm…'

'Mmm…' he agreed sexily as he nuzzled her skin.

'Amnesia…' Annie breathed raggedly. 'Poor Helena. You shouldn't tease her…you shouldn't…'

Her voice faded away into a soft sigh of female pleasure as his touch grew bolder and more intimate and her body responded to him.

In the cot in the nursery the little girl, whose parents' private secret name for her was always going to be Amnesia, smiled contentedly up at the mobile dancing over her head.

*   *   *

'No wonder I could never truly forget you,' Annie sighed sensuously.

'Your dream lover,' Dominic told her.

'The reality is far, far better than my dreams,' Annie assured him lovingly. 'The reality…*my* reality…is you, Dominic…you and Charlotte Alice and our lives together, our future together… The reality is—oh, Dominic!'

The Marriage Demand

PENNY JORDAN

CHAPTER ONE

'DID you really think I wouldn't recognise you?'

The ice-cold darts of numbing, mind-blitzing shock pierced Faith's emotions as she stood staring in horrified nauseous disbelief. *Nash!* How could he be *here*? Wasn't he supposed to be living in America, running the multi-billion-pound empire she had read in the financial press he had built up? But, no, he was quite definitely here, all six foot-odd male animal danger of him: the man who had haunted her nightmares both sleeping and waking for the last decade; the man who...

'Faith, you haven't met our benefactor yet, have you?'

Their *what*? So far as Faith had understood, the huge Edwardian mansion so belovedly familiar to her had been handed over to the charity she worked for by the trustees of the estate that owned it. If she had thought—guessed—*suspected*—for one single moment that Nash... Somehow she managed to re-press the shudder tearing through her and threatening to completely destroy her professionalism.

The Ferndown Foundation, begun originally by her boss Robert Ferndown's late grandfather, provided respite homes for children and their parents who were living in situations of financial hardship.

The Foundation owned homes in several different parts of the country, and the moment Faith had seen their advertisement for a qualified architect to work directly under the Chief Executive she had desperately wanted to get the job. Her own background made her empathise immediately and very intensely with the plight of children living in hardship...

She tensed as she heard Nash speaking.

'Faith and I already know one another.'

A huge wave of anger and fear swamped Faith as she listened, dreading what he might be going to say and knowing that he was enjoying what she was feeling, relishing it, almost gloating over the potential pleasure of hurting her, damaging her. And yet this was a man who, according to Robert, had, along with the other trustees of the estate, deeded the property as an outright gift to their charity—an act of such generosity that Faith could scarcely believe it had come from Nash.

She could feel Robert looking at her, no doubt waiting for her to respond to Nash's comment. But it wasn't Robert's attentive smiling silence that was reducing her to a fear-drenched bundle of raw nerve-endings and anxiety. Grittily she reminded herself of everything she had endured and survived, of what she had achieved and how much she owed to the wonderful people who had supported her.

One of those people had been her late mother and the other... As she looked around the study she could almost see the familiar face of the man who had been such an inspiration to her, and she could almost see too... She closed her eyes as she was flooded with pain and guilt, then opened them but refused to look at Nash; she could almost feel him willing her to turn round and make herself vulnerable to his hostility.

'It was a long time ago,' she told Robert huskily, 'over ten years.'

She could feel her fear sliding sickly through her veins like venom, rendering her incapable of doing anything to protect herself as she waited for the first blow to fall.

She knew Robert had been disappointed by her hesitation and reluctance when he had told her that he was giving her full control of the conversion of Hatton House.

'It's absolutely ideal for our purposes,' he had enthused. 'Three floors, large grounds, a stable block that can be converted alongside the main house.'

Of course there had been no way she could tell him the real reason for her reluctance, and now there would be no need—no doubt Nash would tell him for her.

The sharp ring of Robert's mobile phone cut through her thoughts. As he answered the call he smiled warmly at her.

Robert had made no secret of his interest in her, and had made sure that she was included as his partner at several semi-social events he had to attend as the charity's spokesperson. But so far their relationship was strictly non-sexual, and had not even progressed to the point where they had had a proper date. But Faith knew that that was only a matter of time—or at least it had been.

'I'm sorry,' Robert apologised as he ended his call. 'I'm going to have to go straight back to London. There's a problem with the Smethwick House conversion. But I'm sure that Nash, here, will look after you, Faith, and show you over the house. I doubt I'll be able to get back here tonight, but I should be able to make it tomorrow.'

He was gone before Faith could protest, leaving her alone with Nash.

'What's wrong?' Nash demanded harshly. 'Or can I guess? Guilt can't be an easy bedmate to live with—although you seem to have found it easy enough—and just as easy to sleep with Ferndown, by the looks of it. But then morals were never something you cared much about, were they, Faith?'

Faith didn't know which of her emotions was the stronger, her anger or her pain. Instinctively she wanted to defend herself, to refute Nash's hateful accusations, but she knew from experience what a pointless exercise that would be. In the end all she could manage to say to him was a shaky, proud, 'I don't have anything to feel guilty about.'

She knew immediately she'd said the wrong thing. The look he gave her could have split stone.

'You might have been able to convince a juvenile court of that, Faith, but I'm afraid I'm nowhere as easy to deceive. And they do say, don't they, that a criminal—a murderer—always returns to the scene of their crime?'

Faith sucked in a sharp breath full of shock and anguish. She could feel her scalp beneath the length of her honey-streaked thick mane of hair beginning to prickle with anxiety. When she had first come to Hatton Nash had teased her about her hair, believing at first that its honey-gold strands had been created by artifice rather than nature. A summer spent at Hatton had soon convinced him of his error. Her hair colouring, like her densely blue eyes, had been inherited from the Danish father she had never met, who had drowned whilst on honeymoon with her mother, trying to save the life of a young child.

Once she was old enough to consider such things, Faith had become convinced that the heart condition which had ultimately killed her mother had begun then, and that it had somehow been caused by her mother's grief at the loss of her young husband. Faith acknowledged that there was no scientific evidence to back up her feelings, but, as she had good and bitter cause to know, some things in life went beyond logic and science.

'What are you doing here?' she challenged Nash fiercely. No matter what he might believe, she was not—she *had* not—

Automatically she gave a tiny shake of her head as she tried to break free of the dangerous treadmill of her thoughts, and yet, despite her outward rejection of what she knew he was thinking, inwardly she was already being tormented by her memories. It was here, in this room, that she had first met Philip Hatton, Nash's godfather, and here too that she had last seen him as he lay slumped in his chair, semi-paralysed by the stroke which had ultimately led to his death.

Faith flinched visibly as the nightmare terror of her ten-year-old memories threatened to resurface and swamp her.

'You heard your boss.'

Faith froze as she listened to the deliberately challenging way in which Nash underlined the word 'boss'. Whilst she might have the self-control to stop herself from reacting verbally to Nash's taunt, there was nothing she could do to stop the instinctive and betraying reaction of her body, as her eyes darkened and shadowed with the pain of further remembrances.

At fifteen a girl was supposed to be too young to know the meaning of real love—wasn't she? Too young to suffer anything other than a painful adolescent crush to be gently laughed over in her adulthood.

'As a trustee of my late godfather's estate, it was my decision to gift Hatton to the Ferndown Foundation. After all, I know how beneficial it is for a child—from any background—to be in this kind of environment.'

He started to frown, looking away from Faith as he did so, the hard angry glaze she had been so aware of in his eyes fading to a rare shadowy uncertainty.

He had thought he was prepared for this moment, this meeting, that he would have himself and his reactions totally under control. But the shock of seeing the fifteen-year-old girl he still remembered so vividly transformed into the woman she had become—a woman it was obvious was very much admired and desired, by Robert Ferndown and no doubt many other gullible fools as well—was causing a reaction—a *feeling*—within him that was threatening the defences he had assured himself were impenetrable.

To have to admit, if only to himself, to suffering such an uncharacteristic attack of uncertainty irritated him, rasping against wounds he had believed were totally healed. He had, he knew, gained a reputation during the last decade, not just for being a formidable business opponent, but also for remaining resolutely unattached.

He closed his eyes momentarily as he fought against the anger flooding over him and drowning out rationality. He had waited a long time for this—for life, for fate, to deliver Faith into his hands. And now that it had…

He took a deep breath and asked softly, 'Did you *really* expect to get away with it, Faith? Did you really believe that Nemesis would not exact a fair and just payment from you?'

He gave a wolverine smile that was no smile at all but a cold, savage snarl of warning, reminding Faith of just how easily he could hurt her, tear into the fragile fabric of the life she had created for herself.

'Have you told Ferndown just *what* you are and

what you *did*?' he demanded savagely, causing Faith to drag air painfully into her lungs.

'No, of course you haven't.' Nash answered his own question, his voice full of biting contempt. 'If you had there's no way the Foundation would have employed you, despite Ferndown's obvious "admiration" for you. Did you sleep with him *before* he gave you the job, or did you make him wait until afterwards?'

The sound Faith made was more one of pain than shock—a tight, mewling, almost piteous cry—but Nash refused to respond to it.

'*Have* you told him?' he demanded.

Unable to lie, but unable to speak either, Faith shook her head. The triumph she could see in Nash's eyes confirmed every single one of her growing fears.

Giving her another of those feral, intimidating smiles that made her shake in her shoes but made her equally determined that she was not going to give in to his manipulative method of tormenting her, Nash agreed smoothly, 'No, of course you haven't—from what I've heard from your besotted boss it seems that you managed to omit certain crucial facts from the CV you submitted to the Foundation.'

Faith knew exactly what he meant. Her throat dry with tension, she fought with all her emotional strength not to show him how afraid she now was.

'They had no relevance,' she insisted.

'No relevance? The fact that you only just escaped a custodial sentence; the fact that you were responsible for a man's death? Oh, no, you're staying right there,' Nash rasped as Faith, her self-control finally breaking, turned on her heel and tried to leave.

The shock of his fingers biting into the soft flesh of her upper arm caused her to cry out and demand frantically, 'Don't touch me.'

'Don't touch you?' Nash repeated. 'That's not what you used to say to me, is it, Faith? You used to plead with me to touch you…beg me…'

A low, tortured sound escaped Faith's trembling lips. 'I was fifteen—a child.' She tried to defend herself. 'I didn't know what I was saying—what I was doing…'

'Liar,' Nash contradicted her savagely, his free hand lifting to constrain her head and hold it so that she couldn't avoid meeting his eyes.

The sensation of Nash's lean fingers on her throat evoked a storm of reaction and remembrance. Her whole body started to shudder—not with fear, Faith recognised in shock, but with a heedless, wanton, inexplicable surge of feeling she had thought she had left behind her years ago.

How often that summer she had first seen Nash had she ached to have him touch her, *want* her? How many, many times had she fantasised then about him holding her captive like this? Imagining the brush of his fingers against her skin, picturing the feral glitter in his eyes as his gaze searched her face, his body hard with wanting her.

She shuddered again, acknowledging the naïvety of her long-ago teenage self. She had believed herself in love with Nash and had felt for him all the intense passion of that love, wanting to give herself to him totally and completely, longing for him, *aching* for him with all the ardour and innocence of youth.

'You don't know what you're talking about,' he had dismissed once, when she had been attempting to tell him how she felt and what she wanted.

'Then show me,' she had responded boldly, adding frantically, 'Kiss me, Nash.'

Nash froze in disbelief as he heard the words Faith had unwittingly whispered aloud, repeating her own thoughts. Kiss her? What kind of game was she trying to play? He started to move his hand away from her throat, but as he did so Faith turned her head, her lips grazing against his fingers.

Faith gasped as she felt the warm texture of Nash's flesh against her unguarded lips. She heard the low sound he made deep in his throat, felt him close the small gap that separated them, his body hard and undeniably male against the shocked softness of hers. His hand was pressed into the small of her back, imprisoning her against him, his mouth firm and cool as it covered hers—

Nash felt the shock of what he was doing all the way right down to his toes. Faith's body felt unbelievably vulnerable against his own, all soft womanly curves, her mouth sweet and warm. He could feel the temptation to touch her, give in to her, weakening him. His whole purpose in being here was to see justice done, to make sure she was punished for the crime she had committed. He owed it to his godfather to do that much at least for him—and yet here he was instead—

As he felt Faith's response to him Nash shuddered deeply, fighting to remind himself that the sweet, innocent girl he had so stupidly believed Faith was had never really existed, that the woman she was now knew *exactly* what she was doing and what effect she was having on him. But even telling himself that couldn't stop him from answering the passion in her kiss, the invitation of her softly parted lips.

When Faith felt the hot fierce thrust of Nash's tongue opening her lips, seeking the intimacy of her mouth, stroking sensually against her own tongue, she felt as though she was drowning in wave after wave of increasingly urgent desire. It filled her, stormed her, drew her down to a place of deep, dark, velvet sweetness, a place of hot, bold, dangerous, sensual savagery, a place where she and Nash…

She and Nash!

Faith suddenly realised what she was doing and immediately pulled herself free of Nash, her face flooding with the betraying colour of her distress and confusion, her eyes haunted and dark with the pain of it. She had kissed him as the girl she had been, loving the man *he* had been, Faith acknowledged as she tried to reconcile what she had just experienced

in his arms with the reality of the enmity and distrust
that now lay between them.

As she'd pulled away from him Nash had stepped
back from her. Faith could see the way his chest
was rising and falling with the harshness of his
breathing, and she quailed beneath the bitter contemptuous look he was giving her.

'You're wasting your time trying those tactics on
me, Faith,' she heard him saying cynically to her.
'They might work on other men, but I know what
you're really like…'

'That's not true. I wasn't,' Faith defended herself
passionately. 'You have no right—'

'Where you and I are concerned, Faith,' Nash cut
across her warningly, 'right doesn't come into it.'
What the hell was he doing? Angrily Nash reminded
himself of just what Faith was.

Faith bit her bottom lip.

'My godfather had a right to have the trust he
placed in you respected,' he continued grimly. 'And
he also had a right to expect justice to be done—a
right to have just payment made for his death.'

'I wasn't responsible for that,' Faith protested
shakily. 'You can't make me—' You can't make me
admit to something I didn't do, she had been about
to say, but before she could do so Nash was interrupting her.

'I can't make you what, Faith?' he asked her with
soft venom. 'I can't make you pay? Oh, I think
you'll find that I can. You've already admitted that
you lied by omission on your CV to the Ferndown

Foundation. Given their much-publicised belief in old-fashioned moral standards, you must know as well as I do that there's no way you would have got that job if they'd known the truth. Oh, I'm not trying to say that Ferndown himself wouldn't have still taken you to bed, but I think we both know it would have been a very different kind of business arrangement he'd have offered.'

'I was never convicted.' Faith tried to defend herself helplessly. She felt as though she had strayed into a horrific waking nightmare. Never had she imagined anything like this might happen. She had always known how much Nash blamed and hated her, of course, but to discover that he was now bent on punishing her as he believed the law had failed to do threw her into a state of mind-numbing panic.

'No, you weren't, were you?' Nash agreed, giving her an ugly look.

Faith swallowed against the torturous dryness of her aching throat. Someone had interceded on her behalf, pleaded for clemency for her and won the sympathy and compassion of the juvenile court so that all she had received was a suspended sentence. She'd never known who that person was, and no one would ever know just how heavy she found the burden of the guilt she had denied to Nash. No one— and most of all not the man now so cruelly confronting and threatening her.

'You *knew* I was coming here,' was all she could manage to say, her voice cracking painfully against the dryness of her throat.

'Yes. I knew,' Nash agreed coolly. 'That was a cunning move of yours, to claim that you had no close family or friends to supply a character reference for you and to give the name of your university tutor—a man who only knew that part of your life that came after my godfather's death.'

'I did that because there *wasn't* anyone else,' Faith responded sharply. 'It had nothing to do with being cunning. My mother was my only family, and she…she died.' She stopped, unable to go on. Her mother had lost her long battle against her heart condition two days after Faith had heard the news of Philip Hatton's death, which was why she had not been able to attend his funeral.

'Well, it certainly seems that your tutor thought highly of you,' Nash continued, giving her a thin-lipped, disparaging smile. 'Did you offer yourself to him just like you did to me, Faith?'

'No!' Her voice rang with repugnance, her feelings too strong for her to conceal and too over-whelming for her to notice the glitter that touched Nash's eyes before he turned away from her.

When Robert had been briefing her about the project he had told her that the house was being looked after by a skeleton staff whom the Foundation would keep on whilst it was being converted, and Faith tensed now, as the housekeeper walked into the study.

She wasn't the same housekeeper Faith remembered from all those years ago, and, giving Faith a cold stare, she turned away from her to Nash and told him, 'I've made up your usual room for you, Mr Nash, and I've put the young lady in the room you indicated. I've left a cold supper in the fridge, but if you want me to come in during the evening whilst you're here…'

'Thank you, Mrs Jenson.' Nash smiled. 'But that won't be necessary.'

Faith stared at the housekeeper's departing back, her heart sinking as she recognised the other woman's antagonism towards her. But she had more important concerns to address right now—far more important! Swinging round to confront Nash, she whispered, white-faced, 'You can't stay *here*.'

The smile he gave her sent another burst of white-hot fear licking along her veins.

'Oh, yes, I can,' he told her softly. 'I made it a condition of the hand-over, and naturally the Foundation's board fully understood that I would want to oversee the conversion. Especially since it was being handled by such an inexperienced young architect.'

Faith looked blindly at him. 'But I'm staying here—I have to—it's all arranged. You can't do this to me,' she protested. 'It's…it's harassment,' she accused him wildly. 'It's…'

'Justice,' Nash supplied with soft deadliness.

CHAPTER TWO

'I've instructed Mrs Jenson to put you in your old room.'

Her old room. Hugging her arms around herself for protection, Faith recalled the openly challenging way in which Nash had delivered that piece of information. It had been obvious to her that he was expecting some kind of hostile reaction, but she refused to allow him to manipulate either her actions or her emotions.

Her old room. Pensively she walked across to the small window and looked down at the elegant mini-patchwork of the gardens.

This room had once been part of the house's original nursery, tucked away in the *faux* turret that formed such a distinctive part of the house's architecture. It was an amusing piece of fantasy on the part of its designer, and at fifteen Faith had still been young enough to imagine herself as a fairy tale princess, enjoying the solitude of her private tower.

'I expect you're disappointed that the tower isn't surrounded by a lake,' Nash had teased her when she had tried to express her pleasure at being given such a special room, but to Faith the tower room Philip Hatton had chosen for her was perfect as it was, and she had struggled to find the words to tell him so.

That night, her first night in the room's comfortable and generously proportioned bed, she had closed her eyes and thought about her mother, whispering to her in her thoughts, telling her how lucky she felt, describing the room to her and knowing how much pleasure her mother would have had in sharing with her the wonder of everything she was experiencing. She had wished passionately that her mother could be there with her.

But of course she couldn't. And tears had filled her eyes, Faith remembered, and she had cried silently into her pillow, knowing with the maturity that the last painful and frightening six months had brought her that her mother would *never* see Hatton.

Restlessly Faith moved away from the window. The room had hardly changed; the bed in it looked exactly the same as the one she remembered, although the curtains at the window and the covers on the bed were different. Even the faded old-fashioned rose-coloured wallpaper was the same. Tenderly she reached out and touched one of the roses.

Her bedroom in the tiny Housing Association flat she and her mother had shared had had pretty wallpaper. They had papered it together just after they moved in. She had known how much her mother had hated leaving the small cottage they had lived in since Faith's birth, but the garden had become too much for her and the flat had been closer to the hospital, and to Faith's school, and much easier for her mother, being on the ground floor.

There was something almost frightening about the power one event could have to change a person's whole life, Faith acknowledged now as her thoughts focused on the past. It had only been by the merest chance that she had ever come to Hatton at all.

Shortly after the move to their flat, her mother's doctor had announced that she had to have a major operation and that after it she would be sent to recuperate at a special rest home, where she would have to stay for several months.

At first her mother had flatly refused to agree. Faith had only been just fifteen, and there had been no way she could be left to live on her own for the time the doctors had said her recuperation would take. The doctor's response had been to suggest that the Social Services be approached to find a place for Faith temporarily at a local children's home, where she could stay until her mother was well enough to look after her.

At first her mother had refused to even consider such an option, but Faith had seen for herself just how rapidly and painfully her mother's health was deteriorating, and despite her own dread and fear she had set about convincing her mother that she was perfectly happy to do as the doctors were suggesting.

'It will only be for a while,' Faith had tried to reassure her mother. 'And it will be mostly during the summer holidays. It will be fun having some other girls to talk to...'

And so it had been arranged. But right at the last minute, on the very day that Faith's mother had been due to be admitted to hospital, it had been decided that instead of going to the local children's home Faith would have to be sent to one almost fifty miles away.

Faith could still remember how apprehensive she had felt, but her fear for her mother had been greater. Even worse had been the discovery that she would not be allowed to visit her mother, either after her operation or whilst she was recuperating.

Although on her arrival at the home the staff there had been kind, Faith had felt overwhelmed by the anonymous busyness of the place, and the hostility of one particular group of girls who had already been living there.

She had been allowed to speak to her mother by telephone after her operation, but Faith had determinedly said nothing about the crude attempts of this group of girls to bully her and demand money from her. The last thing she'd wanted was for her mother to worry about *her* when Faith knew she needed all her strength to get better.

A week after she had first arrived at the home Faith had been thrilled to discover that they were being taken out for the day to visit a nearby Edwardian mansion and its gardens. Her father had been an architect, and it had been her secret dream to follow in his footsteps—although with her

mother's meagre income she had known it was unlikely that she would ever be able to go to university
and get the necessary qualifications.

It had taken a little of her pleasure away to discover that the girls who had taken such an open
dislike to her were also going on the trip—as well
as surprising her, since they had all been extremely
and crudely vocal about *their* favourite ways of
spending their time.

Faith had known that her mother would be horrified if she knew about them. Faith had heard them
boasting openly about their criminal activities. She
had even heard whispers from some of the other
girls about them going into the local town and stealing from the shops there.

'Why don't you tell someone?' Faith had asked
the girl who had told her. The other girl had shuddered.

'They'd kill me if they found out, and anyway,
like Charlene says, even if they do get caught they'll
only be sent to a juvenile court.'

'Only!' Faith hadn't been able to conceal her own
shock, but the other girl had shrugged dismissively.

'Charlene's brother's already in a remand home.
She says he says it's great…they can do what they
like. He got sent there for stealing a car. Charlene
hates it here because she says there's nothing worth
thieving—only bits of stuff from shops.'

Faith had been appalled, and even more determined to give the girls in question a wide berth.
They'd seemed to take a delight in taunting and tor-

menting her, but her mother's illness had given her a maturity that had helped her to ignore them and to treat them with a dignified silence.

The theft from her room, though, of the delicate silver brooch her mother had given to her—a tiny little fairy—which had originally been given to her by Faith's father—had been very hard to bear. Especially when Faith had been pretty sure of who was responsible for taking it. She had reported her loss to the home's harassed staff, though she had sensed it was a waste of time.

Hatton was virtually within walking distance of the home, although they had been taken there by coach, and Faith could still remember the wave of delight that had swept her as she'd seen the house for the first time.

Designed by Lutyens, it had a magical, storybook air that had entranced Faith even whilst her quick intelligence had registered the architectural features favoured by the famous designer.

Whilst the other girls had hurried in bored impatience through the house Faith had lingered appreciatively over every room, and it had been when she had sneaked back for a second look at the study that Philip Hatton had found her.

He had been elderly then—in his mid-seventies— thin and ascetic-looking, with kind, wise eyes and a gentle smile, and Faith had been drawn to him immediately.

She had spent the rest of the afternoon with him, listening to him talk about the house and its history, drinking in every word and in return telling him about her own circumstances.

Much to the bemusement of the carer in charge of them, Philip had insisted that Faith was to remain after the others had left, to have tea with him.

'But how will she get back to the home?' the poor woman had protested.

'I shall send her back in my car,' Philip had responded.

Faith smiled now, remembering the lordly air which had been so much a part of him.

Faith could remember every tiny detail of that shared supper.

After sending her upstairs to 'wash her hands', in the kind care of his elderly housekeeper, Faith had returned to the study to find that Philip Hatton was no longer on his own.

'Ah, Faith.' Philip had beamed at her. 'Come in and meet my godson, Nash. He's spending the summer here with me. Nash, come and say hello to Faith. She's a fellow Lutyens fan.'

And so it had begun. One look at Nash, tall, impossibly good-looking, with his muscular sexy body and his shock of thick dark hair, his amazing topaz eyes and his stunning aura of male sensuality, and Faith had fallen headfirst in love. How could she not have done so?

They had dined on fresh asparagus, poached salmon and strawberries and cream—Philip's favourite summer supper, as she had later discovered—and even today the taste of salmon, the smell of strawberries always took her straight back to that meal.

It had seemed to her then that the very air in the room was drenched in some special magical light, some wonderful mystical golden glow, that suddenly she was grown-up, an adult, with both Philip and Nash listening attentively to her participation in their shared conversation.

The misery she had experienced at the home had been forgotten; she had felt somehow like a caterpillar, emerging from its constricting chrysalis to experience the exhilaration and freedom of flight.

It was Nash who had driven her back to the home. Faith could still remember the way her heart had started to race with frantic excitement when he had stopped the car just outside the entrance. It had been dark by then, and in the shadowy privacy of the quiet lane, seated next to Nash in the car, Faith had held her breath. Was he going to touch her...kiss her? Did he feel like she did?

A mirthless smile stretched the soft fullness of her mouth now as she relived her naïve emotions and the sharpness of her disappointment when Nash had simply thanked her for her kindness to his godfather.

'But I enjoyed talking to him,' she had insisted truthfully.

Less than a week after that she had been living full time at Hatton—an arrangement that had been made after Philip had written to her mother, inviting Faith to spend the rest of the school holidays at Hatton as his guest.

She had been speechless…ecstatic, unable to believe her good fortune when the news had been broken to her. If only she had known *then* what the outcome of her stay was to be…

Automatically Faith walked back to the window, pushing her memories away. From up here she had a wonderfully panoramic view of the Gertrude Jekyll-designed gardens that were at their very best at this time of the year. She could well remember the long sunny hours she had spent alongside Philip, weeding out the magnificent long borders either side of the path that led to the pretty summerhouse.

Faith froze as a large car pulled up outside the house and Nash got out. Where had he been? Had she known he was out she would have gone downstairs and got herself something to eat. She didn't want to eat with Nash.

Prior to her arrival Robert had told her that arrangements had been made for her to live in the house, but that she would have to fend for herself so far as meals were concerned.

'The kitchen is fully equipped, and you'll be able to make use of its facilities, but we shall also give you an allowance in order that you can eat out if you wish—and I hope you will wish.' Robert had smiled at her. 'Especially on those occasions when *I* come down to the house for our progress meetings.'

Faith had smiled, but Robert's interest in her was a complication she hadn't allowed for when she had initially applied for her job.

Faith believed she had every right not to inform her prospective employers about the events leading up to Philip's death. But to conceal them from someone with whom she might form a close personal relationship was something she would never consider doing.

To Faith, loving someone meant being honest with them, trusting them, and had she and Robert met in different circumstances she knew there would have come a stage in their relationship when she would have wanted to open up to him about her past.

She liked Robert. Of course she did. And, yes, one day she hoped to marry and have children. But… A troubled frown furrowed her forehead.

Why had Nash had to reappear in her life? She shivered as she remembered the way he had looked at her when he had told her that he was determined to seek justice for Philip's death.

Inadvertently her gaze was drawn downward, to where Nash was striding towards the house, and as though some mysterious force linked them together he stopped and lifted his head, his gaze unerringly focusing on the tower and her window.

Immediately Faith stepped back, but she knew that Nash had seen her.

The summer she had stayed here she had spent more time than she wanted to remember waiting…watching for Nash to arrive. From here there was an excellent view of the drive, and in those days Nash had driven a racy little scarlet sports car.

Although officially he had been spending the

summer helping his godfather, he had also, even then, been working on the business venture upon which he had eventually built his current empire.

In those days whenever he'd seen her watching for him he would stand underneath her window and smile up at her, teasingly telling her that if she wasn't careful one day he might scale the wall to reach her.

Faith had prayed that he might, so deeply in love with him by then that there had scarcely been any room in her thoughts or her emotions for anyone else but him. He had been her ideal, her hero, and as the girl in her had given way to the growing woman her longing for him had increased and intensified.

From hardly daring to look at his mouth, for fear of blushing because of her desire to feel its hard male strength against her own, she had found herself focusing boldly on it, the words she had known she must never speak pleading in silent longing inside her head.

Kiss me.

Well, today, ten years too late, he *had* kissed her, but not as she had longed for him, *dreamed* of him doing then, with love and tenderness, a look of bemused adoration in his eyes as he begged her for her love. Oh, no. The kiss he had given her today had been hard, angry, pulsing with the violence of his emotions and his antagonism towards her.

So why, then, had she responded to it with a pas-

sion that she had never given to any of the other
men she had dated?

The sharp irritation of her inner voice unnerved
her. She had responded to him because her memories had tricked her, that was all. She had
thought…forgotten… She had *believed* that it was
Nash as she had once imagined him to be that she
was kissing. And as for those other men—well, they
had just been casual dates, nothing serious, and she
had kissed them more out of a sense of fair play
than anything else. Kisses were all that she had
wanted to share with them.

Only with Robert had she sensed that maybe…
just maybe something deeper and stronger might
eventually grow to life between them. But these
days Faith was very protective of her emotions, very
cautious about who she allowed into her life. These
days a man like Nash Connaught would have no
chance whatsoever of bedazzling her into making
the same dangerous mistakes she had made at fifteen.

So far as Faith was concerned now, the most important cornerstone for a relationship was mutual
trust. Without that… Without that there could be
nothing—or nothing that *she* would want, that she
would ever consider worth having, as she had good
and bitter cause to know.

In her bleakest moments after the death of Philip
and her mother the only thing that had kept her going had been the knowledge that Philip *had* trusted

her—enough to make that wonderfully unexpected provision in his will for her.

When she had first learned that Philip had left money specially to finance her studies and her passage through university Faith had hardly been able to believe it. Prior to that she had told herself that the only way she had any hope whatsoever of qualifying as an architect would be to find herself a job and then study in her spare time, which she had known meant that her goal would be virtually impossible for her to reach.

But it hadn't just been the discovery that Philip had left her the money that had meant so much to her. What had mattered even more was knowing that despite everything that had happened he had, after all, believed in her. There was, in Faith's opinion, no price that could be put on that. It was a gift *beyond* price; a gift so precious that even now just to think about it filled her eyes with tears and an emotion she knew someone like Nash would *never* in a million lifetimes be able to understand.

Nash, to whom everything was black or white… Nash, who could condemn a person without allowing them to defend themselves… Nash, in whose eyes she was a thief and a murderer…

Angrily Nash headed towards the house. Just for a heartbeat then, seeing Faith standing at the window, the sunlight dancing on her hair, lingering on its stunning and unique mixture of differing shades of blonde, from purest silver to warmest gold, he had been inexorably swept back in time.

He had known right from the moment his godfather had announced that he intended to invite her to spend the summer at Hatton that she spelled trouble, but he hadn't imagined then just how fatally accurate his prediction was going to be. The kind of trouble he had anticipated had had *nothing* to do with theft and…and murder.

His mouth hardened, the expression in his eyes bleak. Like his godfather, he had been totally taken in by Faith, believing her to be a naïve young girl, never imagining… Bitterness joined the bleakness in his eyes. Hell, he had even wanted to *protect* her, believing then that her advances to him were totally innocent and that she'd had no idea of what she was really inviting when she'd looked at him, her face burning hot with the thoughts he could see so plainly in those limpid dark blue eyes.

He had even derived a certain amount of painful amusement from the way she'd looked at his mouth, semi-boldly, semi-shyly, but wholly provocatively, wondering just what she would do if he actually responded to her invitation and gave in to the fierce heat of desire she was creating inside him.

But she had been fifteen, a child, as he had sternly and furiously reminded himself more times than he cared to count during that brief summer, and no matter how much his body might have reacted, telling him in increasingly urgent and physical terms just how *it* viewed her, his mind had known that to give

in to what he was feeling would have been dishon-
ourable and wrong.

She would not always be fifteen, he had told himself. One day she *would* be adult, and then… Then
he would make her pay over and over again for
every one of those naïvely tormenting looks she had
given him, pay in kiss after kiss for all those kisses
he had ached to steal from her but had known he
must not.

How many nights had he lain awake, tormented
by the heat of his own need, virtually unable to stop
himself from groaning out aloud at the thought of
how she would feel lying against him? Her skin
silken soft, her mouth as perfect and perfumed as
Gertrude Jekyll's warmly scented roses, her eyes as
blue as the campanula that grew amongst them.
God, but he had wanted her, ached for her, longed
for her. Hell, he had even been stupid enough to
make plans for his future that had included her…for
their future…

Initially not even to himself had he dared to acknowledge just how much he'd looked forward to
seeing her waiting for him, standing at her turret
window, a modern-day Rapunzel imprisoned away
from him, not by her father but by her age and his
own moral convictions.

It had left a residue of bitterness to be forced to
recognise that the innocence he had striven so hard
to protect from his own desire had been little more
than a fiction created to conceal the real Faith. But
his personal bitterness was nothing to the anguish

and the anger he felt on behalf of his godfather. The anguish, the anger and the guilt. If he had not been so bemused by Faith, nor so wrapped up in the excitement of beginning the property empire that had now made him such a wealthy man, he might have seen more clearly what was happening and what Faith really was.

But there was no way he was going to fall into that same trap a second time.

The shock of discovering that she was working for the very foundation he had chosen to benefit from his godfather's bequest had caused him to take the first flight from New York to London, despite the fact that he had been in the middle of lengthy discussions involving the sale of leases on some of his most expensive properties. His initial intention had been to warn Robert Ferndown of just what Faith was, but then he had heard Robert eulogising about her abilities, and Faith herself, and he had been caught up in a flood of savage anger against her.

It had been then that he had decided to punish her for the crime she had committed, to punish her not swiftly and immediately, with a clean, sharp cut, but to give her a taste of what his godfather had suffered...to keep her on a knife-edge of fear and dread, never knowing when the final blow was going to fall.

He let himself into the house and paused as he walked past the open study door. He could still taste

Faith's kiss on his lips, still almost feel her against his body, feel his own unwanted reaction to her. Angrily he turned on his heel. What the hell was he trying to do to himself?

CHAPTER THREE

FAITH flexed her fingers and moved tiredly away from her laptop. It was still far too early for her to begin her preliminary report on the house, but looking down into the garden had reminded her not just of the pretty little summer house but of the many statues in the garden as well, some of which she knew were extremely valuable.

She would have to check with Robert to see whether or not they were to remain in the garden, and if they were how best they could be protected from damage and theft. Tomorrow she would list them all properly and contact Robert to get his advice.

She tensed as she heard a knock on her door, knowing who it would be and hesitating warily before going to answer it.

'Yes?' she questioned Nash hardly as she saw him standing outside the door.

He had changed his clothes since she had seen him getting out of his car and was now wearing a white tee shirt that clung to his torso in a way that suddenly made her feel far too hot. She could almost feel her face burning as her senses reacted to the maleness of him. As a girl she had adored him, longed for him, *worshipped* him almost, but now, as

37

a woman, she was aware of the air of raw sexuality
that clung to him—aware of it and resentful of it
too.

'The supper Mrs Jenson left is still in the fridge.
She'll be offended if we don't eat it,' Nash told her
abruptly.

The words 'I'm not hungry' were burning on the
tip of Faith's tongue, but before she could say them
her traitorous tummy gave a very audible and very
hungry gurgle.

Unable to meet Nash's eyes, Faith told him
tersely, 'I'll be down shortly. I'm just finishing
something.'

Faith waited until she was sure he had gone before racing to close her bedroom door. Her hands
were trembling violently. Was she imagining it or
could she really scent danger in the air? Danger and
something else—something that was wholly and
hormone-activatingly Nash.

She quickly sluiced her hot face in the bathroom
that adjoined her bedroom, brushed her hair and
reapplied the minimal amount of make-up she favoured. After what he had said to her she could
scarcely believe that Nash had actually bothered to
concern himself about the fact that she had not had
any supper. Or perhaps he wanted to make sure she
ate it where he could ensure that she didn't make
off with the cutlery and crockery, she told herself
cynically.

And yet when she walked into the kitchen and
discovered that it was empty of Nash's presence her

predominant feeling was one of…of what? she asked herself sharply. Not disappointment…no way. No, she was *glad* he was at least giving her the privacy to eat alone, without his tormenting presence.

But as she opened the fridge she realised she was wrong, because Nash was walking into the kitchen.

'Asparagus and salmon,' Faith murmured as she saw the food that had been left for them. Her eyes filmed with tears, forcing her to keep her head down so that Nash couldn't see them whilst she blinked fiercely to disperse them.

Philip's favourites.

Suddenly Faith knew that despite her hunger the food would taste like sawdust to her.

Shakily she closed the fridge door.

'I've changed my mind,' she told Nash. 'I'm not hungry.'

The look of male incomprehension he gave her might have amused her under different circumstances, but when she headed for the kitchen door she saw it change to frowning anger as Nash moved lithely past her to stand between her and her exit.

'I don't know what kind of game you think you're playing—' he began ominously.

Faith felt her self-control starting to fray. It had been a long day, beginning with her being buoyed up with excitement and pride at the knowledge that Robert had entrusted her with such an important project, then going from that to deep, numbing shock when she had first seen Nash. Then had come the trauma of reliving searingly painful memories—and that was without taking into account everything she had experienced when Nash had kissed her.

'*I'm* not the one who's playing games,' she refuted fiercely, her voice trembling with the intensity of her feelings. 'You're the one who's doing *that*, Nash. Why have you come here? Why are you *staying* here? That wasn't part of the arrangement Robert made with the trustees of the estate.'

'You seem to know an awful lot about his business for a relatively new employee,' Nash countered smoothly, and Faith suspected that despite her anger he could tell that underneath it she was feeling very vulnerable. 'But then, of course, you *aren't* just his employee, are you, Faith? Why the hell do you *think* I'm here?' he demanded with an abrupt change of tone. 'Do you really think for one moment that once I learned *you'd* be here I would allow you to stay on your own?

'This house is full of almost priceless architectural features—panelling, architraves, fireplaces, to name just a few items that would fetch thousands if they were removed and sold to some unscrupulous builder who wasn't worried about checking where they'd come from.'

Faith knew that what he was saying was true, but it appalled her that he should actually consider her capable of perpetrating such a crime. Before she could defend herself Nash was attacking her again, although in a very different way this time.

'Are you going to tell *Robert* that you asked me to kiss you?' he asked with acid softness.

'What? I…I did no such thing,' Faith denied with vehement indignation, her face pink with anger.

'Liar,' Nash taunted her. '"Kiss me"—that's what you said to me.' His mouth twisted. 'Although of course it's typical of you that you should deny it.'

Her face was now scarlet with mortification as she had a sickening memory of actually *thinking* those words. Surely she hadn't…*couldn't* have said them out aloud? But she must have done—unless Nash had read her mind, which in truth she wouldn't entirely put past him.

'The next thing you'll be doing is trying to pretend that you didn't enjoy it,' Nash goaded her tauntingly.

Now Faith really *had* had enough.

'I didn't,' she denied flatly.

'No? Well, there's one very sure way to prove whether or not you're telling the truth, isn't there?' Nash retaliated.

The way he was watching her, looking at her like a hungry lion eyeing up its prey, made Faith wish with all her heart that she had never become involved in a verbal battle she knew Nash would not allow her to win.

'Fortunately for me Hatton doesn't have a torture chamber,' she told him with angry scorn.

'I don't *need* a torture chamber to prove you a

liar,' Nash told her smoothly. '*This* is all it's going to take…'

Faith's eyes widened in disbelief as he took hold of her, imprisoning her against his body and holding her captive there as he bent his head.

Grittily she closed her lips tightly together, fiercely refusing to close her eyes, letting them tell him all that her lips could not as they glittered with angry contempt and female pride, daring him to do his worst.

'Open your mouth.' Nash seemed impervious to the intensity of the rage and hostility emanating from her tense body. 'Open your mouth Faith,' he repeated as he drew his tongue-tip oh, so lightly across the closed line of her lips.

The sensual way in which the warm, wet tip of his tongue was stroking almost lovingly against her lips was so shockingly distracting that Faith found her thoughts releasing their hold on her anger and sliding with shaming wantonness to concentrate instead on the sensations Nash's expertly seductive attack was having on her.

If she closed her eyes that sensation magnified a hundredfold, and that surely *must* be the reason she was starting to tremble as treacherously as a young girl experiencing her first real awareness of what a kiss could be. But Nash wasn't even kissing her yet—not really. He was just playing with her, teasing her, *tormenting* her. She could feel his breath against her skin, smell the unique Nash smell of him, feel…

On a low moan of defeat Faith didn't even know she was making, her lips started to part.

Achingly Faith clung to Nash, her mouth moving eagerly against his, her hand sliding behind his head so that she could hold him close to her.

Nash, Nash… Silently she breathed his name in a sharp female cry that held all the pent-up longing of her teenage desire, of the nights when she had lain awake aching for him without knowing exactly what it was she was aching for. She had known about the mechanics of sex, of course, but the actuality of it had still been a mystery to her, and she had passionately believed Nash was the only man who could ever hold the key to unlock that mystery for her.

Had been a mystery?

Faith shuddered and felt the sharp intake of breath Nash made, as though somehow that fierce reaction of her body had affected his.

They were kissing as she had so often imagined they might, their mouths clinging, stroking, tasting, caressing, feasting, and the little murmurs of appreciative pleasure she could hear herself making were running through their kisses in a soft, disjointed paean of pleasure.

Then, abruptly, shockingly, Nash was pushing her away from him, his chest rising and falling sharply as he demanded in a voice that grated against her ears, 'How much more do I have to do to prove you a liar, Faith? Take you to bed? You'd certainly have let me.'

Appalled, sickened, disbelieving, Faith could only stand blank-eyed and shamed as he denounced her. She could offer him no defence nor any explanation. White-faced, her eyes huge and dark with pain and humiliation, she didn't know which of them she hated the most. Him or herself.

Nauseously she waited for the blow to fall, for Nash to tell her that he fully intended to reveal to Robert what she had done, but sinisterly he made no move to do so.

Faith could feel her anxiety start to increase. Her stomach was churning, her head ached and her eyes felt gritty and sore from the tears she refused to allow herself to cry.

'Where do you think you're going?' Nash demanded as she turned on her heel and hurried blindly towards the kitchen door.

'My room. I'm tired and I want to go to bed,' Faith told him shakily. 'Not that it's any business of yours, Nash. I'm not answerable to you. You don't have any control over me.'

There was the smallest pause before he responded, his voice silken with a menace that made the tiny hairs lift on the back of Faith's neck.

'No? Oh, I think you'll find that you are very *much* answerable to me, Faith, and that I have a *great* deal of control over you. If, for instance, I were to tell Robert what you had just done...'

'If?' Faith couldn't manage to keep the note of soft pleading out of her voice as she turned round to confront him.

'I thought you wanted to go to bed,' Nash taunted her smoothly.

He was enjoying this, Faith recognised. Well, she wasn't going to give him the satisfaction of pleading with him…begging him…

'I do,' she agreed fiercely, turning her back on him, walking determinedly towards the door and opening it.

As he watched her departing back Nash finally let out the pent-up breath he had been holding.

Where the *hell* had she learned to kiss like *that*…and who with…?

No other woman had *ever* kissed him like that, as if he was their life, their soul, their one desire. Their soul mate for this life and every life to come, their world…their everything. She had kissed him as though she had waited out an eternity for him…as though she had been starving for him…as though she loved him and only him.

A woman like Faith was a living, breathing mortal danger to a man when she kissed him like that. A woman like Faith…

Angrily Nash tried to dismiss her from his thoughts. Hadn't what she had done to his godfather taught him *anything*? Of course it had! What was she trying to do? Offer him sex to prevent him from telling Ferndown about her?

Alongside his anger and contempt Nash could feel the sharp savage heat that burned through his body. How could he *possibly* want her, given all that he knew about her? He had never merely wanted a

woman for sex. *Never.* And he *didn't* want Faith—
not really. It was just his mind playing tricks on him.
Some bizarre and treacherous effect of seeing her
here at Hatton and reactivating memories of the past.
A past when he *had* wanted her.

How many men had there been in her life since
then? How many men had experienced the dangerous witchery of her? If that kiss she had given him
was anything to go by…no wonder Ferndown was
so besotted with her!

But he had come here to finally put the past to
rest, Nash reminded himself savagely—not to reactivate it.

Upstairs in her room Faith sank down onto her bed,
wrapping her arms protectively around her body as
she rocked herself helplessly to and fro.

Why, why, why had she allowed it to happen?
Why had she betrayed everything that she held most
dear? Why had she allowed herself to forget reality,
and, most important of all, why had she become so
bemused, so intoxicated, so entranced and so lost in
Nash's kiss? She had given in to his hands a powerful weapon for him to use against her, and given
it to him as carelessly and recklessly as she had once
given him her heart and her love.

She should never have come back here—would
never have come back here if she had guessed for
one moment that Nash was going to be here.

Ten years ago he had told her that he would never
forgive her for his godfather's death, but she had

never dreamed that he would pursue her for vengeance in the way he was now doing.

Downstairs in the kitchen Nash looked at the remains of his virtually uneaten meal. Grimly he got up and took the plate over to the pedal bin, removing the food before rinsing the plate and stacking it in the dishwasher.

Salmon had always been one of his godfather's favourite foods. Towards the end of his life it had become increasingly difficult for him to feed himself—a legacy of his stroke—and Nash could remember visiting him on his birthday and finding him close to tears of anger and pride as he had stared at the salmon on his plate.

In the end Nash had fed him himself, dismissing his nurse. It had been the least he could do. Philip had been like the grandfather Nash had never had, his home a refuge to Nash during his schooldays when his own parents had been out of the country. His father had been a foreign correspondent with a national newspaper and his mother a photographer. They, like Philip, were dead now, killed in an uprising in one of the countries they had been reporting from.

Philip had adored Faith, once confiding in Nash that she was the granddaughter he would have loved to have had. He had shown that love for her in his will, which he had altered with Nash's own knowledge and approval only days before he had been attacked. He had made a provision in it for a sum to be set aside from his estate to pay for Faith's further education; Nash knew that had he lived it would have been Philip's intention to finance Faith through a degree.

All three of them had shared a compelling interest in architecture; in fact it had been Nash's own love of interesting buildings which had led to him acquiring his first property whilst he was still at Oxford. He had bought a small row of terraced houses with the money he had inherited from his parents' estate, back then more because he had been amused by their innovative and attractive early Edwardian design than because he had wanted to make money from them by letting them—that had come later.

At least Faith had not lied to Philip about her desire to become an architect. Nash frowned as he remembered how determinedly his godfather had battled with the after-effects of his stroke to make sure Nash knew he wanted his will to stand. People had assumed, because Philip lived in a large house, that he was a wealthy man.

Nash's frown deepened. It was nearly midnight. Time he was in bed.

It had taken Faith a long time to finally get off to sleep, her body tense, her mind racing. And now a dog fox, padding across the gardens, paused and lifted his head, baying to the moon. In her sleep Faith trembled, tormented by the darkness of her dreams, their grip on her so intense that when the fox's cry first woke her she actually thought that she was still fifteen, and was relieved to find herself here in her bed at Hatton, not in her room at the home.

The home!

As she sat up in the bed Faith clasped her hands round her knees and stared morosely towards the window. She had hated the home so much. Or rather she had hated the things she had experienced whilst she was living there.

Her mother's recovery had been progressing much more slowly than anyone had envisaged, and in September, when the new school year had begun, Faith had had to move back into the home from Hatton and attend school with the other girls.

The school her age group had attended had been in the local town—they'd travelled there and back every day by bus—and, as Faith had quickly discovered, girls from the home were considered troublemakers by the staff at school.

When her teachers had discovered that Faith genuinely wanted to work and learn she had earned their approbation and admiration—and the increased enmity of the home's dominating gang of girl bullies.

No one had been more astonished than Faith when, after weeks of tormenting and deriding her, one of the gang had approached her and invited her to join them on a Saturday morning shopping trip into town. Naïvely eager to accept the olive branch she was being offered, Faith had accepted. She'd had no money of her own to spend, but had been happy to take one of the other girl's goods and money to the checkout to pay for them.

It had only been once they were back outside in the street that Faith had discovered their real purpose in befriending her. They had started to shriek with laughter and jeer at her, boasting that they had used her as a decoy whilst they had been shoplifting.

Faith had been horrified, pleading with them to take the stolen goods back—make-up, in the main— which had only made them worse.

'*Pay* for it? Why should we when we can get it for free?' she had been told.

And as Faith had looked unhappily at them she had suddenly been uncomfortably aware of the narrow-eyed attention she was getting from the girl who was the leader of the small group.

Slightly older than the others, with—if the home's gossip was to be believed—a family background of theft, she had marched over to Faith, taking a handful of her hair and tugging it viciously as she'd warned her, 'Don't even think of snitching on us, Miss Posh, 'cos if you do...'

She had stopped whilst Faith had gritted her teeth against the pain. Her eyes had been beginning to water, but she'd been determined not to let the other girl see how much she was hurting her.

''Cos if you do,' the older girl had continued, giving Faith's hair an even more vicious tug, 'we'll just tell them that it was all your idea in the first place. Bet that old geezer up at the big house is filthy rich, isn't he? Bet that place is *loaded* down with stuff. How many tellys has he got?'

Faith had shaken her head and responded honestly, 'I don't know.'

Philip hadn't watched a lot of television, preferring to read.

'Keep much money up there, does he?' her tormentor had demanded. 'I bet he does. And don't tell me you haven't looked or been tempted to take a few quid, Miss Goody-two-shoes,' she had sneered.

'No,' Faith had protested, grateful that the arrival of their bus meant that the other girl had been forced to let her go.

'Just remember,' she had hissed as they got on the bus, 'try telling on us and you'll be for it, good and proper...'

Completely wide awake now, and fully back in the present, Faith hugged her knees.

Her conscience had troubled her very badly over the fact that she had not told anyone in authority about the shoplifting. It hadn't been fear that had stopped her—or at least not any fear of being physically hurt. It had been more her fear of betraying the youthful code of not 'telling tales' that had kept her silent. There *had* been a moment when she had been tempted to confide in one person, though, she acknowledged.

Closing her eyes, she expelled her breath shakily.

The following weekend she had been invited over to Hatton, and Nash had picked her up.

'What's wrong, Shrimp?' he had asked her, in that

teasing manner he'd sometimes adopted towards her which had made her itch to tell him that she was almost grown up, certainly grown up enough to know that she loved him.

'It's...' she had begun hesitantly, but just as she had struggled to find the words to tell him what had happened she'd realised that his attention had been distracted away from her by a stunningly beautiful brunette walking on the other side of the road.

Bringing his car to a halt, Nash had wound down the window and called out a greeting to the other woman.

The smile she had given him had confirmed Faith's view that Nash was just the most gorgeously hunky, sexy man there was, and when the brunette had crossed the road to indulge in some sophisticated banter with Nash, Faith had subsided into her seat, feeling forlorn and unwanted.

It had only been as Nash had finally driven away that she'd realised, despite the girl's open hints, Nash had *not* made any definite plans to take her out, and in the soaring surge of relief and joy that knowledge had brought, the dilemma she had been about to seek his advice on had been pushed to one side.

There had been many occasions in the decade since then when Faith had wondered just how different her life might have been if she had told him.

Just for a second silent tears glistened betrayingly in her eyes, but very quickly and determinedly she blinked them away. She had stopped crying over Nash Connaught a long, long time ago—hadn't she?

CHAPTER FOUR

'END of laburnum tunnel, nymph with water pot'.

As she wrote down her description of the statue she was standing in front of Faith sighed a little ruefully. This morning, when she had initially embarked on her self-imposed task, she hadn't realised just how many pieces of statuary and ornament the garden possessed, nor how much being in it was going to affect her and awaken more memories she had thought long ago safely buried.

But was it being in the garden that had awakened them or was it Nash? Nash and that insane, inexplicable response she had allowed him to steal from her last night?

Stop thinking about it, Faith warned herself fiercely. Stop thinking about *him*!

It was, after all, *Philip* who had first introduced her to the beauty of Hatton's gardens, and Nash had come walking towards them down the laburnum tunnel, the brief darts of sunlight that had pierced its summer-green canopy splashing splodges of lighter colour on the tee shirt he had been wearing—a tee shirt which she remembered far too vividly had openly revealed the smooth tanned column of his throat and the muscular strength of his forearms.

Just watching him then had made her go faint

with love and longing. That had been the occasion, she remembered—how could she possibly ever forget?—when Philip had suggested that Nash should take her to Oxford for dinner.

Faith had been speechless with embarrassment and excitement, scarcely daring to breathe as she had prayed that Nash would agreed.

'Do you like Italian food?' he had asked her.

Faith suspected she would have agreed to like any kind of food so long as she could eat it in his company, and now, recalling the incident, she could vividly see in her memory an image of Nash's face, and the quizzical amusement she had not really recognised then when she had breathed her fervent assent.

Oh, yes, Nash had known exactly how she had felt about him. But then she hadn't made any attempt to hide her feelings...her love...had she?

Nash had driven her to Oxford in his bright red sports car, and if he had felt resentful about the way his godfather had manipulated him into taking her out, there had been nothing in his manner towards her to betray it.

They had been having a good summer weatherwise. The evening had been soft and balmy, Oxford's streets busy with visitors while the colleges were empty of students for the long summer holiday. Nash had parked the car close to his own college, and Faith had studied both it and the other wonderful buildings they had walked past on their way to the restaurant with awed eyes. So much of the country's history had its roots in the early lives of those who had studied here: artists, writers, statesmen and women.

The Italian restaurant had been situated in a pretty courtyard off a narrow lane, and the *patrone*, a jocular middle-aged Italian, had shown them to a table which had afforded them a prime view of the other diners whilst giving them their own privacy.

It had been the first time she had eaten proper Italian food, the first time she had even been to a restaurant really, and Nash had laughed teasingly at her as she had struggled with her ribbons of pasta before moving closer to her and demonstrating the correct way to eat it.

Watching him twirl the pasta onto his fork had been one thing—trying to imitate him had been something else, and in the end...

Helplessly Faith closed her eyes. All too quickly and easily she was fifteen again, seated next to Nash in the restaurant. She could smell the fresh clean scent of his hair...his body... She knew it was Nash's scent because she had sneaked into his bathroom one afternoon when he hadn't been there just so that she could breathe in the special smell she always associated with him. She had even dampened a piece of cotton wool and put some of his shower gel onto it, secreting it beneath her own pillow so that when she went to bed the last thing she smelt at night and the first thing she smelt in the morning was Nash.

'No, not like that.' He had smiled when he'd seen

the way she was fumbling to copy him, adding, 'Here, let me show you.'

And then, unbelievably, his hand had been over hers as she'd held the fork and he'd moved her hand.

'Think you've got it now?' he'd asked her several dizzyingly blissful seconds later. 'Or do I have to feed you?' he had teased.

At fifteen she had been far too young and inno- cent to respond sexually to such a question—and anyway she had known that Nash had not intended it to be a sensual invitation for him to feed her as a *lover*—but she had not been too young to experience a sudden clutching, piercing sensation deep down inside her body, and neither had she been old enough to stop herself from gazing adoringly into Nash's eyes, her heart and feelings in her own.

No doubt *that* had been the reason he had very firmly removed his hand from hers and moved his chair back to its original position, saying crisply, 'Perhaps you should have ordered something it would be easier for you to eat.'

But not even that remark had had the power to quench her euphoric joy, Faith remembered.

The subtle adult nuances of Nash's manner to- wards her, which had been lost on her at fifteen, deep in the throes of the passionate intensity of a love she was longing to have returned, were re- vealed to her in sharp painful clarity now as she reran her mental recording of that time past her now adult awareness.

What she had seen as a uniquely romantic evening shared by two people who were destined to love one another had no doubt to Nash simply been the execution of a duty.

It had been growing dark later, when they had walked back to the car side by side, with Faith as close to Nash's side as she had dared. Nash himself had somehow or other managed to keep a few inches of space between their bodies, but then they had had to cross a very busy intersection, where the traffic lights, for some reason, hadn't been working, and Nash had reached out and taken her hand.

To share such a physical intimacy with him twice in one evening had put Faith on such a high plateau of intense emotion that she hadn't been able to imagine she could possibly feel any happier—unless, of course, Nash had fulfilled her wildest dreams and actually kissed her.

Her wildest dreams?

The reality of Nash's kiss had been more like her worst nightmare, Faith thought bitterly now as she headed for the elegant Italian garden, with its box hedges and formal fishpond.

Philip had told her that the ornaments in this garden had actually originally come from Italy. Boys astride dolphins, with water spouting from the dolphins' mouths, decorated each corner of the pond, which was large enough not to be overwhelmed by the intricate fountain at its centre.

Steps would have to be taken to protect visiting children from the dangers of the pond, Faith acknowledged as she wrote a quick note on her pad before beginning to list the garden's ornaments.

As she did so she noticed that one of the dolphins looked slightly different from the others. Frowning, she went over to make a closer examination of it. Both its colour and composition were different, she recognised as she knelt down to inspect it even more closely.

'If you're planning what I *think* you're planning, you can forget it. Someone's already tried it and that's the result. The dolphin *he* was trying to steal ended up smashed and the one *you're* inspecting is its replacement.'

The unexpected sound of Nash's harsh voice caught Faith off guard. Immediately she stood up and turned to confront him as the meaning of his tautly angry words hit her.

But without giving her a chance to say anything Nash continued coldly, 'What exactly *are* you doing out here anyway, Faith? I thought your task was supposed to be preparing a plan for the house conversion, not checking out the garden—and its contents!'

'I wanted to make a list of all the garden ornaments,' Faith cut across his sarcastic comment in quick defence.

But before she could finish her explanation Nash had stopped her again, exclaiming derisively, 'Oh, I'm sure you did. But unfortunately for you I happened to see what you were up to. As I've already told you, someone else had the same idea before you and tried to make off with these four.' He gestured towards the dolphins.

'I wasn't—' Faith began angrily, but once again Nash refused to allow her to finish what she was saying.

'Your boss has been on the phone for you,' he told her. 'No doubt, like me, he expected to find you doing your job. He asked me to tell you that he'll be here later on today, and no doubt when he does arrive,' he continued smoothly, 'he's going to want a full report on how you've spent your time in his absence.'

She might have registered the sneering double meaning in Nash's speech, but there was no way she was going to give him the satisfaction of letting him know it, Faith decided firmly. And there was *one* point she fully intended to put him right on.

'For your information—' she began determinedly.

But to her fury yet again Nash took the initiative away from her, pre-empting her by saying harshly, 'For my information *what*? I already *have* all the information I need or want about anything *you* might do or say, Faith. Oh, and by the way, Mrs Jenson isn't here to cook and clean for you.'

That was it! Faith had had enough!

'What *is* she here for, Nash? To spy on me? Is that why I caught her in my room this morning?'

Faith could see from Nash's expression that he didn't like what she was saying. Tough! Did he *really* think he could get away with piling insult after insult on her without her retaliating?

'She was probably returning the laundry you'd left downstairs for her to wash,' Nash countered, frowning.

'You mean the laundry I'd left downstairs to put in the washing machine after it had finished the cycle it was on?' Faith corrected him, adding before he could cut her off, 'Wasn't the arrangement my company had with the trustees that whilst I was here I could use the domestic facilities of the house?'

'That doesn't include the services of a housekeeper,' Nash shot back at her.

'I was referring to the washing machine, not Mrs Jenson,' Faith told him sharply, pushing her hand into her hair in helpless irritation as she acknowledged the impossibility of having anything approximating a normal rational conversation with Nash.

But his comments had reminded her of something. 'It would be helpful if I could have a copy of any existing floor plan of the house you might have,' she told him stiffly.

'You mean it will save you the bother of drawing one up yourself—thus allowing you to spend your time far more profitably, from your point of view at least, in checking out the property's more moveable and readily disposable assets. Well, for your information—'

'No. For *your* information,' Faith interrupted him swiftly, copying his own aggressive method of attack, 'let me tell you that the only reason I was looking at the garden ornaments is because…'

As she was speaking a sudden breeze caught at

the pages of the notebook she had put down beside her on the ground, drawing Nash's attention to it.

Instinctively Faith bent to pick it up, but Nash moved even faster, and the expression in his eyes as he studied the list she had made was so contemptuously damning that for some idiotic reason it made Faith want to cry.

'Don't say another word,' Nash advised her as he calmly tore the list she had made in half, and then in half again. 'I'm just glad that Philip didn't live to see what you've become. He *trusted* you, Faith.'

'And I have *never* abused his trust—' Faith began passionately, and then stopped as she saw the way Nash was watching her. What was the point in even trying to talk to him? Instead she simply turned on her heel and walked as quickly as she could back to the house.

Faith was feeling rather pleased with herself. A trip into the local town after her run-in with Nash had produced not only the delicious sandwich she had enjoyed for her lunch but also a very interesting book written by a local historian, which included detailed drawings of Hatton at the time it had been built.

Her mobile started to ring, and as she went to answer it she recognised Robert's number.

'I'm just leaving London now,' he told her. 'So, traffic willing, it shouldn't be too long before I reach you. How are things going? Thanks for your message about the garden ornaments, by the way. I'm

not quite sure what the position is with them. I shall
have to check with Nash, but if they are to remain
in the gardens then we shall definitely have to take
precautions to protect them. Missing me?' he asked
her softly then, in a very different tone of voice.

He started to laugh when Faith didn't immediately
reply, telling her even more softly, 'You don't have
to tell me now. You can *show* me later instead.'

He had rung off before Faith could say anything.

Faith's next encounter with Nash came shortly afterwards, when she went into the kitchen to make
herself a cup of coffee. She was just pouring the
boiling water onto the coffee grains when the back
door opened and Nash walked in.

'Before you say a word,' she told him, 'I bought
the coffee myself, and I have the trustees' agreement
to use the kitchen,' she added sarcastically. 'Presumably that was a trustees' meeting you were too busy
to attend,' she finished, with mock sweetness.

'Faith—' she heard him saying as she turned
away from him to return the milk—*her* milk, which
she had bought with her own money—to the fridge.
Whilst Nash might have taken it upon himself to set
the terms for the hostilities between them, she was
determined to show him that there was no way she
was going to balk at them, or run away in ignomin-
ious defeat.

'Perhaps I should ask Robert to mention to them
the…difficulties I'm encountering in working here.

Although they have gifted Hatton to the Foundation...' she began.

Faith wasn't used to having to make threats or respond to other people's hostility, but she felt that Nash had left her with little choice.

It comforted her to remember that Nash was not the only trustee of Philip's estate, although she had no real idea who the others were. Whoever they were she certainly had every reason to be grateful to them. Without the extra funds they had made available to her she would never even have been able to consider continuing her studies, as she had done. Nor would she have spent a brief working holiday in Florence—a job which had been organised for her thanks to the very kind offices of one of the trustees, according to her university tutor.

She had had no idea then that Nash was one of their number, and she could well imagine how it must have infuriated him to do anything of benefit for her. But she also knew that he would have adhered scrupulously to the terms of Philip's will. That was the kind of man he was.

'Faith.' Nash stopped her in a grim voice, a voice so determined that it forced her to listen to him.

'I just wanted to tell you that I've put a set of plans of the house in the study for you. They're on Philip's desk.'

Nash was actually speaking to her as though she were a normal human being instead of some loathsome monster. Faith opened her mouth and then closed it again, but the good manners her mother had been so insistent upon forced her to thank him, even though she resented having to do so.

It was much later in the afternoon, whilst she was working on the plans upstairs in her room, that she saw Robert arrive. Putting her work to one side, she went downstairs to meet him.

'Sorry it's taken me so long to get here,' he apologised when they met in the hallway. 'The traffic was appalling.'

'Well, at least you're here now,' Faith offered.

'Mmm…but not for long, I'm afraid,' Robert told her ruefully. 'We're having major problems with the Smethwick House conversion and it looks like I'm going to have to leave you pretty much to your own devices down here until we get them sorted out. Don't look so worried,' he told her with a smile when he saw her expression. 'I have every faith in you.'

He might, but Nash most certainly didn't, and it was Nash she was going to have to deal with on a day-to-day basis, Faith recognised as Robert went on to explain that he had booked a table at a local riverside restaurant.

'We can talk properly over dinner,' he told her, 'but first I need to have a word with Nash. I'm glad he's decided to stay on here for a while. The house is quite remote and I don't like the thought of you being here on your own.'

It was a new experience for Faith to have a man act so protectively towards her. Nash, of course, would have taken a completely different stance, insisting that it was the others who needed protecting from *her*, not the other way around.

After arranging to meet Robert back downstairs in an hour's time, Faith returned to her room to continue with her work.

She began to check the sizes of the upstairs rooms on the plans, noting down those which were large enough to be converted into family-sized rooms and those which were better suited to single occupation.

The downstairs snooker room would, no doubt, be something that the Foundation would want to retain, but she put a question mark over the tennis court, recognising that it might be too expensive to renovate and maintain.

Totally engrossed in what she was doing, Faith was shocked to glance at her watch and realise what time it was. She had barely fifteen minutes left in which to get ready to meet Robert.

Somehow she managed it, snatching a quick shower and changing into a cool black linen dress, and brushing her hair before applying a fresh dusting of make-up.

Despite her blonde hair her skin tanned well, and the hot summer had given it a golden sheen. Her dress, although demure, was sleeveless, revealing the slim tanned warmth of her bare arms and legs.

A bright fuchsia-coloured pashmina which had been an uncharacteristic impulse buy in the sales provided her with a wrap, just in case the evening should prove cool. Faith stroked the silky texture of the wrap gently as she draped it over her shoulders.

Just touching it made her feel very feminine and extravagant. Her mother would have loved it.

She hesitated before opening her jewellery box and putting on the tiny gold-set diamond ear-studs that had been a twenty-first birthday present—and a very unexpected one at that.

She could still remember vividly her shock and speechless delight when she had opened the registered parcel and read the note inside.

'Congratulations on your twenty-first birthday and on the excellence of your academic work', the note attached to the small jeweller's box had read, and instead of any signature there had simply been a typed and very formal, 'The estate of the late Philip Hatton'.

Tears shone briefly in Faith's eyes now as she put the earrings on. That gesture by the anonymous trustees had meant so very much to her, and she could still remember what a thrill it had given her to wear them going out with her university friends to celebrate her birthday.

Robert was waiting in the hallway, smiling admiringly up at her as he watched her descend the stairs.

Although he lacked Nash's arrogantly male brand of sexuality, Robert was a very attractive-looking man—a nice man, Faith acknowledged as she smiled back at him.

'You look good in black,' he complimented her as she reached him. 'It suits you.'

Out of the corner of her eye Faith could see Nash

emerging from the drawing room, and she knew he must have overheard Robert's compliment, even though he chose not to acknowledge either it or her.

She could tell from Robert's behaviour towards her that as yet Nash had said nothing to him about her past, or rather his interpretation of it, but she knew it would only be a matter of time before he did, which meant that she would have to tell Robert herself first. She felt her stomach starting to tense in tight, anxious knots. The shame of what had happened would always cast a dark shadow over her life and she hated the thought of having to resurrect it.

The restaurant Robert took her to was busy and very obviously trendy and expensive. It was the sort of place where private conversation was virtually impossible, and Robert gave her a rueful look as they were escorted to their table.

'I hadn't realised it was going to be as busy as this. I asked Nash to recommend somewhere but I don't think he can have fully understood me.'

Robert's mention of Nash gave Faith the opening she had been looking for. Tentatively she asked him, 'Do you know how much longer Nash intends to remain at Hatton? After all, now that the trustees have handed it over to the Foundation there isn't any real reason for him to be there.'

No reason at all, in fact, other than to torment her, Faith reflected inwardly.

'Well, at the moment the trustees—or rather Nash, should I say, since he is the *sole* trustee of his late godfather's estate— What is it?' Robert asked Faith in concern as she made a small sound of shocked disbelief.

'Nash is the sole Trustee?' she repeated.

'Oh, yes,' Robert confirmed. 'And it was his own idea to get in touch with the Foundation. Apparently he feels very strongly about the needs of children from deprived backgrounds, but, as he's told me himself, he wants to be sure that the Foundation is the right beneficiary for Hatton before fully handing it over. I must admit I'd hate to lose the house at this stage. It's done me no end of good with the rest of the board to be able to say I've secured Hatton for the Foundation.' He gave her a rueful smile. 'Most of them have known me since I was a schoolboy and I'm afraid they still tend to treat me as one.

'I'm looking to you to impress Nash with our plans for converting the house, Faith. I've heard good things about your work and I can well understand why.'

Every word Robert said was adding to Faith's anxiety. How long had Nash been the sole trustee of Philip's estate? she wondered dazedly. Not very long, surely.

'I told Nash of your concern about the garden statues and ornaments, by the way,' Robert was continuing. 'I said you'd told me you were going to make a list of everything. At the moment, like the house and its contents, everything is covered by insurance paid for by the estate, but once Hatton passes legally into our hands that will become the

Foundation's responsibility. I did ask Nash if he had thought of removing some of the more valuable artefacts, but he says he wants them to remain with the house.

'I'm counting on you to do a really first-class job for me here at Hatton, Faith,' Robert repeated. 'An awful lot hinges on our successful acquisition of the house—for both of us. Like I've already said, it will be a real feather in my cap, and I shall make sure that you are suitably rewarded.

'I don't suppose the fact that you and Nash know one another is going to do us any harm either,' he chuckled, so patently oblivious to what Faith was actually feeling and thinking that she felt dangerously close to hysterical laughter as she recognised the weight of the responsibility he was placing on her.

'Robert…I don't think…' she began, carefully and quietly searching for the right words to explain the true situation to him, but he reached across the table gently taking her hand in his and squeezing it.

'Stop worrying,' he told her. 'I *know* you're the right person for the job. After all, I was the one who made the decision to employ you. You can do it, Faith; I know you can. The rest of the board might have thought we should take on someone older— and male—but I know that you're going to prove them wrong and me right.'

Faith's heart sank lower with every word Robert uttered. How *could* she tell him now? How *could* she let him down? She had had no idea that the hand-over of Hatton to the Foundation hadn't fully gone through—or that Robert had had to battle against his co-board members to take her on.

There was only one option left to her now, only one thing she could possibly do—even though it was something that went totally against everything her pride was urging her to do and had been urging her to do for the last twenty-four hours. She was going to have to appeal to Nash, beg him to listen to her for Robert's sake, because of what she felt she owed him for his support of her and for the sake of all those who would benefit from what the Foundation would do with Hatton.

'Not hungry?' Robert asked her solicitously as she pushed her food around her plate.

'I ate a large lunch,' Faith fibbed wanly.

Why was life doing this to her? Why?

CHAPTER FIVE

NASH looked irritably at his watch. Hadn't Faith realised when she had left the house with Robert that, since she didn't possess a set of keys to Hatton, *he* would have to wait for her return before he could lock the house up for the night?

His irritation increased as he recalled the look of male expectancy and desire in Robert's eyes when he had told him during their meeting that he was taking Faith out to dinner.

'There are several things I need to discuss with her, and since we both have to eat we might as well do so together.'

But Nash knew his own sex well enough to know that Robert's real reasons for taking Faith out for a meal were a thousand miles away from practicality—and Faith had obviously had more than business on her mind, as well, to judge from the way she had been dressed when she'd left the house.

The black dress she had been wearing had looked expensive, and the wrap she had draped around her shoulders had had a silky sheen—but not as silky as Faith's softly tanned skin; diamonds had sparkled in her ears...

A bitter, almost tormented look darkened Nash's eyes as he thought about Faith's earrings, but Faith herself would have been stunned if she had known just what was putting that look there.

From the study, where he had been purporting to be 'working' for the last hour, Nash had an excellent view of the darkening driveway that led away from the house to the main road—the driveway down which Faith would have to return.

He had been caught off guard when Robert had brought up the subject of the garden statuary, claiming that Faith was concerned for their security—her concern not just that they could be stolen but also that they could be inadvertently damaged by the children and their parents.

'I have to confess I hadn't realised how valuable and irreplaceable some of the pieces are,' Robert had admitted ruefully. 'And Faith is right. If they are to remain we shall have to find some way of protecting them. We'll need to catalogue them, and then—'

'I already have a list of them,' Nash had informed him brusquely. 'The insurers insist on it.'

Had he misjudged Faith? A stark look darkened Nash's eyes. Here he went again, looking for excuses for her…looking for…

He closed his eyes. Only he knew and only he would ever know just what he had gone through when he had returned home early following a business meeting in London, acting on a hunch…an instinct…something that had felt too urgent to analyse, to discover his godfather lying on the study floor with Faith crouching over him, his wallet in her hands and a look of mixed fury and guilt in her eyes as he'd broken through the circle of girls standing protectively around her to confront her.

Later, as he had waited at the police station whilst Faith and her fellow thieves were being charged—after a two-hour delay since apparently as they were all under age and juveniles they could only be questioned and charged in the presence of a parent or guardian—the police sergeant had commiserated with him and told him not to blame himself.

'These girl thieves—sometimes you'd think butter wouldn't melt in their mouth,' he had offered comfortingly. 'But we see the other side of them, and, believe you me, they can be just as violent and abusive as the lads, if not more so.'

'But my godfather loves Faith,' Nash had protested, still unable to fully take on board what had happened. 'I just can't believe she would do something like this to him.'

What he had really been saying was that he too loved her, and that he couldn't believe she would do something so damaging to *him*, to what he had believed they would one day share—when she was old enough.

'You'd be surprised,' had been the sergeant's dark response. 'Seems from what the others have said that the one who you found holding your godfather's wallet was the ring-leader. She'd put the others up to it. You say she was staying at the house during the summer?'

'Yes,' Nash had agreed numbly. 'She came on a

visit from...from the home, and my godfather invited her to stay. He felt sorry for her. Her mother...'

The sergeant had sucked in his breath and shaken his head.

'Got a bad reputation, has that home. There've been complaints about girls from there stealing from local shops. They go in a gang—' He'd broken off as the head of the children's home and the WPC accompanying her came back into the waiting area.

Unable to stop himself, Nash had hurried towards them, demanding, almost begging, 'Faith...? Has she...? Is she...?'

'She still refuses to admit that she was involved,' the home's head had told him tiredly. 'And I have to admit I would never have thought... But she is a very intelligent girl, and sometimes they're the very ones... They're so much more aware than the others, you see,' she had added simply. 'They have so much spare mental energy with nowhere to go.

'She would have seen the opportunities, of course, when she visited and stayed with your godfather, and I imagine that the temptation must just have been too much for her, especially in her circumstances. Her mother has been ill for a very long time and they have been living in considerable financial hardship...that often breeds a dangerous form of resentment.'

She had looked down at the floor and then told Nash uncomfortably, 'She has asked to see you. She says...' She'd stopped. 'She claims that she is the victim of the other girls' malice and that she was trying to protect your godfather, not steal from him. But the other girls are adamant that *she* was the one who planned the whole thing, and I have to admit that does make sense.'

'I don't want to see her,' Nash had refused immediately, knowing that he would carry with him for ever, engraved on his mind and his emotions, the scene which had met his eyes when he had walked into Philip's study.

The telephone cord had been cut, but thankfully Nash had had his mobile telephone with him—they had been relatively rare in those days, and he had only decided to buy one himself because, as yet, he hadn't any proper office facilities.

He had rung the emergency services, having first locked the girls and himself in Philip's study. One of them had produced a knife, but he had very quickly removed it from her.

Whilst they had screamed and hurled threats and abuse at him Faith had remained completely silent, and it had only been after the crew had started to carry Philip out to the ambulance and the police had taken charge of the girls that she had finally said anything.

White-faced with terror as she had stared from the police to him, she had begged him to listen, begged him to understand, begged him to believe that she had had nothing to do with what had happened.

'You were holding Philip's wallet,' he had reminded her grimly.

'I was trying to *help* him,' she had protested.

'Don't believe her,' one of the other girls had screamed. '*She's* the one that made us come here…told us it would be easy pickings. She was the one who said the old man was going to be on his own.'

Silently Nash had looked at Faith. Despite all the evidence against her he had desperately wanted to believe that she was innocent, but the look of guilt in her eyes had given her away.

Ignoring her pleading cries to him as the police ushered all of the girls out of the house, he had turned to follow the ambulance crew.

At the hospital they had told him that Philip had suffered a stroke—brought on, they suspected, by shock. He would live, they had assured Nash, but as to how serious the after-effects of his stroke would be they had no way at that stage of saying.

Had Faith shown the slightest degree of remorse, offered him any kind of explanation instead of lying so blatantly to him, he might have given in and agreed to see her. As it was…

'What will happen to her?' he had asked the police sergeant.

'She'll be put in a remand home until they can go before a juvenile court, then it's up to the court to decide what their sentence will be and whether or not it will be custodial.'

Nash had closed his eyes, torn in two by his conflicting emotions. *He* should have been there, with his godfather, to protect him. If he had been…

Bleakly he had turned to leave. He still hadn't been able to believe what Faith had done, and he'd known if he hadn't seen the damning evidence with his own eyes he would *never* have believed it. His godfather had trusted her, loved her…and he himself…

A bitter look had darkened his eyes as he'd made his way to where he had parked his car.

She was fifteen—he had believed her to be naïve and innocent, in need of protection from the desire she had made so obvious she felt for him, from his own increasingly hungry need to respond to it.

How *could* he have been such a fool? She had probably deliberately set out to delude and deceive him right from the start. Physically she was mature for her age; mentally she was as intelligent and knowledgeable, if not more so, as a good many of his own peers.

He had enjoyed their dinner-table debates, enjoyed the passion she brought to every aspect of her life, and he had enjoyed looking forward to the day when the barriers between them could be properly lifted and he could show her just how he wanted and intended to respond to all those sexy, innocent little messages of longing and provocation she had been sending him all summer.

He hadn't just wanted her physically. He had *loved* her, Nash acknowledged grimly now, and her deceit had hurt him, come close to destroying him on just about every level there was.

His godfather's stroke had badly affected Philip's

powers of speech, which he had never fully recovered, and whenever anyone had tried to question him about the incident he had become distressed, saying only, 'Faith… Faith…'

Rather than risk him having a second and even more serious stroke, Nash had insisted that he was not to be questioned any further.

Faith had been lucky to escape a custodial sentence, the authorities had told Nash. That escape had been in the main because it had been her first offence, and because of the plea for clemency that Nash himself had made for her.

Even now he loathed acknowledging that he had been guilty of such a weakness, but the thought of her being sentenced had eaten into him like acid and, despite his anger and contempt, and the bitterness he had felt towards her, he had still interceded on her behalf.

It was what Philip would want, he had told himself, knowing as his godfather slowly struggled to make himself understood that he refused to accept that Faith was in any way to blame, insisting that the other girls had used her…forced her…

Nash had longed to be able to share Philip's belief, but he had known better. He had, after all, seen the guilty expression in Faith's eyes as she'd crouched over his godfather, as well as heard the condemnatory accusations of her co-conspirators.

It hadn't really come as any surprise to Nash when a second and more serious stroke had indeed followed Philip's first one, quickly followed by his death. He still believed that it was the original attack that had caused it—and for what? A paltry few pounds? Because, despite what other people might have believed, Philip had *not* been a wealthy man. He had owned Hatton and its grounds, yes, but a series of bad investments after his retirement had eaten into his capital, and in the latter years of his life it had been Nash who had financed him...who had financed...

He froze as he saw Robert's car heading down the drive.

As Robert brought his car to a halt on Hatton's drive Faith prepared to get out. They had spent longer than she had expected and it was almost midnight.

'I'll see you to the door,' Robert told her, opening his own door.

What Robert had told her had given her a good deal to think about, and her eyes were as shadowed as the garden as she walked towards the house.

'Not so fast,' Robert protested as he hurried to catch up with her and then reached for her hand before Faith realised what he was intending to do.

'I know we haven't known one another very long, Faith, but something tells me that you're a very special person,' Robert murmured, his voice becoming even softer and lower as he repeated huskily, 'A very special person.'

Faith knew instinctively that he was going to kiss her, and as his lips brushed hers with tender warmth, his hands holding her gently, she closed her eyes.

This was how a kiss should be—giving, tender, caring—so why wasn't she feeling anything other than the warmth of Robert's lips against her own? Why wasn't she experiencing the heart-racing, nerve-tightening, stomach-churning intensity of emotion and sensation she had experienced when Nash had kissed her?

Guilty at her own lack of response, she allowed Robert's lips to remain on hers for a few more seconds before gently pulling away.

'Too soon?' Robert asked ruefully, and Faith was glad that the darkness hid the guilt in her eyes as she nodded her head before turning towards the house.

'Don't worry over what I told you tonight,' Robert urged her as he opened the door for her and then stood to one side to allow her to walk past him and go through it.

How could she *not* worry, though? Faith asked herself after she had closed the door behind him. She had once read a book which suggested that an individual was confronted with the same problem over and over again in life, until they found a way of dealing with it.

At fifteen she hadn't been mature enough or strong enough to deal with the harsh realities of the problems Nash had caused her, and now... What was life trying to tell her, to do to her, by making her go to Nash and ask for his clemency?

Faith knew that professionally she was more than capable of doing the job Robert had entrusted her with for the Foundation. In her mind's eye she could already see the faces of the children and their parents when they arrived at Hatton.

Philip had had a very privileged but a very lonely childhood, and she knew how much it would have meant to him to know that this house, *his* house, would be filled with children and giving them so much pleasure. *That* was what must have priority, Faith told herself fervently—the fulfilment of Philip's wishes.

'Fantasising about your lover?'

The unexpected sound of Nash's voice reaching her from the darkness of the moonlit hallway made Faith give an audible gasp.

'Robert *isn't* my lover,' Faith denied unguardedly.

Nash looked away from her as he went to lock the door. He had unwittingly witnessed the kiss Robert and Faith had shared as he'd walked past the study window. There was no doubt in Nash's mind about the role Robert wanted to play in Faith's life—and in her bed—and Faith certainly hadn't been objecting.

As she heard Nash locking the door Faith took a deep breath. There was no point in putting off what she had to do, nor in lying awake half the night worrying about it when Nash was here now.

Before she could lose her courage, she told him quickly, 'Nash, if you've got the time there's something I'd like to discuss with you.'

The slightly nervous, almost conciliatory tone of

her voice, so different from the anger and hostility she had shown him so far, alerted Nash's suspicions.

'It's late,' he told her. 'And I've spent the last hour waiting for you to come back so that I can lock up. Can't whatever it is wait until tomorrow?'

Faith knew that normally such a reaction from anyone, never mind Nash, would have immediately crushed her. But tonight she was so on edge, so uptight and anxious, that she dared not allow herself to hesitate.

'No. I really do need to speak to you now,' she told him.

As she watched him Nash hesitated, and then frowned before striding over to Philip's study and pushing open the door.

'No. Not in there,' Faith refused quickly.

'Where, then?' Nash asked her. 'Your *bedroom*?'

Faith was too overwrought to recognise the sarcasm and bitter cynicism underlying his words, and she certainly had no idea what was going through his mind or what he was feeling. Her one desire was to get her unwanted appeal to him over and done with as quickly as possible.

'Yes, yes…my bedroom is fine,' she agreed almost eagerly, hurrying towards the stairs.

Now what the hell was she up to? Nash wondered cynically as he followed her.

It was Nash's turn to hesitate as Faith pushed open her bedroom door and hurried inside, switching on the light and then turning to confront him as he followed her in and closed the door.

Just for a minute she was tempted to ask him to leave the door open, then mentally reprimanded herself for her foolishness.

At twenty-five she might, for reasons best known to herself, still be a virgin, but there was certainly no need for her to *act* like one.

'Well?' Nash demanded sharply. 'I'm waiting. What is it that's so important it can't wait until tomorrow?'

'Robert told me tonight that it isn't definite yet that the trustees—that *you*,' she forced herself to amend, 'will definitely gift Hatton to the Foundation.'

Nash stared at her, perplexed.

'You brought me up here to tell me *that*?' he asked grimly.

'No,' Faith admitted, bowing her head, unable to bring herself to look at him as she told him in a low voice, 'I hadn't realised it until tonight, but Robert has put himself in a very vulnerable position with the rest of the board by employing me. Apparently I wasn't their choice.'

She stopped and nibbled nervously on her bottom lip.

'I would hate to feel responsible for anything that might jeopardise Robert's position or the Foundation's acquisition of this house.'

For a moment her passionate belief in the work of the Foundation overcame her own anxiety and dread.

'Hatton would be so perfect as one of the

Foundation's homes. I *know* how much it would have meant to Philip to see it put to such a use, and I know too how much it meant to me to be allowed to stay here. I shall always be grateful to Philip.'

'Grateful? You can say that and expect me to believe it after what you did?' Nash demanded gratingly.

Faith's face burned. She itched to defend herself, to throw caution recklessly to the four winds and tell Nash just how wrong he was about her without caring how much such a claim on her part might antagonise him. But of course she could not afford to do that—not now.

Instead she had to content herself with a heartfelt, 'You'll never know how much I regret what happened to Philip, Nash. How much I wish...' She stopped as her throat clogged with emotion. 'Please,' she begged him. 'Please, Nash, we're both adults and we both loved Philip. Surely we can put aside our differences for his sake...for the sake of what he wanted for Hatton?'

'Our *differences*?' Nash threw harshly at her. 'My God, you make it sound as though we've had an idiotic quarrel about some minor incident, not—'

'I do *know* how you feel about me, Nash,' Faith told him quietly. 'I know you feel that I deserve to be punished, even though—' She stopped and made herself focus on the matter in hand, not her own feelings. 'What I wanted to say to you is that if that punishment is going to affect Robert and the Foundation, and Philip's plans for the house, then...'

'Then what?' Nash challenged. 'What will you do then, Faith?'

'Whatever it takes not to have that happen,' Faith told him simply and truthfully. 'I'll do whatever you want, Nash, just so long as you don't stop the Foundation from having Hatton.'

Whatever he wanted! Nash could hardly believe what he had just heard. Faith was offering herself to him in return for his silence.

A furious, savage, destructive anger swept down over him, a culmination of all the years of pain and loss, a dangerous implosion set in motion by the kiss he had witnessed and his own reaction to it.

Years ago she had offered herself to him with what he had then believed to be the innocence of youth—an offer he had truly thought came from love. But he had been so very, very wrong...and only he knew of the nights, the *lifetime* he had lain awake aching for her, wanting her, swearing that he would burn his need for her out of his heart and flesh himself rather than give in to it.

Did she really imagine for a single second that he would take her up on her offer—an offer that proved irrefutably just what kind of person she was? Of course he wasn't going to, not even for the satisfaction of teaching her a much-needed lesson. But he surely had the right to exact *some* payment from her.

'And what does *Robert* think about your...offer... to me?' he asked her silkily.

Faith frowned. Hadn't he been listening to her?

'Robert doesn't know anything about this,' she told him quickly. 'And he mustn't know either.'

Faith was worried that if Robert *did* know he might insist on doing something chivalrous, which might damage his own position, and that was the last thing she wanted.

'So this is to be a personal...*arrangement*...a private agreement?' Nash suggested.

'Yes,' Faith agreed immediately, holding her breath as she waited for Nash to ask her what she intended to do if he didn't agree. Once she had answered that question, informed him that she would hand in her notice rather than prejudice the Foundation's work, she knew there would be no going back. But to her surprise Nash did not ask the question she had been expecting.

As the silence between them grew Faith fiddled nervously with one of her earrings, expelling a sharp sound of distress as it came loose and fell to the floor, dropping down on her hands and knees to look for it.

The images, the temptation, the *torment* of seeing her in such a pose caused Nash to grind his teeth in furious self-denial. How on earth had he *ever* imagined her to be innocent?

As she searched the floor her head was on a level with his groin, the distance between them less than a metre—much less than a metre, he recognised as she crawled closer to him. Totally against his will he could feel his body reacting to her. Angrily he tried to control the fierce upsurge of desire hardening his body, turning away from her as he did so to conceal the evidence of the effect she was having on him.

Suddenly he could see her lying naked in his bed, all silken skin and open arms...

Ten years ago he had dreamed of gently and tenderly initiating her into the pleasure of lovemaking, but now he suspected she could well be the one teaching *him*. Then, at twenty-two, he had considered himself to be reasonably sexually knowledgeable and accomplished, but after he had met Faith—

He had been living in New York the year Faith was twenty-one, dating an 'uptown' woman several years his senior who had made no pretence about her reasons for wanting him in her bed, and *only* in her bed, since she'd had her own very successful career.

They had been planning to have a weekend together out of the city at the Hamptons. She'd had friends who had a house there they could borrow. The day before they had been due to go he had received his yearly report on Faith's progress via the third party through whom he was financing her education, in obedience to his godfather's wishes.

Only he and Philip's bank knew how little money Philip had left, how impossible it would have been to pay for Faith's education out of that money.

The report had been glowingly full of praise for her—not just for her scholastic work but also for the extramural activities she'd been involved in: raising money for children's charities, giving her limited spare time to help teach young children to read. There had even been a mention of her upcoming twenty-first birthday.

To this day Nash had no idea just why he had gone out and bought her those earrings. He had told himself that it was because Philip would have wanted him to do it. Small the diamonds might have been, but they had been the best quality that Tiffany's could supply, set in twenty-four-carat gold. He had mailed them to England before leaving for his weekend at the Hamptons.

His companion had been scornful and vocal about his body's embarrassing failure to respond to her, and although eventually they *had* had sex, sex was all it had been—a joyless, grimly fought for physical coupling which hadn't afforded either of them very much pleasure.

'Oh…thank goodness…' he heard Faith exclaiming now, as her face broke out into a relieved smile and she picked up her earring.

'For God's sake, get up,' Nash commanded. 'I don't need demonstrations of your sexual skills, Faith.'

Her sexual skills! Faith's face burned as she realised just what he meant.

'And as for your *offer*—well, let's just say that the jury is still out, shall we?' Nash told her.

Faith closed her eyes as she stood up. Why on earth had she bothered to try to appeal to him? It was plain that he fully intended to go on tormenting her.

Nash frowned as he heard his own words. What was he saying? There was *no way* he intended to even *consider* the sordid bargain Faith was trying to strike with him.

But something was driving him, savaging him. Something he didn't want to name and couldn't bear to acknowledge.

As Nash turned to walk towards the bedroom door Faith hurried after him. There was something she still had to ask—how long had he been the sole trustee of Philip's estate?

But before she could say anything Nash had turned round, asking her bitingly, 'What is it you want, Faith? This?'

And then he was kissing her, covering her mouth with his, savaging it, destroying the fragile fabric of the illusion she had created for herself that somehow there could be peace between them.

'No!' she tried to deny, reaching out to push him away. But Nash simply swung her round, pressing her up against the door as he cupped her face to prevent her turning away from him.

'Yes,' he reinforced rawly, driving the word into her as he parted her lips with his tongue, thrusting it so powerfully into the vulnerable sensitivity of her mouth that her whole body quivered in shocked recognition of the sensuality of his action.

Imprisoned against the closed door, with the full weight of his lower body resting against her, Faith struggled to combat her own feelings. If Nash's actions had shocked her, then her own reaction to them was even more shocking, and made her even more angry.

Instinctively she knew that never in a thousand lifetimes could Robert make her feel like this, make her experience such a fierce, female clawing and urgent need to match the raw sexuality of Nash's behaviour.

Was *this* the price Nash intended to demand for his silence, his acquiescence to the Foundation's acquisition of Hatton? *Her?* The use of her body in whatever way he chose to use it?

Faith burned with shame and bitter fury—and with another emotion, far stronger than the combined strength of the other two. An emotion that stripped her pride bare and lashed the flesh from her emotions, leaving them raw and bleeding. She *wanted* Nash.

CHAPTER SIX

THE black dress lay in a pool of darkness at Faith's feet and the diamonds she had replaced in her ears shone through the butterscotch and cream of her hair. Her skin gleamed with its own living, breathing warmth, covered only by the nude-coloured camisole she was still wearing. But Faith herself was oblivious to the sensuality and torment she presented to Nash. Every hedonistic and wanton urge she had ever possessed was combining with the emotion she had fought so hard to conquer and deny, causing her to cling urgently to him as she returned the fierce passion of his kiss.

It was as though when Nash had released her from her dress he had also released her from her inhibitions; the fury and bitterness she had originally felt as he kissed her had burned away to nothing but the sheer power of her response to him.

As a girl she might have dreamed of him kissing her, of them being lovers, but as a girl she had been far too immature to ever dream of anything like *this*—this raw, hungry, aching, overpowering need for him which was filling her, driving her, compelling her.

Beneath her fingers she could feel the fabric of his shirt, a barrier to what she really wanted to touch and feel, and she gave a small female growl of thwarted longing, her body tensing with the frustration of not being able to touch him as she so much needed to do, skin to skin, flesh to flesh.

As her fingertips found the opening at the front of his shirt her growl turned to a soft purr of pleasure, but *he* was the one who was trembling from the effect of what she was doing, Nash recognised helplessly as his body reacted immediately to her touch.

He tried to remind himself of why he was here, of why he was doing this, but Faith's fingers were tugging frantically at his shirt buttons and instinctively he started to help her.

'You feel so good…'

Helplessly, totally lost in what she was feeling, Faith moaned the words into his mouth, the movement of her lips against his a series of soft, erotic little flutters that made him shudder from head to toe.

God, but he wanted her…craved her…needed her… He had always known it would be good between them, but had never dreamed it could be like this…

How could just kissing someone make her feel as though her whole body was about to explode? Faith wondered dizzily.

With Nash's help she had finally unfastened his shirt. Greedily she stroked her hands over his naked chest. She wanted to touch him, stroke him, kiss him, lick him, breathe in the pheromone-laden scent of him that was already affecting her so headily.

The only reason he was doing this, Nash told himself, was to remind himself of just what she was, to see just how far she was prepared to go.

Pain streaked the fiery intensity of his longing for her. He couldn't possibly still love her—not knowing what she was, what she'd *done*. But the way she was touching him was driving him crazy...drowning out any kind of logic or reason.

Nash hadn't stopped kissing her from the moment he had pushed her up against the door, Faith recognised giddily. She felt almost drunk, drugged by the way he was making her feel, by the way he was making her need him. Her lips clung to his as the hot, hard weight of his lower body moved against hers, keeping her pinned where she was and reinforcing with every movement how powerfully male he was.

Once, a long time ago, she had broken all the rules, turned her back on convention and, driven by her teenage hormones and her love, had gone to Nash's room, creeping into its darkness to find her way to his bed.

All she had wanted to do was be with him, to have him hold her, love her, but as he had sat bolt upright in the bed she had seen in the silvery light of the moon that he was naked, and a wild, wanton female urge had overtaken her, driving her to beg him to kiss her.

Then, for a moment, she had almost thought that

he might as he had leaned closer to her. She had held her breath and closed her eyes, trembling from head to foot when his hands had closed over her wrists. But the words he had eventually spoken had not been soft, sensual words of love, but a harsh command to her to open her eyes.

When she had complied he had told her firmly, 'This has got to stop, Faith, for both our sakes. You're young and you don't really know what you're asking...or doing,' he had added more gently. 'I promise you that one day you will thank me for sending you away tonight.'

Thank him... Shamed and in despair, Faith had fled from his room to cry herself to sleep in her own bed. But now, as she remembered that incident, she acknowledged that Nash had been right. At fifteen she *had* been too young for the intensity of the raw passion they were now sharing.

Now, she sensed with a surge of erotic female power, there was no way that either of them was going to be able to stop.

Emboldened by her own thoughts, she pulled Nash's shirt free of his jeans.

A long, slow shudder of pleasure rolled through her as she touched his naked torso. But just touching him wasn't enough. She wanted to look at him, taste him, fill her famished senses with the sensual reality of him, with the knowledge that he wanted her, needed her, as powerfully as she did him.

Dragging her mouth away from his was almost a form of torture, but worth the momentary sense of loss it caused her when her awed gaze slid with hedonistic enjoyment over his body.

No film star could ever come anywhere near matching Nash for sheer heart-stopping, hormone-inducing, raw masculine sensuality, Faith decided. He was everything a man could be, everything a man *should* be, and yet, for all the hot, passionate intensity and impatience of her desire, there was still a part of her that was suddenly and sweetly over-whelmed by loving tenderness.

Responding to those emotions, she kissed the top of her finger and gently placed it against the mas-culine outline of his throat, and then replaced it with her lips, her mouth, slowly starting to kiss her way downwards.

Nash felt as though he had opened a door and walked into his deepest and most private fantasy—only in *that* Faith had interspersed her kisses with words of love.

Ten years old that fantasy might be, but, as he was discovering, it still had the same power over him now as it had done then.

'Faith,' he groaned, taking hold of her and de-manding, 'How would you like me to do that to you? To tease you, torment you, lie you down on that bed and slowly kiss my way all over your body?'

As she tilted her head back so that she could look into his eyes Faith knew that her own were betraying her, but she was beyond caring.

'You want that?' Nash was asking her thickly.

'You want me to kiss your breasts, your nipples, your belly…' His voice dropped to a low, raw growl of male arousal. 'That special secret place? Do you want that, Faith?' he demanded. 'Do you want me to kiss you there, to taste you, lick you, make you want to give yourself completely to me?'

Faith couldn't speak. She could barely move; her whole body was held in thrall to the heavy, hot pulse of sensation inside it, that Nash's words had aroused.

Nash couldn't believe what he was saying— thinking…*wanting*… He was like a man possessed, taken over by some alien power—the power of love…

As the words slid into his mind he pushed them away. This had *nothing* to do with love. This was justice. This was—

Faith had started to kiss him, tiny hungry darting kisses that covered his face, his throat, his mouth.

'Take off your clothes, Nash,' she begged him. 'Take me to bed. Show me…teach me…'

Teach *her*! Nash wanted to tell her that he doubted there was anything he could *possibly* teach a woman like her, but she was reaching for the belt on his jeans, fumbling with the clasp, and the feel of those slim feminine fingers fluttering helplessly against his body was doing the kind of things to him that would have brought a stone statue to life.

Even so, he still tried to cling to sanity. He started to say gruffly to her, 'We need—'

But Faith shook her head, interrupting him, telling

him in a desire-laden whisper, 'I need you, Nash. I need you so much…so *badly*…'

Her hand had been resting on his waist as she unfastened his jeans, and now, without him even being aware of her having moved, he felt it sliding inside them. He could feel as well as hear the sound of the aching groan inside his head as her touch grew bolder.

Faith shuddered as the movement of her hand caused Nash's jeans to drop lower and his body to tense. Beneath her fingertips she could feel the crisp thickness of his body hair.

In retaliation Nash slid down the delicate straps of her camisole, exposing the full, taut roundness of her breasts. Her nipples were already hard, responding to the hungry touch of his hands.

As he bent his head, unable to resist responding to the temptation they were offering him, Nash drew a long, shuddering breath. They were behaving like two hormone-crazy teenagers, so hot for one another that they couldn't wait for the comfort of a bed— but they *weren't* teenagers. They were…

The shudder that tormented Faith's body as Nash's lips closed over her nipple drove the ability to think about anything other than what they were sharing completely out of his head. He swept Faith into his arms and carried her over to the bed.

Feeling that she had escaped into the most beautiful dream, Faith watched as Nash removed the rest of his clothes, her eyes soft with love.

As a teenager she had hardly dared to allow herself to imagine being with Nash like this, and as an adult she had closed down that part of herself that was her sexuality. Now those barriers had melted like wax in the heat of the sun, and the sensation that raced and rolled and thrust through her unprepared body as she stared at Nash caused a flutter of such sexually explicit sensation to begin to unfurl, deep inside her, that she gave a small half-shocked, half-bemused little gasp.

'Faith?' Nash questioned her softly, but she shook her head and looked away from him, suddenly as shy and self-conscious as though she had still been fifteen.

Whatever else Faith might lie about she wasn't hiding her desire for him, Nash recognised. But then some women were like that, weren't they? Highly sexed…easily aroused…

Nash leaned forward and kissed Faith's mouth. Her lips clung eagerly to his, her breasts filling his hands, her skin satin-soft.

He kissed her breasts and then her nipples, sucking on them gently, afraid to give way to the full force of his desire in case he hurt her. He kissed the soft warmth of her belly and teased his fingers between the thighs she was keeping unexpectedly tightly closed, moving higher and deeper, feeling her body relax and admit him to the sweet, warm wetness that was waiting for him.

He couldn't wait much longer. Just touching her like this was driving him crazy. In fact, he couldn't wait *any* longer!

'Open your legs,' he whispered to her as he kissed her.

Open her legs! Suddenly Faith felt nervous, afraid of somehow disappointing him. After all, this *was* her first time. She was inexperienced, unknowing.

Hesitantly she started to part her thighs, and then, as Nash started to move slowly over her, against her and then within her, all her doubts and fears fell away and she was climbing, flying, soaring free, a part of Nash as he was a part of her, two equal parts of one perfect whole.

This was what she had been born for, what she had been *destined* for…this and Nash…

As she felt the gathering force of her arousal Faith closed her eyes, Nash's name rising from somewhere deep down inside her, its taste on her tongue unbelievably sweet, its sound on her lips a paean of love and welcome.

Unable to stop herself, she wrapped herself around him and whispered passionately, 'I'm so glad I waited for you, Nash—for this…us… I couldn't have borne it to happen with anyone else…not the first time—' Or any other time, she'd wanted to say, but Nash spoke first.

'What?' he demanded roughly.

She could feel Nash's shock, feel the almost painful momentary cessation of his body moving within hers. The thought of losing him, of losing 'it' now that she was so close, panicked and drove her. Frantically she moved her body against the stillness of his, once, and then again, and again—until with a raw groan Nash was moving with her, for her, carrying them both so swiftly towards the edge of her known universe that Faith could only cling on to him desperately as the feeling engulfed her, sweeping her into its own vortex.

As he heard Faith cry out Nash shuddered, caught up in the undertow of the sharply conflicting emotions savaging him.

Faith had been a virgin! That was impossible…unbelievable… But his body knew differently, had somehow sensed the truth about her even before she had told him herself. But where his mind had registered the danger of what he was doing once he had heard the words, his body had reacted very differently. And even before Faith herself had so recklessly urged him on he had known that he couldn't control his body's desire for her.

Nash closed his eyes and then opened them again, moving away from Faith as he got off the bed and started to reach for his clothes.

Faith's virginity altered none of his feelings about what she had done to his godfather. How could it? He had no idea why she hadn't had any previous lovers—although he did know it couldn't have been from any lack of offers. Had she been saving it until she met the right man? A man rich enough to give her the lifestyle she wanted? A man such as Robert Ferndown?

If so, then why throw away such a valuable bargaining counter now, and with him?

To buy his silence? A long shudder ripped through him. Did she *really* think…?

It no longer mattered what she thought, or what he felt. How could it? What mattered now was what they had done.

'What is it? Why are you going?' Faith demanded anxiously as Nash pulled on his clothes. *Why* was he leaving her when he should be holding her, loving her?

Her body felt weak; she was in both physical and emotional shock, unable to comprehend anything other than the fact that Nash was deserting her.

Nash waited until he had reached her bedroom door before asking his question.

'Why?' he demanded emotionlessly. 'You're twenty-five, Faith, a woman.'

What was he trying to say—that she was too old to be a virgin, that he wished she had not been?

Faith felt as though someone had cut her emotional veins and she was slowly bleeding to death, slowly growing colder and colder, emptier and emptier of the love that had burned so hotly and fiercely in Nash's arms. Ten years apart from him hadn't been enough to destroy it and neither had the accusations he had flung at her or his misjudgement of her. No, she had had to wait for now, in his *arms*, to have her love destroyed, murdered, as he had so often accused her of murdering his godfather.

From somewhere she managed to find enough pride to respond stiffly to him.

'It wasn't a conscious choice.' She gave a small,

careless shrug and a bitter little smile. 'I'm sorry if it wasn't what you were expecting—'

Nash stopped her savagely. 'You should have *told* me.'

'I did…' Faith reminded him quietly.

'Not *then*. My God… *That* was too late, Faith,' he grated, underlining his meaning and adding crudely, 'By the time you told me I doubt that a chastity belt could have stopped me!'

'*I* wasn't the one—' Faith began defensively, but immediately Nash stopped her again.

'*You* were the one who offered me sex in return for my…silence,' he told her sharply. 'You're unbelievable—do you know that? What were you thinking? That I'd stop and that your virginity—your prize bargaining counter—would remain intact? Was *that* why you pretended to be so eager to touch me, Faith—because you were planning to make sure that things never got as far as penetration, that I wouldn't be able to last that long?'

Faith listened to him in disbelief. She had *never* offered him sex. What was he *talking* about? And as for the rest of what he had said—a deep, angry tide of colour swept over her.

'I suppose it's too much to hope that you're using some form of birth control?' Nash continued wearily.

One look at Faith's face confirmed his worst fears.

Faith could feel herself starting to shiver. Now, with her body empty of the sensual urgency and need which had driven her, she couldn't understand how she had behaved in the way she had. As she forced herself to meet the hard, angry topaz glitter of Nash's gaze her own fell away.

'I…I can't be pregnant,' she began to stammer, 'Not after just the once…'

The sound of Nash's laughter shocked her even more than his rejection of her.

'I don't *believe* this,' she heard Nash saying forcefully. 'And from you, the girl your tutors praised to the skies for your maturity and intelligence…your sense of responsibility, your compassion for other people.'

'You read my tutors' reports?' Faith's forehead began to pleat in suspicion.

'They were with your references for the job,' Nash told her after a brief pause. 'Not that *that* matters now,' he added dismissively. '*Now* you and I have rather more urgent things to worry about—don't we?'

Red-faced, Faith turned away from him. He was right, of course he was right, and she didn't know why she was behaving so stupidly.

As he opened her bedroom door Nash hesitated.

'Does Ferndown know about…your virginity?' he asked her abruptly.

The hot colour in Faith's face became a burning wave of anger.

'What business is that of yours?' she began, biting her lip as she saw the look Nash was giving her. 'No! No, he doesn't,' she admitted reluctantly.

CHAPTER SEVEN

IT WAS five o'clock in the afternoon. Faith hadn't seen Nash in nearly two days—since that night when he had left her bedroom, in actual fact—and for some reason the emptiness of the large house was now beginning to prey on her a little—the emptiness of the house or the absence of Nash?

The former, of course, Faith insisted firmly to herself as she tried to return her concentration to her work.

Yesterday morning when she had come downstairs to find a note in the kitchen from Nash, saying that he had gone away 'on business', her immediate reaction had been one of overwhelming relief.

What had happened between them that night was something she wanted to seal up and hide away somewhere, with a large 'Danger—do not open' label on it.

Absent-mindedly she started to doodle on her notepad, a horrified expression widening her eyes as she saw the entwined hearts symbol she had drawn.

What was the matter with her? She didn't love Nash—not any more—and he most certainly did not love *her*. But she had...

Her face burning, she stood up and walked over to the study window. It was being here at Hatton that was the cause of her problems and responsible for what had happened—being here at Hatton with *Nash*. Only Nash wasn't here now, so she ought to be able to concentrate on her work instead of...

Had Nash really left 'on business', or had he left because he wanted to put some distance between them, to underline to her that he didn't want her in his life?

Faith tensed as the study door opened, her heart thumping, but it was only Mrs Jenson the housekeeper.

'I'm off now,' she told Faith.

As she tried to smile in acknowledgement Faith was sharply conscious of the other woman's unspoken hostility towards her. She had sensed it the first time they had met, and she didn't think it was just her imagination that it had become somehow more brazenly threatening in Nash's absence.

Hadn't she got enough problems to contend with without worrying about Mrs Jenson? Faith asked herself as the housekeeper turned to leave, and returned her attention to her work.

Whilst she worked she tried to visualise Hatton in its converted state, but worryingly such a vision refused to form for her. Instead the only person she could see living here at Hatton was Nash.

The only person?

Agitatedly Faith turned round. Surely it was only natural that when she visualised Nash she should also visualise a family, *his* family, with him? she tried to defend herself.

Maybe. But was it also natural that she should visualise that same family—those two little girls, those two strong-jawed boys—with Nash's unmistakable topaz eyes and her own Scandinavian hair colouring?

It was just her memory playing tricks on her, Faith insisted with inward mental indignity. It was just because once, a long time ago, when she had been too naïve and silly to know better, she had fantasised that one day she and Nash would have such a family. It meant nothing now. *Nothing...*

Her eyes clouded as reality forced her to acknowledge an anxiety she had been pushing to the back of her mind.

Lost, deep in thrall to the wonder of making love with Nash, irresponsibly she had not given a single thought to what the result of that lovemaking might be. Without a previous sex life there had been no need for her to consider such things.

She *couldn't* be pregnant, she tried to reassure herself. Apart from anything else she was well past the age when something like an accidental pregnancy was allowable. She was a woman, responsible for her own life—and for a new life which she and Nash might have created?

Her mobile rang, interrupting her thoughts, and the sound of Robert's voice made her uncomfortably aware of just how what had happened with Nash was likely to be viewed by other people—and especially Robert himself.

'I just thought I'd ring to see how things are going,' he explained.

Quickly and professionally Faith outlined to him what she was doing.

Was the business Nash had left to conduct anything to do with the Foundation and the house? Faith did not feel that it was her place to ask, and Robert already sounded harassed and preoccupied.

'How's the Smethwick contract going?' Faith asked him.

'Not very well,' he admitted. 'I'm having lunch with the other members of the board tomorrow and I suspect I'm going to be asked to come up with a solution to the delay. I don't suppose Nash has said anything to you about Hatton?' he asked Faith hopefully.

Faith was still feeling guilty about Robert and the problems he was having later in the evening as she cleared away her supper things and then made her way back to the study.

They were having a wonderful spell of good weather and she was tempted to spend the evening outside in the garden. But she had run into a problem with her work on the conversion of the house which she wanted to get to grips with.

Large as it was, in terms of a family house, Faith was concerned that the costs involved in its conversion to a respite home would be too high in relation to the number of people it would ultimately be able to house.

The wonderful Jekyll gardens were not designed for children to play in, and to destroy them in order to create something that was suitable seemed almost sacrilege.

Faith was still trying to find an acceptable solution to the problem several hours later, when Nash arrived back.

As she saw him getting out of his car her first inclination was to hide herself away in her room; her face was already starting to burn a self-conscious pink. But her life had given Faith both courage and the determination to stand up for herself. Why *should* she hide herself away? What had happened between them had, after all, taken two, even if…

She discovered that she was holding her breath as Nash opened the front door.

She had left the study door slightly ajar; surely he would guess from the fact that she had the light on that she was working here, even if he had not seen her from the drive. And he would, of course, be as reluctant to see her as she was him.

Faith heard the breath rattle betrayingly in her lungs as Nash disproved her anxious theorising by pushing open the study door and walking in.

In the dark-coloured business suit he was wearing he looked even more dauntingly and overpoweringly male.

The remembered torrid heat of their lovemaking seemed to engulf Faith as she tried to match the subtle domination of his body language.

'I know it's late but there's something we need

to discuss,' he told her brusquely as he pushed something towards her across the desk.

'What's this?' Faith asked him uncertainly, eyeing the piece of paper uneasily. She had no idea what it was, but the look on Nash's face was enough to set all her own internal alarm bells clanging.

'It's a special licence,' Nash told her grimly.

'A what?' Bemusedly she looked at him.

'A special licence,' Nash repeated in a clipped voice, adding before she could say anything, 'I know the bishop—he was a close friend of my father's—and he agreed exceptionally to grant us a licence to get married. I've made all the arrangements. The service will take place tomorrow morning at eleven. I've already seen the vicar. He was—'

'Married?' Faith interrupted him in a shocked voice. 'No! *No!* We can't! That's not possible,' she objected. Her heart was pounding. She felt dizzy...disbelieving...filled with panic and yet somehow distanced from what was happening, as though she was merely an onlooker watching her own emotions, observing her own reactions.

But Nash was speaking once again, telling her sharply, 'I'm afraid it isn't merely possible, Faith, it's essential. You and I *have* to get married. We don't have any other option.'

Faith could feel other emotions beginning to filter through the protection of her shock now: painful, hurting, damaging emotions that were almost too much for her to bear. Emotions she couldn't allow herself to even acknowledge, never mind examine.

'Why?' she asked Nash, her voice high with defensive panic. 'We don't—'

'Do you *really* need to ask me that?' Nash cut across her with grim cynicism. 'You could be pregnant.'

Faith closed her eyes and took a deep steadying breath. No, of course, she didn't.

'Are you trying to suggest that we should get married because of a baby I may or may not be carrying?' she questioned him sharply.

'Because you may be carrying *my* baby,' Nash agreed harshly, 'and because…' He walked over to the study window, keeping his back towards her as he told her coldly, 'No matter what my opinion of you might be, Faith, I have my own moral code. An old-fashioned moral code by modern standards, perhaps, but it was Philip's code, and in many ways he had more of an influence on my childhood than either of my parents.'

He paused and then turned round, catching Faith off guard so that there was no time for her to conceal the pain she knew must be in her eyes as he continued mercilessly, 'Had you been more…experienced…'

'You're saying we have to marry because I was a *virgin*?' Faith demanded, her disbelief colouring her voice. 'But that's…that's archaic, Nash.'

'To *you*, I dare say it is. But the fact remains that according to *my* moral laws it is the right thing, the *only* thing I can now do.'

Faith took a deep breath.

'And if I refuse?' she asked him, holding her head high as she forced herself to challenge his control of what was happening.

'I can't allow you to do that, Faith,' Nash told her sombrely, maintaining the kind of blistering eye contact with her that would normally have left her raw with pain and despair. 'If it helps to sweeten the pill for you just try reminding yourself that you've played the bargaining counter of your virginity extremely well, and that *my* wealth is far in excess of Ferndown's—although I dare say I shall keep a much tighter hold on it where you're concerned than he would.'

Faith couldn't speak. She couldn't think; she couldn't even breathe so deep and traumatising was what Nash had said to her.

She was, she discovered vaguely, trembling… shaking. Not with fear but with anger…temper… rage…fury…pride…that Nash should dare to speak to her as he had. But somehow she managed to control the desire to give vent to her feelings and instead to say, as calmly as she could, 'There may not be a child.'

The look he gave her was as vitriolic as pure acid.

'Because it was your first time?' he derided her, watching in grim satisfaction as her face flooded with colour. 'As I've just told you,' he continued coldly, 'that is *not* the whole issue.'

'Yes, I know. You're doing this because I was a virgin,' Faith repeated flatly. She couldn't keep the furious disbelief out of her voice. 'Nash, that's…

that's—' She stopped, unable to find the words to convey her feelings to him. 'What if I *wasn't* really a virgin? What if you just thought that I was?' she challenged.

'You're getting hysterical,' Nash told her dismissingly. 'Overreacting...'

'*I'm* overreacting?' Faith exploded. Why was she bothering arguing with him when it was plain that he had made up his mind and that he wasn't going to change it?

Well, she didn't have to go along with his plans...his orders. She was a free agent. She could walk out of this room, get into her car and...

'Don't even think about it,' she heard Nash advise her warningly, somehow managing to place himself between her and the door, as though he had read her mind. 'Tomorrow morning you and I are getting married,' Nash repeated. 'And whatever has to be done to achieve that *will* be done.' He gave a small brief shrug. 'I'm surprised you're making such a fuss. After all, you're getting what you've already proved you want.'

His words, uttered with such a careless lack of compassion, caused Faith to feel as though her heart was being squeezed in a giant vice.

Had he guessed, then? Had she *shown*...? Did he dare to think that just because she had been foolish enough to give in to her desire for him she was still idiotic enough to harbour her teenage infatuation for him? Did he even, perhaps, think that she'd still

been a virgin because of him…because of wanting
him…loving him?

Faith opened her mouth to tell him furiously that
he was wrong and then closed it again, her body
going weak with relief as he added, 'You wanted to
marry for money, Faith, and that's exactly what you
are doing.'

Money. Nash thought… Shakily she closed her
eyes, too caught up in her own feelings to deny
Nash's insulting insinuation.

'Oh, and just in case you *should* try to do anything stupid, perhaps I should warn you now that
until we are married I shan't be letting you out of
my sight.'

'Until… But that means…' she began to protest,
and then stopped.

'Yes?' Nash encouraged her.

'We aren't going to get married until tomorrow.
What are you planning to do, Nash? Sit up all night
outside my bedroom door to make sure I don't escape?'

Faith realised the moment she looked at him in
the silence that followed that she had dangerously
overreached herself in attempting to challenge him.

'*Outside* your bedroom door?' The look he gave
her was pure purgatory. 'Don't be naïve, Faith.
Since we've already anticipated our marriage vows
there's precious little point in us not sharing the
same bed, and it will certainly make it easier for me
to ensure that you don't do anything…foolish…'

'By what?' Faith challenged him furiously, 'Handcuffing me to—?'

She stopped as Nash purred dangerously, 'Don't tempt me. Is bondage something you like to fantasise about, Faith?' he asked her shockingly.

'No,' Faith denied immediately.

'No? So you don't like the idea of emotionally enslaving a man…of making him long for your love. Bondage needn't be just physical,' he added tauntingly.

'I don't like the idea of any relationship where the two people in it don't meet as equals,' Faith managed to find the courage to tell him. She couldn't believe that any of this was really happening. That Nash really intended they should marry, for the most idiotic, impossibly antiquated reasons she had ever heard.

And by special licence—like two desperate lovers whose greatest need was to be together.

Well, she was certainly going to feel and look the most unbride-like bride the local vicar had ever married, she told herself defeatedly, considering the workman-like clothes she had brought to Hatton with her.

If it had been anyone other than Nash who had proposed such an impossible alliance she would have argued and fought to get them to change their mind. But, as she had good cause to know, once Nash had adopted a position, an attitude, a *judgement*, nothing and no one could shift him from it.

'You can't possibly want this marriage,' she protested in one final attempt to persuade him to see reason.

'This has nothing to do with what I *want*,' he retaliated immediately. 'It's what I *have* to do.'

'But we don't love one another, and if there's no child...' Faith protested.

'You'll what?' Nash asked cynically, misunderstanding her question. 'Take a lover? If you do, Faith, you'd better make sure that he really wants you and that he can afford you, because I shan't tolerate any unfaithful wife—and with our past history...'

Their glances met and clashed, but to her intense fury and chagrin Faith discovered that hers was the first to fall away.

Nervously Faith pulled the bedclothes up to her chin and lay facing the bedroom door. She had taken two of the herbal sleeping tablets she occasionally used and was praying that she would be fast asleep before Nash carried out his threat to join her.

She had no chance of escaping. Nash's car was blocking her own in and he had the keys to the house. A tiny inner voice warned Faith that she wasn't making as much attempt to escape as she should, but she dismissed it as illogical and unhelpful.

What was she supposed to do—jump out of her bedroom window?

And besides, if she *should* be pregnant... She had grown up without her father and, even worse, she had seen at first hand how much her mother had missed having the support of the man she loved. The husband and the father who had not been there had cast a shadow over both their lives.

Her tablets were beginning to take effect. Faith could feel her thoughts slowing down, her eyelids growing heavy. Tomorrow she was going to marry Nash. A soft tremor ran through her body. Nash… His name was on her lips as she finally slid into sleep.

Downstairs Nash stood motionless in front of the study window, looking out into the now dark garden.

He knew that to a lot of people—no doubt to Faith herself, included—what he was doing would seem old-fashioned and unnecessary. But Nash believed in taking his responsibilities seriously, and what could be more of a responsibility to a man than the knowledge that he could have fathered a child?

It had shocked him and caught him more off guard than he liked to acknowledge to discover that he was Faith's first lover. If he closed his eyes he could even now visualise her as she had been at fifteen. But it had been a woman he had held in his arms two nights ago, a woman he had made love with.

A woman who had not previously activated her sexual self and yet, for some reason, had chosen to do so with him. *Him*—the very last man she might logically have chosen. Why?

Irritably he turned away from the window. When had there ever been a logical reason for what Faith chose to do? She had kept her virginity to use as a bargaining counter—and then thrown it away on him.

Perhaps, like him, she had found herself in a situation over which she had had no control. Perhaps, like him, she too...

She too what? Explosively he cursed under his breath and frowned as he caught sight of his briefcase. He had brought it in with him from the car. Almost reluctantly he opened it and removed a small file from it, taking out the papers inside and spreading them out on Philip's desk.

The contents of the reports from Faith's tutors were so familiar to him he could almost have quoted them verbatim. She'd been a hard-working, dedicated scholar, determined to do her best. 'A young woman with integrity as well as intelligence', was what one of her tutors had written about her.

How easily she had deceived them. As easily as she had deceived his godfather... Nash's glance fell on a separate piece of paper. Frowning, he reached for it.

It was a letter which Faith had written to the trustees shortly after she had been informed of Philip's bequest. In it she expressed her surprise and gratitude and made a promise that she would do everything in her power to repay Philip's faith in her—'You cannot know how much it means to me to know that Philip believed in me and in my innocence…'

Her *innocence*! If only she *had* been innocent.

She had *known* of his concern for Philip's health. He had talked to her about it only days before she and her little gang had broken into the house, his anxiety having caused him to drop his guard and confide in her. And in doing so had he unwittingly been as instrumental in what had happened to Philip as she had been herself?

She had *known* that he was going to be away from the house and that Philip would be on his own. He had told her so himself. And she had known too of the older man's increasing frailty. There had been certain little warnings. Philip had complained on a couple of earlier occasions about a 'weakness' in his arm—a classic sign that he might even then have been suffering from very minor strokes, according to his doctor.

What had Philip thought when he had first seen her…when he had first let her in? He would have been pleased to see her, delighted by her unexpected visit, Nash knew. How many times had he tormented, tortured himself, imagining what Philip must have gone through when he had finally realised the truth? That Faith's visit had not been motivated by love but by greed. And for what? Philip had never kept more than a hundred pounds in cash in the house—never!

A hundred pounds.

Nash could still remember his godfather's solicitor's bewilderment when Nash had told him what he intended to do.

'You want to pay for this young woman's education and you want her to believe the money has come from your late godfather's estate?'

He had been bemused…perplexed, dubious even, but Nash had been insistent—and insistent, too, that Faith was to believe that her inheritance was being handled by several anonymous 'trustees'.

At first it had given him a certain grim sort of pleasure to know that he had so much control over her life…her future…to know that, if he should so choose, with one word he could destroy her. He could take away from her the golden opportunity she had been given. And while Philip's death and his own feelings of guilt about it were still raw, Nash had needed that kind of savage mental satisfaction.

Later, as the reports had started to come in from her tutors, praising Faith not just for her dedication to her work but also for the way she herself was as a person, his feelings had changed, veering between contempt and anger that she should so easily deceive them and a dark, bitter sense of loss.

His own weakness towards her had infuriated him then and still did now. Why the hell couldn't he accept what she was instead of wishing…wanting…? What if she *was* carrying his child? How was he going to protect that child from the disillusionment of knowing what his or her mother was?

He didn't know, but somehow he would have to find a way.

Picking the papers up from the desk, he replaced them in the folder and locked it in his briefcase. He took it out to his car and opened the boot, placing it inside and at the same time removing the other contents of the boot: a large hat box embossed discreetly with the name of a very expensive milliner, a dress bag bearing the name of an even more expensive designer, plus a box containing a pair of shoes with heels so high and spindly they had made his eyebrows arch. But the exclusive store's personal shopper had been insistent and so he had given in.

After carrying them back into the house he locked the door and then took them upstairs.

When he walked into her bedroom he saw that Faith was sleeping with all the innocence of a young girl.

Putting the packages down on the floor, he left the room.

Downstairs in Philip's study he poured himself a glass of whisky, lifting it to his mouth and then putting it down again untasted. *That* wasn't going to solve his problems.

Faith woke up abruptly. Last night she had forgotten to close her curtains and now the sun was shining in. Nervously she turned her head, but to her relief the other side of the bed was empty, its pillow undented. And then she saw the packages on the bedroom floor.

What on earth…?

Pushing back the bedclothes, she slid out of the bed and padded towards them.

She opened the shoebox first, her eyes widening as she saw the delicate cream satin stilettoes. They were in her size, though she would never have bought anything so fragile nor so expensive. She turned to the hat box, holding her breath as she eased off the lid. She had to remove several layers of tissue paper before she could lift out the hat.

Disbelievingly she stared at it. Cream, like the shoes, it was a froth of fine straw and raw silk. A wedding hat. Her heart slammed heavily against her ribs. Very carefully she restored it to its box. Her hands were shaking and she had to blink several times. Not because she was crying. No. The only tears she was likely to shed today would be tears of rage and resentment—and not because Nash had touched her emotions. How on earth could he? How on earth could she be foolish enough to let him?

She stared at the dress bag for several minutes before she could bring herself to unzip it.

The dress and coat inside it were also cream—exactly the right shade for her particular colouring and the right kind of style for her build. At the bottom of the dress bag was a small cache of tissue-wrapped items—underwear and sheer hold-up stockings. Nothing, it seemed, had been forgotten. Nothing overlooked to equip her for her role of bride.

For a moment Faith was tempted to bundle the

whole lot up and fling them out of her bedroom window. How *dared* Nash do this? How *dared* he make a mockery of everything that a wedding day should be? How *dared* he compel her into making meaningless vows for a marriage that was a desecration of everything that love should rightfully be?

It was early, not even seven o'clock yet. Quickly she showered and then pulled on her own clothes— a soft cotton top, jeans—slipped her bare feet into her shoes.

They were going to have another hot day.

The hat, the dress and the shoes were all back in their original containers. It was a struggle for her to carry them all but somehow she managed it.

Nash was sleeping in the same room he had always used. Faith was so angry that she didn't even bother to knock warningly on the door, simply thrusting it open and marching in, going over to the bed, where she dropped everything carelessly onto it, and at the same time announcing furiously, 'You may be able to force me to marry you, Nash, but there's no way that you can force me to do so wearing…wearing *these*.'

Nash was sitting up in his bed, his face darkening.

'So what *are* you going to wear?' he asked her sarcastically. 'Your jeans?'

'I'm not a child or a doll, to be dressed up to…to suit your whims,' Faith exploded.

Behind her anger lay tears, and the sharp, despairing misery she was determined she was not going to allow Nash to see. Her wedding outfit was something she should have chosen herself, with excitement and pride and joy and love. Not…not something Nash had felt obliged to buy because he knew she wouldn't have anything suitable in her wardrobe. And if he had really loved her it wouldn't have mattered to either of them what she wore when they exchanged their vows, because all that would matter would be their shared love.

Their *shared* love? She *didn't* love Nash.

'I'm not wearing that outfit, Nash,' she reiterated.

'No? Then what will you do when our son or daughter asks to see our wedding photographs?'

Wedding photographs! What photographs? Faith wanted to challenge him, but irresistibly she had a mental image of the child Nash had conjured to life with his words. Their child…Nash's daughter or son—and hers.

A hot, sweet, dangerously yearning feeling spread through her, transfixing her.

'I've brought you your tea, Mr Nash, and the papers. Oh—'

Faith could feel the heat burning her skin as the housekeeper came into the room. The knowing smirk she was giving them made Faith cringe. There was something about the woman that she really did not like. It made her feel not just acutely uncomfortable but somehow vulnerable as well. It was obvious that Nash, though, did not share her feelings, nor her embarrassment. 'Thank you, Mrs Jenson,' he greeted the housekeeper. 'You can be the first to congratulate us. Faith and I are getting married this morning—aren't we, darling?' he added, and he leaned forward and took hold of Faith's hand, drawing her down towards him before Faith could stop him, his mouth brushing with deliberate slowness against her own.

The speculation in the other woman's eyes as she sidled towards the door was almost more than Faith could bear.

'*Why* did you have to tell *her*,' Faith asked Nash angrily as soon as she had gone.

'Would you have preferred her to think we were just having sex and to spread it all over the village? You may not care very much about *your* reputation, Faith, but I can assure you that I care a great deal about mine.'

'I now pronounce you man and wife...'

Faith was shaking from head to foot, tiny shudders of tension and emotion running seismically through her body.

The sunlight through the stained glass windows of the old Norman church glinted on the rings she was wearing—a single solitaire diamond of breathtaking clarity that somehow reminded her of her earrings, and a matching plain gold band. They were married. She was Nash's wife.

Nash's *wife*! Another deeper shudder shook her.

All those years ago when she had fantasised about marrying Nash she had never imagined she would do so feeling like this.

She was wearing the clothes Nash had bought for

her. Not because of anything Nash had said but because in the end she had felt that the vicar of a small country church might find it offensive that she should choose to be married in jeans and a tee shirt. It had been for his sake, out of respect for his feelings and for the church itself, that she had changed her clothes.

'I can't remember the last time I married a couple by special licence,' the vicar was saying, and Faith could tell from his voice that he believed he had just married a couple who were desperately in love.

Desperately in love! Once that had been *exactly* how she had felt about Nash.

Once!

Certain memories of the way she had responded to Nash in bed, the way she had felt about him, refused to go away.

But that didn't mean that she still loved him, she tried to reassure herself, fighting against her inner panic. How *could* she after what he had done?

The atmosphere inside the church was one of peace and timelessness, a quiet, gentle benediction. A sense of the faith of the people who had worshipped here for so many generations touched her soul, Faith recognised as she paused to draw strength from her surroundings.

No marriage should ever be entered into like this, in mutual distrust and hostility.

She couldn't bring herself to look at Nash as they left the church together.

CHAPTER EIGHT

'I'LL be off then, now. I've finished upstairs. Wednesday is always my day for upstairs, although it's taken me longer than usual seeing as I've had the *two* beds to change.'

Faith frowned as she heard the mocking note underlining the housekeeper's words, but she refused to let the older woman see that she had recognised it.

No doubt it *would* seem odd to her that a newly married couple should sleep not just in separate beds but in separate rooms.

She grimaced to herself as she remembered the furiously angry words she had flung at Nash on the day of their marriage.

'I might have to share a life with you from now on, Nash, but there's *no way* ever we will share a bed.'

'Then it's just as well I wasn't planning to invite you to do so, isn't it?' Nash had returned after the briefest of pauses.

'No. You've already *done* what you wanted to do, haven't you?' Faith had lashed out at him, driven by a sense of desperation and pain she'd been unable to control.

'If you're trying to insinuate by that comment that

I knew you were a virgin and that I deliberately—'
Nash had begun dangerously, before stopping and
shaking his head.

'We're married now, Faith,' he had told her flatly,
'which means that there's hardly any point in trying
to provoke me into changing my mind, is there?'

'But we *will* be having separate rooms, won't
we?' she had insisted stubbornly, holding her breath
as she'd waited for him to argue with her.

Only he hadn't. Instead he had simply shrugged
his shoulders dismissively and responded, 'If that's
what you want.'

Of course it was what she wanted... It had been
then and it still was now—wasn't it?

It was probably only her pride that was making
her feel so...so somehow lacking as a woman just
because of Mrs Jenson's smirked comment. Anyway, Faith had far more to worry about than the
housekeeper's views on her marriage.

Far more!

It was a hot, sultry day and Faith was tempted to
blame the heat for the problems she was having in
trying to concentrate on her work. Another few days,
no more than a week at most, and she should know
if the night she and Nash had spent together was
going to result in a child.

Instinctively she glanced down at her left hand.
Her rings were slightly loose, and she twisted her
diamond solitaire 'engagement' ring absently.

'Why have you given me this?' she had challenged Nash as he had driven back to Hatton from the church.

'They came as a pair,' he had responded with a dismissive shrug.

A pair…

She and Nash were now a pair, in the eyes of the rest of the world and the law.

She had tried to ring Robert earlier in the week to tell him that she and Nash were married but had been told by his secretary that he was up in Scotland visiting an elderly cousin who had been taken ill.

'He's asked me to hold everything but the most urgent messages,' she had informed Faith.

Helplessly Faith looked at the plans she was supposed to be working on. No matter how hard she tried she just couldn't get properly motivated. Every time she started to make practical notes on how the house could best be adapted to suit the Foundation's needs she started to visualise Philip showing her around it, the pride in his eyes as he had done so.

Abandoning her work, Faith went upstairs and removed her tee shirt, tying on a brief halter-necked top before going outside into the garden. Nash was away on business and she had the house to herself. Absent-mindedly she bent down to remove a weed from the long border.

Half an hour later there was a growing pile of weeds next to her on the gravel path and she was diligently occupied in adding to it.

The sky had taken on a brassy hue and the air

had become heavy. The weather was forecast to break later in the week, bringing much needed rain.

Nash frowned as he walked into the empty study. There was no sign of Faith in the house but her car was parked outside.

His frown deepened as he scrutinised the plans she had been working on. They were for the ground floor of the house and he could see from her notes that she was concerned that the existing kitchen facilities would not be adequate for the Foundation's needs.

She had done a small but detailed plan, showing how some of the house's larger rooms could be divided to provide the facilities the Foundation would need. Nash reached out to turn them over and tensed as he saw the plans Faith had put beneath them.

These were very different from the ones she had been working on. They showed the ground floor of Hatton very much as it still was, but with the addition of a pretty conservatory and the alteration of the old butler's pantry and scullery area next to the kitchen to provide a large airy family room. Nash studied what she had done for a long time before sliding the top drawing back over it.

The deal he had been putting together in New York was a complex one but it was finally getting close to completion, Nash thought, then paused as he reached the top of the stairs, glancing out of the window that looked out onto the garden. He could see Faith busily weeding. Her brief halter top exposed the smooth tanned flesh of her back. She had tied her hair up out of the way.

It had been a long flight from New York and it had been his intention to have a shower and go straight to bed—so why was he turning round and heading back down the stairs?

Faith didn't know just what it was that made her stop what she was doing and turn her head to look down the long walkway. Some sixth sense? Some instinct? The instinct of a woman for a certain man?

Her heart slammed against her ribs as she saw Nash. He had taken a shortcut from the house to the walkway and was standing just in front of the small gazebo which commanded a view of the entire length of it. A little unsteadily Faith got to her feet.

The air was so oppressive and heavy that it seemed to physically press in on her, and the sun had disappeared, swallowed up by a warning bank of heavy cloud which was slowly darkening the sky.

Faith gave a small shiver as she saw it. It was the kind of sky that presaged thunder. She knew her fear of thunderstorms was illogical, but that didn't stop her dreading them.

Nash watched her as she stood irresolutely glancing from him to the sky. Once she would have run to him, her face lighting up with joy at the sight of him as she flung herself into his arms. Here, in this very gazebo, she had clung to him, lifting her mouth temptingly towards his as she'd told him, 'Oh, Nash…I'm so glad you're back. I've missed you.'

The kiss he had given her had been just the merest

brush of his mouth against her cheek, unlike the one he had *wanted* to give her, plundering the soft sweetness of the lips she was offering him, cupping her face, stroking the silky softness of her throat, removing from her body the thin top she had been wearing and slowly caressing her breasts, watching the pleasure shine brilliantly in her eyes as he did so before whispering to her how much he loved and wanted her.

Grimly he pushed aside his unwanted memories and walked towards Faith.

Why was he looking at her like that? Faith wondered warily. Was he thinking that she ought to be inside working and not out here? She flinched as she heard a faint roll of thunder in the distance.

Nash heard it too. Faith, he remembered, was terrified of thunderstorms. Irritably he pushed away his feeling of relief that he had reached Hatton before the storm. Why the hell should he feel any need or desire to protect her?

'I think I'll go back inside,' Faith told him, her eyes on the darkening horizon.

Her hair was starting to come loose and she reached up to remove the band she had secured it with, unintentionally unfastening the tie on her halter top at the same time. Her concentration was more on the growing storm than on what she was doing.

It was only when she felt her top starting to slide free of her body that she realised what she had done, and held it protectively against her breasts with her hand. With the straps tangled in her now loose hair,

discreetly retying them wasn't going to be possible—and anyway it was obvious from the way Nash
was looking at her that he realised what had happened.

'I applaud your modesty, but is it really necessary?' he asked her dryly. 'Women sunbathe topless
openly in public, Faith, and it would be a very secluded person these days who isn't familiar with the
sight of naked female breasts. And besides...' He
stopped, but Faith knew what he had been going to
say.

He had been about to remind her that he was no
stranger to her naked body—and not merely the
sight of it either!

He had been walking alongside her, but now he
was standing behind her, one hand lightly touching
her naked shoulder as he told her, 'Keep still for a
minute and I'll refasten it for you.'

It was a mundane enough remark, and a mundane
enough action, surely—merely tying two pieces of
cloth together, that was all. But as he refastened her
straps his fingers brushed against her skin, sending
messages that were far too dangerously sensual
shooting through her. Her body felt too sensitive,
too aware of him. She could feel the frantic race of
her heartbeat, driven by a mixture of fear and pain,
and her tension was exacerbated by the distant slow
roll of the still thankfully distant storm.

What if Nash were to bend his head now and
gently kiss the slope of her shoulder before turning
her round to face him? Beneath her top Faith felt

her nipples harden, whilst a hot coil of desire began
to tighten deeper within her body.

If things were different between them wouldn't
she now be turning to *him*, smiling teasingly up at
him whilst she silently invited him to kiss her, touch
her…make love with her…?

Why was she thinking like this? Had Mrs
Jenson's comment to her earlier affected her more
than she had thought? Had it somehow challenged
her as a woman to such an extent that she felt she
had something to prove?

'There…'

'Thank you.' Her voice was curt, her body
screaming with tension. Why was Nash still holding
on to her? She could feel his breath against her skin,
so warm, so close that it was almost as though he
was whispering the softest of kisses against her naked shoulder. Frantically Faith fought to remind herself of the reality of her situation. If she did have
something to prove, surely that something was that
she was in no danger whatsoever of succumbing to
her teenage feelings for Nash?

The thick sulphurous silence of the garden was so
oppressive that even the bees had gone silent.

'Have you told Ferndown yet?'

Nash had released her as he spoke and automatically Faith spun round to face him.

'If you mean have I told him about…that…
that…about our marriage,' she answered, 'Then,
no…I haven't.'

'Faith—' Nash began, and then stopped as a low, growling roll of thunder made her flinch.

'We'd better get inside. With any luck the storm will bypass us here,' he told Faith as they hurried towards the house. 'My solicitor's coming out to see me later. Otherwise—' He stopped speaking, his mouth suddenly grim.

Otherwise what? Nash asked himself with inward scorn. Otherwise he'd stay with her, protect her, hold her…take care of her?

As Faith lifted her hand to pull open the house door the diamond in her engagement ring caught the light and glinted brilliantly. He had ordered it specially from Tiffany's, and he had lied when he'd said that it was part of a matching set.

Once she was inside the house Faith felt less afraid. She couldn't hear the storm now. It was, mercifully, still too far away.

Faith started up nervously from her chair as she heard the unmistakable sound of thunder. It was ten o'clock in the evening and she was on her own in the house watching television—or rather trying to— in an attempt to distract herself from what was happening outside. The local weather forecast had predicted that the storm would pass them by, but the increasingly loud claps of thunder Faith could hear above the noise of the television didn't sound as though it was doing any such thing.

Nash had taken his solicitor out to dinner. She had been invited to join them, but of course she had refused. She had seen the curiosity in the older man's eyes when Nash had introduced her to him as his wife.

Why had Nash had to do that? She had felt such a hypocrite accepting his good wishes. His late cousin had been Philip's solicitor, he had informed Faith.

And so, of course, he would know about Philip's bequest to *her*, for which she owed such a debt of gratitude.

Another roll of thunder shook the sky. Unable to stop herself, Faith rushed to the window and opened the curtains. The storm had brought an early murky dusk, and as she peered out anxiously into it a jagged fork of lightning splintered across the sky.

The storm was in the distance and she had nothing to fear, she knew. It would bypass the house. But she just wished it would hurry up and do so.

She had been caught in a bad thunderstorm as a small child and she suspected that that was the original cause of her now almost phobic fear of thunder. Her desire to run and hide was totally illogical, she told herself firmly as she forced herself to leave the window and go back to her chair.

If she turned the television up loudly enough she wouldn't even hear the thunder, and anyway it would soon be gone—except that half an hour later Faith knew that it wasn't going away. It was coming closer and closer.

In the restaurant in Oxford where he had taken his solicitor Nash broke into the older man's fond reminiscences of Philip.

'I'm sorry,' he apologised, 'but I'm going to have to go. Faith is terrified of thunderstorms, and contrary to the forecast this one seems to be moving closer to us.'

They had travelled to Oxford in separate cars since David Lincoln lived on the other side of the city, and within minutes of calling for the bill Nash was back in his own car and speeding towards Hatton.

Switching on the radio, he heard that the storm had changed direction and that it was proving to be worse than the original forecast.

Frowning, Nash put his foot down on the accelerator. It was only natural that he should be concerned, he told himself. After all, Faith could be carrying his child.

But as fast as he drove, the storm was faster. He could see it illuminating the sky in front of him, hear its savage ferocity, and he knew from the time lag between the vivid pyrotechnics of the lightning and the threatening rolls of thunder that the centre of the storm was still some miles away.

Another jagged flash of lightning tore open the sky before it earthed.

Nash cursed as minutes later his car headlights picked out the tree it had hit, the huge branch now blocking the road.

Quickly reversing his car, he drove back the way he had come. The only alternative route he could take was a circuitous one that would add well over another half an hour to his journey.

He glanced at his dashboard clock…

Faith trembled as another bolt of lightning exploded in the darkness outside her bedroom window. Anxiously she started to count, waiting for the follow-up burst of thunder.

Ten seconds…twenty… The storm was miles away yet—miles away.

She was perfectly safe. There was no need for her to panic. Hatton had withstood nearly a hundred years of summer storms.

But it was built on the highest piece of land locally; its tall, decorative chimneys reached up into the sky. The fury of the storm left Faith in no doubt about its need to find an escape…a prey to vent its pent-up energy upon. Around her bedroom window was the frame which had once held the metal bars that all nursery windows of a certain era had been fixed with. If the lightning should find and strike it…

As though in some malign way it had read her thoughts, a sudden vivid flash of lightning illuminated her bedroom window.

Faith could feel her fear overwhelming her as fast as the storm was threatening to overwhelm the house.

There had been a storm the summer she had stayed here. Nash had found her crouched on the landing, her hands over her ears. He had taken her to his room, talking to her, soothing her, staying with her until the storm had passed.

Nash!

Faith screamed his name as the thunder crashed and rolled outside, drowning out the sound of her terror. She was a creature of the elements now, incapable of any kind of logic, driven by instinct and fear.

Wrenching open her door, she raced along the landing, her breath coming in painful rasping sobs as she finally reached Nash's bedroom. The room was in darkness, a silent stronghold of peace and safety, somehow inviolate from the storm.

In here she would be safe, Faith knew instinctively. As she closed the door she could hear the storm raging ever closer.

Shaking with the nauseous intensity of her fear, she crawled into Nash's bed, wrapping the bedcovers tightly around herself.

'Come on,' Nash had urged her gently all those years ago when the storm had finally died away. 'It's gone now. You can go back to your own bed.'

'I don't want to go,' Faith had protested. 'I want to stay here with you.'

And she had clung to him as she spoke, silently willing him to let her stay. Against her ear she had heard his heartbeat, accelerating as she moved, and her own heart had lurched yearningly against her ribs as she'd prayed that he would let her stay, let her show him how much she loved him, how grown up she was...how ready to be his.

But instead he had shaken his head and told her firmly, 'You *can't* stay here, Faith—you know that…'

And then, before she'd been able to say another word, he had picked her up in his arms and carried her back to her room and her own bed, for all the world as though she was still a little girl and not the fully grown woman she had wanted him to see her as.

Another crash of thunder engulfed the house, blotting out even the sound of her own scream. Frantically Faith reached for Nash's pillow, pulling it over her head.

Safe beneath its darkness as the thunder momentarily abated, she realised that the pillow carried Nash's scent.

As she breathed it in a huge wave of feeling rolled over her. Tears filled her eyes. Things could have been so very different between them if only Nash had believed her, trusted her, loved her. Her mind stepped back to the night that had destroyed her dreams…

She had visited Hatton the previous weekend and Nash had told her that he was going away. It had simply never occurred to her that there was a hidden agenda behind the questions she had been asked at school about whether or not Nash would be there.

'No,' she had replied, never dreaming what was being planned. It had only been by chance that she had actually found out. Another girl who had overheard a snippet of conversation had alerted her to what was going on.

It was three miles from the home to Hatton, and she had run all the way, arriving with a stitch in her side, terrified that she might be too late to warn Philip of what was going to happen.

The front door had been open—evidence, it had been claimed later, that *she* had been the one to organise everything and that Philip had unsuspectingly let her in. She had heard voices coming from Philip's study. When she had rushed in she had found Philip collapsed on the floor with the gang ransacking his desk and, most sickeningly of all, one of them standing over him, holding his wallet.

Frantic with shock and anguish, Faith had gone to protect Philip, getting between him and his attacker and snatching his wallet out of her hand as she'd done so. And it had been whilst she had been crouching protectively beside him that Nash had arrived.

At first she had been too relieved to see him to realise what interpretation he was putting on the situation.

Even when the ringleader of the gang had deliberately lied to him, claiming that she, Faith, was the one responsible, the one who had organised their break-in, it had never dawned on her that Nash would believe it.

The ambulance and the police had arrived together, and Faith had become almost hysterical with shock and disbelief when she had realised that, far from being allowed to go in the ambulance with Philip, she was going to be taken to the police station with the rest of the gang.

Once there she had pleaded to be allowed to see Nash—so sure even then that she would be able to make him see the truth, so sure that there had to have been a mistake, that it would be totally impossible for him to believe that she would do *anything* to hurt Philip.

But Nash had refused to see her, refused to believe her.

Virtually overnight she had grown up, become the woman she had so much wanted to be—and that woman had made a vow to herself that the love she had felt for Nash was going to be totally destroyed, ripped out of her...

Faith gave a gasp as the whole house seemed to reverberate with the intensity of the thunder, bringing her back to the present and reality. She was too terrified now to scream, too terrified to do anything but lie frozen with fear in Nash's bed, her only source of comfort and strength his familiar scent.

Nash cursed as he opened Hatton's front door. The storm was virtually overhead now, and it was, as the reporter on the local radio station had just said, the worst to strike the area in over twenty years.

Calling out Faith's name, Nash checked Philip's study and then the kitchen, before racing up the stairs two at a time. Her car was outside so he knew she was in the house, and he guessed that she would have taken refuge in her bedroom.

The door to it was open but the room itself was empty. The bedclothes were half on the bed and half off it, indicating that Faith had, at some stage, gone to bed. But where was she now?

No light shone beneath the door of the bathroom but Nash checked it anyway, still calling her name. Fear of the kind he knew Faith suffered allied to a storm as bad as the one they were having was a dangerous combination. If she had panicked and perhaps run outside she might have fallen, be lying somewhere terrified...hurt... It was pitch black outside, and as he'd come in it had started to rain.

'Faith...?' No reply.

Had she been panicked into leaving the house? There was a flashlight in his car but he would need a more protective coat.

As he reached his bedroom and realised that the door to it was open Nash felt his heart lurch against his chest wall.

Ten years ago, in the middle of a summer storm, Faith had sought refuge with him in his room. But things had been different then. His room was the last place she would go now in search of sanctuary and safety—wasn't it?

Hardly daring to breathe he stood still, his breath leaking from his lungs in a long, slow, painful rasp as he saw the almost impossibly small bump she made in the middle of his bed.

She had curled herself up so tightly that her outline beneath the bedclothes was almost that of a child.

As his eyes accustomed themselves to the darkness of the room he saw his pillow and the way she was clutching it tightly to her, her face buried beneath it.

The storm had reached its crescendo: lightning so intense that it actually hurt his eyes to see it, followed almost immediately by a burst of thunder so loud that even Nash himself winced.

The small tight bundle that was Faith shook so much the whole bed shook with her.

Pity and an emotion far too dangerous for him to name arced through him.

Sitting down on the bed, Nash reached for her.

At first Faith thought she was dreaming, that in fact she had actually been killed by the thunderbolt and that she was now in a place where dreams, fantasies, somehow came true. How else could she be here in Nash's arms whilst he tenderly wrapped his bedding around her shivering body, at the same time telling her that she was safe and that there was nothing to worry about because the storm would soon be over?

'No, don't look,' she heard him commanding her as she stared towards the window and saw the greedy darting flicker of lightning, as quick and as deadly as a serpent's tongue.

Overhead the thunder still pounded the house, but Nash was gently pushing her head into the curve of his shoulder, holding her, his actions unbelievably tender and more than distracting enough to take her mind off what was happening outside.

'The storm will soon be gone,' he was telling her again soothingly, his arms tightening around her as she flinched against another roll of thunder.

Ten minutes later, with the sound of the rain outside louder than that of the dying growl of the thunder, Faith tried to persuade herself that he was right.

'I would have been here sooner but there was a tree across the road,' Nash was telling her.

He had thought about her…come back because of *her*?

The warm Nash smell enveloping her was so much stronger when it came from Nash himself, and its almost magical ability to comfort her was making her reluctant to move away from him. The very thought of going back to her room, where she knew she would lie awake all night dreading the return of the storm, made her shake inside with anxiety.

All those years ago when the storm had died away Nash had insisted on returning her to her room. Now Faith could feel him starting to move away from her.

'No.' She clutched immediately at his sleeve. 'Don't make me go back go my own room, Nash,' she begged him. 'The storm might come back.'

'You want to stay *here*?'

It was too dark for her to see his expression but she could hear the sombreness in his voice.

Under more normal circumstances pride would have driven and dictated her answer, but there was no room for pride inside her now.

'I want to stay here,' she admitted, taking a deep shuddering breath before adding, 'And I want to stay with you. I want to stay here with you, Nash,' she reinforced, as though she was afraid he might not understand her need. 'Just until the storm's gone,' she whispered. 'Just for tonight.'

As he exhaled slowly and carefully into the darkness above her downbent head, with the soft warm weight of her in his arms, Nash gave in.

'Just for tonight,' he agreed huskily.

CHAPTER NINE

'YOU won't go to sleep and...and leave me awake on my own—will you?'

Faith's anxious question reached Nash across the darkness that separated them, her little-girl nervousness tugging at his heartstrings. He had managed to persuade her to relinquish his pillow and to allow him to go to her room to get two more, but by some unfortunate mischance whilst he'd been gone the storm had made a dying rally, returning to shake the sky, and he had found her virtually paralysed with terror as she crouched on the bed.

The discovery that she was naked beneath the bedclothes she was holding in a death-like grip had made him wish he had thought to bring more than just her pillows from her room, but when he tried to move away from her to go back she refused to let him go, clinging to his arm with the fingers he had gently removed from the bedding.

'I have to get undressed, Faith,' he told her ruefully. 'I need a shower and a shave.'

He saw her head turn in the direction of his *en suite* bathroom.

'If it makes you feel any better you can come with me,' he offered teasingly, trying to distract her from her fear.

Reluctantly she let him go.

'You won't be long, will you?' she urged him as he headed for his bathroom.

'No. I shan't be long,' he assured her.

Like her, it was his habit to sleep naked. But tonight... A little grimly he wrapped a towel around his lower body before heading back into the bedroom.

Faith was exactly where he had left her.

Now, lying in the same bed with her, so close to him that he could feel her breathing as well as hear it, Nash wondered wryly if she had *any* idea just how unlikely it was that he would be able to sleep. Perhaps it was as well that she didn't!

The storm had gone, leaving the air cooler and fresher. Faith stretched sinuously, luxuriating in the pleasurable warmth of the large bed and her body's awareness of the protective presence of Nash. A sleepy, sensual and wholly womanly smile curled Faith's mouth as her relaxed senses responded to the knowledge of Nash's proximity.

Instinctively Faith snuggled closer to him, her hand curling possessively round his arm, the breath leaving her lungs on a long sigh as her lips nuzzled the warm flesh of his throat.

In her half-asleep state it was easy for Faith to abandon the barriers she had put up against her feelings and allow her deepest and most sensual self to have its way.

This was Nash as she had so much longed for

him to be all those years ago, and subconsciously her body registered that fact, pouring through her veins a soothing reality-diffusing elixir that was a mixture of emotion and desire and one other very powerful ingredient which her deepest self knew and recognised.

'Mmm…'

As she stroked the bare skin of his arm and gently tasted the warmth of his throat with her half-open lips her whole body was washed with a sweetly languorous wave of female pleasure.

'Mmm…'

Faith moved even closer, her body touching Nash's as her fingertips gently explored him.

Nash had barely slept, unable to snatch more than a few seconds of rest before forcing himself back awake just in case… Just in case what?

Certainly not just in case Faith started doing what she was doing right now. *No…* What he had been afraid of was that *he* might be tempted to…

After the accusations she had flung at him on their wedding day he had told himself that he would never allow himself to be tempted to touch her again, no matter how much he might want to do so. Lovemaking wasn't something he wanted to feel he was forcing on her—it was something that should be shared, like love itself.

He tried to grit his teeth against the raw moan of pleasure her touch was commanding.

Helpless to stop his body's reaction to the stroke of her gently explorative fingertips, he did the only other thing he could, reaching out and taking hold of her arm, lifting her hand away from his body. As he did so the naked warmth of her breasts brushed against his skin.

A long, slow uncontrollable shudder of reaction ripped through him, the groan he was unable to silence causing Faith to open her eyes.

She was in bed with Nash! Wonderingly she gazed at him, her eyes soft with emotion, her body still far too powerfully affected by the hormones his proximity had released to listen to any cautionary warnings of her mind.

Had she any idea just how powerfully sensual the way she was looking at him was? Nash wondered despairingly as he felt his self-control melt beneath its heat.

'Nash.'

As she whispered his name Faith leaned forward, her lips parting in a deliberate and irresistible invitation to be kissed. When he hesitated, the look in Faith's eyes deepened and darkened, and she moved even closer to him, the top half of her body resting on his as she brushed his mouth with hers.

A virgin she might have been, but when it came to tempting a man she most definitely knew how to be all woman, Nash acknowledged as he closed his arms around her and opened his mouth over hers.

Faith felt as though she might melt from the sheer intensity of the heat engulfing her as Nash kissed her.

His eyes, like hers, were open, focusing on her,

hypnotising her into a state of physical and emotional responsiveness that totally swept away her inhibitions.

She might be completely awake now, mentally completely aware of what reality was, but her body was still lost in the sensual spell that this night-long proximity to Nash had woven around it.

'Nash...'

As he lifted his mouth from hers she raised her hand and gently touched his lips. His body moved against her. One of them was shaking. It had to be her. She felt as though she was sinking, drowning in the depths of Nash's gaze.

His lips caressed her fingertips, his tongue-tip stroking each one individually before his fingers curled around her wrist and his mouth moved downwards into her palm, making her quiver, then along her arm, lingering on the sensual spot just inside her elbow and making her tremble almost violently as his touch generated a response that threatened to devour her.

She could feel it right down to her toes, all the way up her spine to where the tiny hairs at the nape of her neck were lifting in a sensual signal as old as time itself.

In the shadowy light she could see the pale curve of her breast and the darkly flushed tensely aroused peak of her nipple, already aching with its need to feel the erotic suckle of Nash's mouth.

Beneath the bedclothes her belly tightened, her hips moving, lifting as she pressed herself closer...

closer; and an almost violent spasm of pleasure racked her as she felt the hard, hot pressure of Nash's arousal.

And all they had done was kiss…just once… And she wanted more…all of his kisses…all of him…

Nash tried reminding himself of all the reasons why he should not give in, but his mind was listening to a very different kind of argument, one that said she was his, they were married, this was his destiny—this and whatever might result from their intimacy—and that the debt of responsibility he would owe the child they might conceive would outrank the debt of responsibility he owed his godfather.

They might conceive? But it was too late for his brain to issue an urgent warning, his body, his heart, his *soul*, were already in thrall to a far more elemental urgency.

Faith felt as though she finally understood what it was to experience ecstasy, to reach a place that made her feel immortal and, even more awe-inspiring, made her feel that she and Nash were finally meeting as equals.

There were no more barriers between them. They weren't just touching naked flesh to naked flesh, but naked soul to naked soul. And instinctively, immediately, she knew, in the very heartbeat of time, that it had happened. She felt the fierce, final surge of Nash's desire within her, carrying her forward to her own sharp high plateau of infinite pleasure, and knew that this time they *had* created a new life.

Nash couldn't sleep. Anger, guilt, despair and a helpless longing for things to be different denied him the peace that Faith was enjoying.

Like her, he had been sharply aware of the soul-baring intimacy of what they had shared. Like her, too, a part of him had experienced the awesomeness of the beating wings of destiny hovering over them. But now that moment had gone he was once again facing the same emotion-churning dilemma he had faced so many times before. He was still unable to reconcile what he felt for Faith in terms of his love for her with what he knew cerebrally he ought to feel—because of what she had done.

If he allowed himself to love Faith he would end up hating himself. If he forced himself to hate her he would—

Restlessly he got out of bed. All his adult life he had made his own decisions and stuck to them. Now, though, he acknowledged that he needed help. Now he needed the wisdom and compassion that had been Philip's.

He showered and dressed, leaving the house whilst Faith still slept. He needed to be on his own to wrestle with his own demons. Being with Faith distracted him too much, made it impossible for him to think of anything other than how much he loved her.

There! *Finally* he had admitted it, allowed himself to acknowledge it…to face it…

No matter how much guilt or anguish it cost him to accept it, his desire for Faith, his love for her, was no different now than it had been before her cruelly heartless attack on Philip.

Conscience, logic, pride might insist that he should feel differently, that he should loathe her for what she had done and despise himself for wishing he could find some way of excusing her, but they all weighed as feathers in the scales that tipped so heavily in favour of his love for her. A love that might be weighted with sorrow and guilt, but a love he couldn't ignore or defy.

In his bed, holding her, responding to the sweet sensuality of her, he had seen the woman he'd always believed the girl he had known would become. All sweet, wanton allure laced with uninhibited passion, and yet somehow, at the same time, touched with an innocence and an honesty that made him ache with love for her.

She was a mystery, a conundrum, a question he could find no logical answer for. It was as though in hurting his godfather she had somehow stepped totally outside her own character and behaved in a way that was alien to her true nature.

Grimly he mocked himself for his own thoughts as he got into his car and started the engine.

Philip was buried near Oxford, in the peace and tranquillity of the small graveyard of the church where his parents had been married, and where they were also buried. As he drove there Nash remembered how he had half-hoped, half-dreaded that Faith would come to Philip's funeral, only learning later that her mother had died virtually at the same time as Philip.

He remembered too how that first year he had missed the anniversary of Philip's death, returning from New York several days later to find that someone else had visited the grave ahead of him, that that someone had planted it with Philip's favourite flowers and left a bunch of scented roses which had just begun to fade.

He had known who they were from even before he had read Faith's message.

To Philip in remembrance.
Dearly loved and dearly missed. Your faith in me has lightened my darkness and your inspiration will guide me all my life.
Faith.

Nash rubbed his hand across his eyes as he remembered the tears he had shed. Tears of anger and self-denial, tears that had burned his eyes like acid rather than washing them free of pain.

Her duplicity had infuriated him, and he had been sorely tempted to seek her out and tell her just *who* was paying for her precious education, just *who* she had to thank for the second chance at life she had been given. But of course he had done no such thing.

An eye for an eye, a tooth for a tooth, and a heart for a heart? Did Faith have a heart? Nash wished he knew.

*   *   *

A little nervously Faith emerged from her own bed-room and headed for the stairs. She had woken up an hour ago, her body so sensually relaxed that she had immediately blushed with self-consciousness as she'd remembered just *why* it felt that way.

At first she had assumed that Nash was in his bathroom, but when he had not emerged she had managed to pluck up the courage to leave his bed and check for herself.

She had no idea just why he was allowing her the privacy to come to terms with what she had done, but she was supremely grateful that he was. Faith was not going to try to deceive herself. *She* had been the one to institute their...intimacy. *She* had been the one to turn to Nash, to touch him, to kiss him...to...to...

Her face was well and truly on fire now. She tried desperately to think rationally. But what was reason or logic when her body was still languorous and hedonistically relaxed with pleasure and her heart was overflowing with the most intense kind of emo-tion?

She and Nash had made love. Made *love*. Not merely had sex. They had made love as they had surely been destined to do, and just as soon as she could Faith was going to sit him down and *make* him listen to her whilst she explained to him just what had happened that fateful night. This time somehow she would *have* to find a way to make him accept. Because... A little self-consciously her hand covered her stomach, but there was delight and joy in the smile that curled her mouth as she drew in and then expelled a shaky breath of awareness.

This wasn't just something she was doing for herself because she was finally prepared to admit that she still loved Nash, she told herself determinedly. It was something she *had* to do for the sake of the child she was so sure they had conceived. They owed it to their child to give him or her not just their individual love but also their *shared* love.

Their *shared* love? Strong-mindedly Faith refused to allow herself to even suspect that Nash *didn't* share her feelings. Surely after what they had experienced together he *must*.

Instinctively she felt for her rings and then frowned. She was wearing her wedding ring but where was her 'engagement' ring? Had she taken it off last night during the storm without realising what she was doing?

She was halfway down the stairs when she heard the front doorbell. The sight of Nash's solicitor standing outside momentarily disconcerted her, but she made him comfortable in Philip's office before going in search of Nash—only realising when she did so that Nash's car was missing.

'It doesn't matter,' David Lincoln assured her. 'I just wanted to return some papers to him. He forgot them last night.' He smiled at Faith. 'He was very anxious to get back to you.'

His skin pinkened a little. 'So very romantic, and what one might describe as a perfect ending. I have to confess when he first told me what he intended to do all those years ago I was a trifle uncertain—but, Nash being Nash, he was insistent. "It was Philip's wish that Faith should complete her education," Nash told me, and he fully intended to make that possible despite the fact that there just wasn't the money in Philip's estate to allow for such a bequest.

'Of course you'll know all about that now,' he told Faith warmly. 'I must confess I was never really sure just why Nash was so insistent that his involvement was to be kept a secret, or why he wanted you to believe that several trustees were administering your bequest when in fact Nash was the only one—paying for your education out of his own pocket.'

Stunned, Faith let him continue to sing Nash's praises.

Nash had paid for her to go to university, not Philip. *Nash* had supported her during the years she had been studying, learning. Nash...

A horrid feeling of nauseous light-headedness engulfed her, a sense of shock and disbelief; a sharp coldness was replacing the delicious warmth she had woken up with. Nash *owned* her. Nash had *bought* her...and last night he had no doubt simply been claiming his repayment.

An icy wave of desolation and loss swept over her. She felt as though something infinitely precious had been taken away from her, although it took her several minutes to analyse what it was.

What had made Philip's gift so very special to her had been her belief that it proved he had known her innocence. But now... Had Philip even *wanted* to help her, or had that too simply been another lie created by Nash?

As he parked his car outside Hatton's front door Nash took a deep breath. Had the hard-won peace and purposefulness he had felt as he knelt beside Philip's grave deserted him or was it still there? Had he finally laid the past to rest and accepted that if he wanted to move on he must draw a line under the events leading up to Philip's death?

He loved Faith, no matter what she was. He knew that. He knew too that as a girl she had loved him. And, earlier, in his arms he had felt...*she* had felt... But in order to give those feelings a chance he had to put aside his own bitterness and guilt.

Today, kneeling on the soft earth in the churchyard, he had felt somehow that Philip was giving him his blessing, urging him to build a new life for himself and for Faith as well. And for the first time since it had happened Nash actually felt able to admit to his own feelings of guilt at not being there when Philip had most needed him—guilt he had previously offloaded onto Faith. Whether or not they could turn their relationship around he didn't know, but what he did know was that they needed to talk.

Faith had seen him arrive, and she was waiting for him when he walked into the hallway.

'I want to talk to you—'

'We need to talk—'

Both of them spoke at once, and then both of them stopped.

'Will Philip's study be all right?'

Faith heard and recognised the unexpected, almost tender tone to Nash's voice, and just for a second her resolve wavered. Perhaps she had misunderstood.

Nash was already ushering her into Philip's study, his hand remaining in the small of her waist as he paused to close the door, almost as though he couldn't bear to totally relinquish his physical contact with her.

She didn't wait for Nash to finish closing the door before she burst into speech, demanding sharply, 'Is it true that *you* financed me through university, Nash? That there *was* no bequest from Philip?'

Nash frowned as she hurled her angry questions at him like missiles flung heedlessly in a furious attack. Her anger was as mystifying to him as the cause of her questions.

'What makes you think—?' he began, but Faith cut him short.

'Your solicitor was here. He told me. He seemed to think that this—' she held up her left hand, showing him her ring finger, her voice filling with contempt '—is the culmination of some romantic fantasy between us. If only he knew the truth. The only reason you would ever pursue me is for revenge.

'Is that why you did it, Nash? Out of some perverted desire to exert control over me, to buy my future so that you could hold the power to destroy both it and me if you chose?'

Faith knew that her voice was becoming wilder and wilder, like her claims, as her imagination tormented her with increasingly shocking motives for what Nash had done.

'It was Philip's wish that you were given the chance to fulfil your ambitions,' Nash told her quietly, once he had had time to realise what had happened.

'He *told* you that, did he?' Faith demanded bitterly. 'He *said* he wanted you to pay for me to—?'

'No,' Nash was forced to admit. 'He wanted to do something to help you. He had it written into his will...' Nash stopped and looked away. 'Unfortunately in the end he wasn't able...either physically or financially...to make the provisions he wished to make.'

'So *you* made them for him,' Faith persisted fiercely. 'Why?' she demanded sharply. '*Why* did you do it, Nash? *Was* it because you wanted to have some kind of hold over me? To be in a position to go on punishing me for Philip's death?'

The accuracy of the accusations she was hurling at him startled Nash, and shocked him too. Hearing his own emotions put into words gave them a rawness, a blind cruelty and lack of charity that left a bitter taste in his mouth. Was it too late for him to plead with her for understanding and clemency, or would she respond to him in the same way he had once responded to her when she had pleaded with him for those very same things?

How often through the years had that knowledge haunted him…that *regret*? But how could he explain to her now and expect her to understand that he had refused to see her simply because he had been so afraid that he might weaken, because he had believed so passionately that he owed it to his godfather not to do so.

As she waited for his response Faith twisted her wedding ring round her finger.

Broodingly Nash focused on it, and as she recognised what he was doing Faith went still. Nash was looking at her hands, her rings. Only she wasn't wearing her engagement ring because she hadn't been able to find it as yet. Her engagement ring— with its uncanny similarity to the earrings Philip's 'trustees' had given to her to mark her twenty-first birthday…the earrings she had valued and treasured with such joy and love.

Anger and betrayal flooded her in equal measure.

'*You* bought my earrings,' she told Nash. '*You…*'

Nash winced as he heard the bitterness and loathing in her voice.

'It was what Philip would have wanted me to do,' he told her, just as he had always told himself.

'How *could* you?' Faith demanded in a raw whisper. 'How *could* you do something like that and yet at the same time still believe that I was responsible for Philip's death? Can you even begin to *imagine* how it makes me feel? Knowing that everything I am I owe to you. My education, my qualifications, Florence, my job!'

'You got your job on your own merits, Faith.'

'No,' she denied. 'I got it on your money. Your money and the education it bought for me. Have you *any* idea how much I hate knowing that, Nash? How much I *hate* knowing that everything I am I owe to your charity? Is that what you wanted? To be able to stand and gloat? How much you must enjoy knowing how easily you could destroy me! Was that why you took me to bed, Nash, because you felt you owned me?'

Nash could see the tears of fury and shame in her eyes and he closed his own, mentally cursing the appalling timing of his solicitor's innocent disclosures.

Whatever he tried to say now Faith was going to misinterpret it, and she was certainly in no mood to listen to what he *had* wanted to say to her. As for that new beginning he had so wanted to ask her to make...

'I wasn't the one who instigated what happened between us,' he tried to remind her, and knew that he had said the wrong thing as he saw the look on her face.

'I hate you, Nash. I *hate* you,' she told him furiously, before whirling round and running up the stairs, away from him.

CHAPTER TEN

FAITH walked tensely across the hallway. Robert should be arriving soon. He had telephoned her the previous evening to say that he was going to make a flying visit to see her.

'Just to touch base, really,' he had told her, adding ruefully, 'Unfortunately there won't be time for anything else.'

'How is your cousin?' Faith had asked him.

'He's fine,' Robert had responded. 'He's nearly ninety, and he's determined to make it to his centenary.'

He had had to ring off to take another call before Faith could say any more.

What was she going to tell him about the problems she could see confronting them with the conversion of Hatton? She desperately wanted to be able to give him some good news, but she was becoming increasingly concerned about the suitability of Hatton for the Foundation's purposes.

The success of this project was so important to Robert, and Faith wanted it to succeed for his sake. Perhaps another more experienced architect might be able to see an answer that was hidden from her?

As she heard a car pulling up outside she hurried

towards the front door, pausing as the sunlight caught the gold of her wedding ring.

That was something else she was going to have to tell Robert. But tell him what? Certainly not that she was trapped in a marriage that was no marriage at all and never would be, nor that she prayed passionately at night in bed—the bed she slept in alone—that she had been wrong about that spark of life she had felt ignite when she and Nash had made love. Made *love*! Who was she kidding? *She* might have thought they were making love, but what Nash had been doing was collecting an interest payment on his investment.

They had barely spoken to one another since her outburst on discovering the hidden role he had played in her life. Or rather she had made it virtually impossible for Nash to speak to her, either by avoiding him or simply walking away from him when he did try to approach her.

Only this morning he had walked into the kitchen whilst she was there, and she had seen from the look on his face that he fully intended to make her listen to him. She, though, had been equally determined not to do so, and as she had stormed past him he had taken hold of her arm—not in a painful grip, exactly, but there had been enough force there to ignite her own still smouldering fury.

Fortunately for her Mrs Jenson had arrived before Nash could say anything, giving her the opportunity to escape. But Faith had seen the look in his eyes as she had done so, and she knew she was pushing his self-control into its danger zone.

But why should she care?

The sunlight glinting on her wedding ring as she opened the door for Robert reminded her that she had still not found her missing engagement ring.

'Mmm…it's good to breathe clean air instead of city fume-choked stuff,' Robert commented appreciatively as he followed her into Philip's study.

The look he was giving her was even more appreciative, Faith recognised as he smiled at her.

'How are the plans coming along?' Robert asked her eagerly.

Faith paused, going over to the desk instead of closing the study door as she had been about to do.

'I'm having rather a few problems,' she admitted. 'The kitchen…'

She lifted her hand to show Robert the kitchen area on the plans on the desk, and went silent as she saw he was looking at her wedding ring.

'Nash and I are married,' she told him uncomfortably. 'It was… We didn't… I don't…'

Her voice trailed away as she saw how shocked Robert was.

'I knew the two of you had a…history,' he responded manfully, 'but I didn't…'

He shook his head whilst Faith watched him with a mixture of anxiety and guilt. There had been nothing serious between them, and she had no reason to feel guilty, but nevertheless she was aware that her

news wasn't something he had expected or wanted
to hear.

To her relief he immediately rallied and told her
ruefully, 'When I asked you to use your influence
to persuade Nash to finalise the Foundation's acquisition of Hatton I didn't expect you to go to *those*
lengths, you know!'

Gratitude towards him for the way he was trying
to ease the situation for her filled Faith, but outside
in the hallway, where he had been on his way to
speak to Robert, Nash froze.

His immediate instinctive interpretation of
Robert's comment filled him with bitter anger. Faith
had used him—used his love for her for her own
ends.

Faith gave Robert a shaky smile as she shook her
head.

'I wish I *could* do something to help you,' she
admitted. 'You've been so kind to me, Robert.'

To her chagrin her eyes filled with tears, and she
knew that Robert had seen them.

'Hey, what's all this?' he demanded softly, closing the space between them and giving her a comforting hug.

Faith had her back to the door and her face buried
against Robert's shoulder, so she didn't see Nash
stride into the study. But Robert did, immediately
releasing her as he said self-consciously, 'Oh, Nash.
I understand that congratulations are in order. Faith
has just been telling me your good news.'

'So I can see,' Nash agreed curtly, giving Faith a

look of icy contempt before turning away from her to tell Robert, 'Perhaps once you've finished ''congratulating'' her you could spare *me* five minutes? There's something I want to discuss with you.'

Faith saw Robert drive away from her bedroom window. She had gone there to leave the two men to their discussions following Nash's arrival in the study.

Her face burned with a mixture of anger and resentment.

Nash had had no right to look at her the way he had, with that...that contempt, that almost murderous loathing. It had been obvious from Robert's reaction that he'd felt he was confronting a savagely jealous husband, but *she*, of course, had known better.

How much longer must she wait before knowing whether or not she had conceived Nash's child? How many days' grace should she give herself? She knew there were home tests one could do, but surely it was still too early for that?

She froze as her bedroom door crashed open and Nash strode in.

'So Ferndown asked you to used your ''influence'' with me, did he?' he demanded without preamble. 'Don't bother denying it, Faith. I overheard the pair of you.'

'And, typically of you, Nash, you immediately leaped to conclusions and made judgements based on those conclusions. Does it ever occur to you that you could possibly misjudge something? No, of course it doesn't,' Faith told him scornfully, answering her own question. 'All Robert wanted was to know what the Foundation's position was with regard to Hatton. He didn't realise… He didn't know…'

'He didn't know what, Faith? He didn't know just what lengths you'd go to…just how *dedicated* you can be? Unlike me! I have your tutors' reports, after all, and yet I still fell for it. I still let you— How many times were you prepared to have sex with me before you asked for what you wanted?'

'How *dare* you say that?' Faith choked furiously. 'I didn't…'

'You didn't what?' Nash demanded. 'You didn't go to bed with me as a calculated manoeuvre…out of self-interest and greed? If it wasn't for that, Faith, then what was it for?' he asked her with frighteningly savage softness. 'Was it for this?'

He moved as swiftly as a big cat on its prey, all raw male energy, strength and muscle as his body enveloped her, imprisoning hers with ease.

Don't touch me, she wanted to cry—but the words remained locked in her throat, just as the angry fists she wanted to beat against his chest in a frantic bid for freedom remained locked at her sides.

Was it her own anger that was paralysing her so completely? Faith wondered dizzily. Or was it Nash's unleashed male power?

'You're my wife, Faith,' she heard him saying as his mouth covered hers. 'Mine…'

His—bought and paid for! The wild ferocity of her own reaction shocked Faith, but she was totally unable to control it—just as she was totally unable to control the sharp bite of her teeth against Nash's mouth as she fought against the possession of his kiss.

But as fire met fire and the resulting conflagration was driven by the wind nothing could stand in its way to stop it.

Faith was conscious of Nash's thick curse as her teeth raked his lip. She could taste his blood on her tongue and feel the savagery of his hands as he held her, dragging her further into his body, not pushing her away, his mouth opening with shocking demand over hers.

Scarcely knowing what she was doing, Faith raked her nails down his forearm, twisting and turning as she fought to break free of him. And yet, for all her fury, somewhere deep down inside her body there was a growing sense of excitement, of arousal, of a dangerous, previously unknown instinct.

She felt as feral, as filled with conflict of needs and urges, as a she-wolf, Faith recognised breathlessly. Panting with heat and desire for the male who wanted to mate with her and yet at the same time snarling her aggression and hostility towards him as her enemy.

In Nash too she could sense the same feelings. Hostility crossed with desire was a volatile, explosive mix of emotions—a need by both of them to prove who was the stronger emotionally.

This was the dark side of the tender intimacy with which she had given herself to him before, and as she fought against him Faith knew that if she were to win and he let her go there would be an ache deep down inside her that desperately needed to be satisfied; that could only be satisfied by Nash.

Faith leaned closer to Nash, tipping back her head to expose the vulnerable softness of her throat. Her body arched back over his arm, her mouth swollen from the savagery of their angry passion.

As he looked down at her Nash could feel his muscles bunching like those of an animal, coiled to spring forward for the kill. He could see the pulse quivering in her throat, and the urge to cover it with his mouth, take it…take *her*…was so strong he could hear it roaring in his own ears.

Why *should* he act with conscience or listen to any voice pleading clemency? Hadn't Faith by her own actions put herself in a position where she didn't merit either? He could take her now, fill her with the urgent possessive heat of his body and take them both to a white-hot place that for a breath of time would taste like heaven. But then, afterwards, he would have to live with what he had done, what level he had allowed himself to be dragged down to.

Abruptly he released her.

Unsteadily Faith reached out to stop herself from falling, her eyes wide with shock and disbelief as she saw the distance Nash had put between them.

A part of him had known all along just what he

was inviting by giving in to the dark urge that had driven him to keep Faith in his life, Nash recognised, as the red mist of his anger faded to be replaced by a sickening sense of self-loathing. Wreaking vengeance on her might not have been an obsession, but he had certainly been guilty of believing that he owed it to Philip to see that she was never allowed to forget what she had done.

Turning on his heel, he strode towards the door.

Silently Faith watched him go. They had come so close to the edge of an abyss. Faith shuddered in shock as she realised how close.

What had so nearly happened between them just now must never, ever be allowed to happen again. She couldn't remain here now, anyway. Not even if… Her hand touched her stomach as she made a silent apology to the child she might be carrying for depriving him or her of a father.

Once she was back in London she would get in touch with Robert and tell him about her past, and then she would start looking for a new job—abroad, perhaps, where she could make a fresh start, where there would be no Nash to torment and hurt her. And no escape either from her own realisation of just how strong her love for him was.

How she could love him still she had no idea; all she knew was that she *did*.

Meticulously Faith looked round her room.

Yes, everything was packed—not that there had been much to pack. Her wedding outfit and its accessories had been carefully returned to their boxes and would be left for Nash to dispose of as he pleased. If his mood yesterday was anything to go by he would probably burn them at the stake on an effigy of her, Faith decided wryly. Her work was in her case ready to be returned to Robert. There was only one task she had yet to complete.

Very carefully she removed her wedding ring and placed it in the box that held her earrings.

Nash had left the house earlier—she had no idea where he had gone, was only glad that he had. This way at least she could leave with some semblance of dignity, without breaking down and crying to him, pleading with him as she had done all those years ago.

She frowned as she started to close the small jewellery box. She still hadn't found her engagement ring. Perhaps Mrs Jenson the housekeeper might have come across it when she had been tidying up. Very slowly and carefully Faith made her way downstairs to go the kitchen.

Nash frowned grimly at the building in front of him. It was derelict now, a burden to the council who owned it, its windows broken and its grounds overgrown. It had always looked a bleak, institutionalised sort of place to him, and he had felt desperately for Faith having to live there. A children's *home*! Home was the last thing it looked like.

He had no idea why he had driven here, or what answers he had been hoping to go find. What an-

swers, after all, were there? How *could* he love a
woman who made him despise himself for doing so?
At Philip's graveside he had told the older man that
she had been young, misguided, and that whilst he,
Nash, would never forget, he wanted to put aside
the past and forgive, make a new start for Faith, for
himself—and, perhaps most importantly of all, for
the child they might have created. And then he had
heard her conversation with Ferndown! Once again
Faith had condemned herself.

The look in his eyes was as bleak as the place in
front of him as he turned and walked away from it,
back to his car.

'Mrs Jenson, I wonder if I could have a word
with…' Shock froze Faith to the spot as she stared
at the woman standing next to the housekeeper.

'Charlene,' she whispered in disbelief.

'Aunt Em said you'd turned up here,' the other
woman smirked. 'What a turn-up for the books, eh?
Who'd have thought it, after what you done? Bold
as brass, some people are… Wait 'til it gets out in
the town that there's a murderess living here…'

Faith had had enough.

'That's not true,' she denied swiftly. 'You know
perfectly well that I had *nothing* to do with what
happened. It was you and the rest of your little gang.
You lied about me, blamed me…implicating me
when *I* was trying to protect Philip.'

For a moment the horror of the past threatened to
overwhelm Faith. She was still in shock from walk-

ing into Hatton's kitchen and discovering there the very person who had been responsible for the break-in, the very person who had callously threatened and frightened Philip. She flinched as the girl she had known as Charlene Jenks laughed.

'You asked for it, Miss Too-good-to-be-true, running telling tales on us, trying to get us into trouble. You deserved everything you got,' she added viciously, her eyes suddenly sharp little spikes of malice. 'I can still see your face when the police hauled you away along with the rest of us. ''Nash, don't let them take me,''' she mocked, mimicking Faith's soft voice. '''Nash, you can't believe I would ever hurt Philip...''

'But he did believe it, and why shouldn't he have done? You made it all so easy. There you were, caught red-handed with the old fool's wallet in your hand. All we'd done was follow your instructions, we said. You were the one who planned it all. You were the one who knew he'd be in the house on his own, who knew how to get in. You just knocked on the door and told him it was you, didn't you? And he let you in. That's what we said and everyone believed us. Including your precious Nash!'

'Stop it! Stop!' Faith protested, covering her ears, her face white. 'How could you have done it? How *could* you have frightened him...hurt him like that?'

Faith's voice shook with emotion as she spoke. Outside the half-closed kitchen door Nash stood in silence, his body rigid with shock.

He had walked into the empty hallway and de-

cided to head for the kitchen to make himself a cup
of coffee, but as he had approached the doorway he
had heard the women's voices coming from inside
the room and he had stopped—and listened. At first
his heartbeat had accelerated, pounding fast with
shock. Now it had slowed down to heavy, agonised
thuds of anguished despair.

Faith was innocent—just as she had claimed all
along. How she must hate him now.

Inside the kitchen Charlene Jenks was still taunting Faith.

'It was easy… Until we got caught, thanks to you
bursting in like that and ruining everything. Still, we
made you pay for it.' She started to scowl. 'Trust
you to get off with it, though. Course, we all know
who was responsible for that. He must have had the
hots for you even then, your precious Nash, to speak
up for you the way he did. Heard all about it, we
did—how he'd begged the magistrate to treat you
leniently. Going to bed with you even then, was he?
And you under-age? Just wait until we spread that
tale around the town.'

Faith came out of the shock Charlene's revelations had given her.

'Don't you dare even think about spreading those
kind of lies about Nash,' she told her passionately.

Nash had interceded for her! *Nash* was the one
who had spoken up for her…saved her from being
sentenced…

On the other side of the door, Nash had heard
enough. Pushing it fully open, he strode into the

kitchen, ignoring the housekeeper and turning to confront Charlene.

'Just *one* more word, *one* more threat, and you'll find yourself having to explain to the police,' Nash told her grimly. 'And as for you,' he told Mrs Jenson as Charlene started to back away from him, her face pallid with shock and apprehension, 'you're fired— and don't even think about asking for a reference.'

'I haven't done anything,' the older woman began to protest truculently. 'It was our Charlene that wanted to come up here. Said she'd got an old score to settle.'

Maliciously she glowered at Faith, but when Nash moved towards her Faith shook her head, saying immediately, 'No, Nash, ignore her.'

'Let me warn you,' she could hear Nash saying as he walked them towards the back door, 'I fully intend to go to the police and register a complaint against both of you.'

Faith could tell from his tone that he meant what he said, and she could see that they could too.

Her shock was wearing off now, and by the time Nash had closed the kitchen door and they were alone she had finally managed to steady her quivering limbs.

'What can I say?' Nash asked her bleakly.

'You weren't to know,' Faith responded, her voice as dry as death. 'All the evidence was against me. I was there, next to Philip, holding his wallet. They said I was the one to plan everything, that it was my idea.'

'You asked me to listen…to trust you…'

Faith looked away from him in silence.

'I should *never* have left Philip that night,' Nash castigated himself harshly. 'I *knew* how weak he had become, but my damned work…'

He said the words with such guilt and self-loathing that Faith's heart ached for him. Tentatively she lifted her hand in a gesture of comfort, and then let it fall again.

'In insisting that *you* feel guilt, Faith, what I was doing was trying to sidestep my own guilt. I needed to be able to blame you because it stopped me from blaming myself.'

'Why did you intercede for me?' Faith asked him in a low voice. She couldn't bring herself to look at him whilst she waited for his response, twisting her hands together and feeling the heavy, driven thud of her own heart.

'Why the hell do you think?' Nash asked in a gritty, emotion-laden voice. 'You must have sensed how I felt about you, Faith, and how—' He stopped, and Faith lifted her head and searched his face, her eyes huge and dark.

'I know how I felt about *you*,' she admitted shakily. 'You were kind to me, but…' She hesitated, trying carefully to pick her way safely through the minefield of self-doubt and fear that distanced her, separated her from the shining beacon of her growing hope.

'Kind!' Nash made an explosive sound. 'Kindness wasn't what I wanted to give you, Faith. What I *wanted* to give you, share with you, was...' He looked down at her and she could see the hot male glitter in his eyes. Immediately her own senses sprang into response.

'I wanted you, Faith,' Nash told her rawly. 'Wanted you in all the ways a man of my age had no right to want an under-age child.'

'I *wasn't* a child. I was fifteen,' Faith protested.

'Fifteen, sixteen—eighteen, even. It wouldn't have made any difference,' Nash told her grimly. 'You were too young, too inexperienced for what I wanted with you.'

Stunned, Faith told him fiercely, 'Sexual experience isn't everything. It isn't a barometer of how a person can really feel when...'

'I'm not talking about *sexual* experience,' Nash informed her. 'I'm talking about your experience of *life*, your right to experience life *for* yourself and *by* yourself. If I had given in to my feelings for you then, to my need for you, my *love* for you...'

He paused whilst Faith's heart leaped frantically against her chest wall at the sound of the word 'love'.

'It wouldn't just have been the law of the land I'd have been breaking if I'd given you my love then, Faith. It would have been my own moral code as well, the one Philip taught me.'

'Perhaps if Philip had made a full recovery from his stroke and been able to tell you what had happened...'

'Why should I have needed Philip to tell me?'

Nash asked her harshly. 'I should have known for *myself.*'

'Why did you pay for my education?' Faith asked him quietly. '*Was* it just because you wanted to have power over me?'

'It was what Philip wanted,' Nash told her shortly, but Faith was sure he wasn't telling her everything.

'The earrings you bought me,' she persisted, 'for my twenty-first birthday...'

'Your tutors' reports stressed how hard you'd worked. I knew you had no family,' Nash told her curtly. 'Hell, Faith, what is it you want me to say?' he demanded when she made no response. 'That I bought them because there wasn't a day when I didn't ache for you...there wasn't a *night* when I didn't wish I could forget what had happened to Philip?'

'Did you offer Hatton to the Foundation because of me?' she asked him shakily in the fraught silence that followed his passionate outburst.

Nash shook his head. 'Not consciously. But...'

'But?' Faith pressed.

'The truth sits between us, Faith. I can never forgive myself.'

'In this instance surely any forgiveness is within *my* gift rather than yours?' Faith pointed out wryly.

But although she held on to her breath, and her hope, Nash made no attempt to reach for the ladder she had thrown him to cross the gulf between them.

'The best thing we can hope for now is that there isn't going to be a child,' he told her heavily. 'We should be able to end our marriage reasonably easily.'

Desperately Faith demanded, 'And what if I don't want to end it?'

Nash sighed and walked over to her.

'Do you think I haven't guessed what you really want?' he asked her tautly.

Faith held her breath again, waiting to hear him tell her that no matter how much she still loved him he could not return her feelings. But to her bemusement he continued harshly, 'I have to set you free to make your own life, Faith.'

What on earth was Nash saying? He must surely know that *he* was all she wanted. This must be his way of being tactful, of saving her pride. But her pride was the last thing she cared about now. And yet as Nash walked towards the kitchen door and away from her, for some reason she didn't ask him the one question that could potentially have kept him with her. What if, as she suspected, she *was* pregnant? Would he still want to end their marriage then?

Outside in the garden Nash stared unseeingly into the distance. It was too late for him to regret his behaviour now, but not too late for him to suffer the reality of his own shame. All those years ago he hadn't believed her because he had been afraid of doing so, afraid of his love for her and what it might do to them both. It had been easier to tell himself that she wasn't worthy of his love when the truth was that he hadn't been worthy of hers!

*   *   *

There was nothing for her here at Hatton now, Faith acknowledged as she headed for her bedroom. She ought to be feeling glad, triumphant, proud that Nash had finally accepted her innocence, and not... Not what? Not aching with love and need for him, not wishing that he still loved her?

Automatically she touched her wedding ring, and then frowned as she suddenly remembered that she *had* been wearing her engagement ring on the night of the storm, when she had fled to the sanctuary of Nash's room and Nash's bed...

Emotional pain did the most extraordinary things to a human being, Nash acknowledged as he made his way towards his bedroom and contemplated the wasteland his life had now become.

As he opened the door he saw that Faith was sitting on his bed, her face turned slightly away from him. He could see a single tear glisteningly rolling over her cheek as she studied the rings on her hand.

'What are you crying for?' he asked her harshly.

Faith started as she saw him. She had found her ring underneath Nash's bed, where it must have rolled.

'For what might have been,' she told Nash sadly and honestly. 'If...'

'If what?' Nash prompted her.

'If you hadn't stopped loving me, Nash,' she told him steadily.

'*Stopped* loving you?' Nash exhaled sharply. 'I have *never* stopped loving you, Faith,' he told her thickly. 'I couldn't—no matter how many times I wished to God that I could.'

'But you hated me as well.'

'I hated my own inability to control my love for you,' Nash corrected her. 'It's ironic, I suppose, that after years of fighting against myself, when I finally managed to make my peace with myself and confess to Philip that not even the loyalty I owe him could stop me from loving you, I should discover that *I* was the one who was guilty of the real sin.'

Faith started to frown.

'I don't understand—' she began, but Nash stopped her.

'The night of the storm…when you…when we… I decided then that it was time to lay the past to rest. I went to Philip's grave…'

The night of the storm! Suddenly Faith knew what she had to do. She must be the embodiment of her own name. She must have courage and conviction.

Slowly she stood up and walked over to where Nash was standing. When she reached him she said softly, 'The night of the storm? When I kissed you like this…?'

And she put her arms round him and stretched up to reach his mouth, slowly and very deliberately caressing it with all the power and determination of a woman in love.

'Faith…' Nash protested on a low groan. 'You mustn't…'

'Why not?' she whispered boldly, feathering the

words tormentingly against his aching mouth. 'I'm your wife and you're my husband...my love...the father of my child...'

As he opened his mouth to protest she closed her own over it, kissing him with passion and love.

He moved, lifting his hands to her arms, and for a moment she thought he was going to push her away. But then his hands slid over her arms and he was drawing her closer, taking control of the kiss from her. Tenderly she yielded it to him.

'Tell me that you love me,' he demanded thickly in between kisses.

'Not until *you've* told me,' Faith responded, smiling.

Abruptly Nash released her, and for a moment she thought she had got it wrong, overplayed her hand... And then he was entwining his fingers with hers as he commanded, 'Come with me. I want to show you something.'

By the time they reached the gazebo at the end of the walkway Faith was almost out of breath. It was a perfect summer evening, balmily soft, scented with roses and lavender.

'The first time I stood here and saw you,' Nash told her softly, 'I knew how much I loved you, how much I would always love you—and I do, Faith.'

'Tell me again how you felt that first time you saw me,' she urged him.

'Tell you?' Nash questioned. 'I've got a much better idea. Why don't I show you instead?'

'Out here in the garden?' Faith whispered, semi-shocked but more excited.

'Out here in the garden,' Nash agreed, and he drew her to him and began to kiss and caress her.

EPILOGUE

'PHILIPPA. It's such a pretty name.'

Faith smiled warmly at Robert Ferndown's fiancée Lucy as both Robert and Lucy cooed over baby Philippa where she lay snugly in her father's arms.

She was three months old and today she was being christened, at the same church where Faith and Nash had been married.

They had asked Robert and Lucy to be godparents—a strong bond of friendship had begun to develop between the four of them, and Faith was looking forward to attending their marriage later in the year.

'I do so envy you Hatton,' Lucy had told Faith the first time Robert had introduced her to them.

Faith had smiled.

'It *is* a lovely house,' she had agreed serenely, turning away from the other girl to watch Nash.

She had still been pregnant with Philippa then. It had been Christmas, and for their first Christmas together Nash had sent away the army of builders who had taken over Hatton after he had decided that instead of giving the house to the Foundation he and Faith should make it their family home.

'We shall need an awful lot of these,' Faith had

laughed, patting her bulge when he had told her, 'to fill it!'

'So…?' he had teased back, lifting one eyebrow.

'Robert will be disappointed for the Foundation,' she had warned him.

'I've got something else in mind for Robert,' Nash had informed her.

'Oh? What?' she had asked, staring at him in bemusement when he told her.

'The old children's home where I…? But…'

'I've made enquiries and the council is willing to sell it to me. The house can be demolished and a new one built—a proper home—not an institution.'

'And you'd do that and give it to Robert? Oh, Nash…'

'Don't you dare say "Oh, Nash" to me like that in your condition,' he had warned her. 'You temptress…'

Philippa stirred in her father's arms. They had named her for Philip, a loving tribute to him.

'If you keep on gazing adoringly at her like that I'm going to get jealous,' Faith warned Nash untruthfully as she left Lucy to slip her arm through her husband's.

'Wait until tonight,' Nash whispered to her as they walked towards the church. 'And then I'll show you just how little cause you have to feel neglected or jealous. You will always be first in my life and in my heart, my darling, darling Faith.'

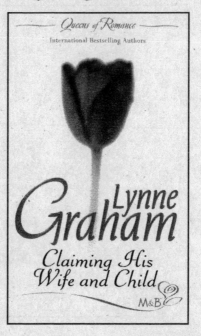

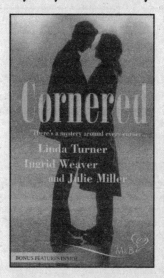